To Andy,
Enjoy!

NIGHT HERON

By Marilinne Cooper

PRELUDE

JUNE 15, 1950 – WINNIE

On the very first night of their marriage, Winnie began to understand that being a wife to Travis would be nothing like she had anticipated. When he opened the door to the bathroom of their luxurious hotel suite while she was still undressing, her alarmed eyes met his in the mirror. He observed the reflection of her slim curves in white lace bra and underpants, his gaze lingering on the matching garter belt holding up expensive, sheer silk stockings.

"Travis, go away, I'm not ready for you yet!" She held her silk wedding nightgown modestly across herself.

Winnie didn't know how well she would come to know the look he had in his eyes as he reached forward and gently but firmly removed the shimmering garment from her hands.

"I don't want you to wear this." He tossed it into a corner of the tiled floor. "I want you to come to me just as you are now."

"Like this?" She giggled in nervous disbelief, trying to ignore the hair–raising tingle on the back of her neck.

"I find a partially dressed woman much more exciting than–" He cut the sentence short, before revealing too much about his own experience. "Come, my dear." Extending his hand to her, he tried to lead her out into the bedroom.

"I– I can't do it like this, Travis. At least turn the lights off or close your eyes until I get into bed."

Travis laughed, enjoying the game. "What happened to Winnie Scupper, my sophisticated woman of the world?"

Caught between his warm moist palms, Winnie's hands were cold and trembling. "You know I'm still a virgin, Travis, even if I am thirty." She looked up at his handsome, chiseled features and was suddenly chilled by the feeling that she didn't know her new husband at all. "This is my wedding night." She was embarrassed by the pleading tone of her own voice. "Can't we do this the way I want to?"

Travis's smile didn't fade; instead it seemed to harden onto his face. "This is my wedding night too," he replied. "I'm your husband now and if I think I know what's best, you will have to do what I say."

He dropped her hands. Caressing her smooth dark hair, he removed the clips that held it off her forehead. "I'm going out into the bedroom to wait for you. In one minute I want you to come out dressed exactly as you are now. Except..." He held out the white satin pumps she had worn with her wedding dress. "Put these on and then come out." He pressed the shoes into her unwilling grasp and kissed her gently on the lips. "I'll be waiting for you."

Winnie sank to the cold bathroom floor, burying her face in her arms. She was terrified of the man she had just married.

They had met the previous December, on a crowded commuter train into New York City. She had been carrying a large flat box which contained the stained glass window she had just completed for a wealthy customer on Fifth Avenue. When an impeccably dressed gentleman rose to offer her his seat, she could not help but flash him a dazzling smile of thanks. The man, looking down at her, saw how the smile changed her serious expression into one of extraordinary beauty, and he was instantly intrigued.

4

"What's in the box?" he asked, noting her red cashmere coat was trimmed in black mink and that the earrings sparkling in her earlobes were undoubtedly real diamonds.

"A window. Of stained glass. It's what I do. I make them." Winnie was embarrassed at how flustered this attractive stranger made her feel. She was nearly thirty, an old maid not a young girl. Pulling off her soft leather gloves, she fumbled in her purse for a printed business card.

"Winnie Scupper. Artisan in the Fine Art of Stained Glass. Work on Display at the Christopher Street Gallery or in progress at the Bedford Hills Studio," he read aloud. His eyebrows lifted as he appraised her again. "Must not have much time to spend with your family." He had already noted that she was not wearing a wedding ring; a multi-faceted ruby in an ornate old-fashioned setting graced her long, slender finger.

"I'm not married," she replied stiffly. It had been so long since she had flirted with the opposite sex, she barely realized how leading his questions were.

"A beautiful woman like you?"

"I was engaged to someone but he was killed in the war." Winnie didn't like talking about Charles but there was something magnetic about this sophisticated stranger. Maybe it was merely the fact that the number of eligible men in Westchester County had been substantially lower in the post-war years. To cope with her grief over Charles, Winnie had thrown her entire soul into glasswork. The few men she had dated were boring and had not seemed worth the energy she had put into dressing up and making light conversation.

"Oh, I'm sorry. You live in Bedford Hills?" he asked as he neatly tucked the card into his inside coat pocket.

"Yes. And you?"

"I'm just here on a business for a few days."
Stealing a look at him, Winnie could see no briefcase or
attaché.

"What do you do?"

He laughed smoothly. "Nothing as interesting as
stained glass, I assure you. That's a lovely ring; antique
isn't it?"

"Yes, it was my grandmother's." She was
impressed that he would notice her ring and recognize
its value. Unconsciously, she let down her guard a little
more, and gave him another smile.

She was about to speak again when the train
began slowing down for the next stop, the brakes
squealing loudly. When it finally came to a halt, all the
standing passengers fell forward and then abruptly
back. To keep his balance, the stranger grabbed for the
armrest of Winnie's seat, and his hand pressed against
her own momentarily. She felt a thrill of excitement
stab her like a sharp spike from her chest down to her
abdomen. Gasping softly, she looked away from him and
out the window, pretending to scrutinize the crowd of
people waiting on the station platform.

She had been so sure she would never have this
feeling again, this sudden arousal that seemed to
promise love, passion and sexual fulfillment all at once.
And to have it come over her so suddenly with a strange
man on a train! It was whorish and unthinkable.

As new passengers began pushing through the
aisle of the already crowded coach, once again his body
was thrust against her shoulder and his chin grazed her
hat, knocking it askew. She could smell his cologne
mixed with the faint aroma of pipe tobacco and she was
overcome by the very maleness of it. It made her body
feel like a thousand loose puzzle pieces coming apart,
floating in space and not quite able to be reassembled
again.

Even the aisle was crowded now. As the train
began slowly chugging out of the station, the man

retained his position of overwhelming closeness. "I didn't realize so many people would be heading into Manhattan at this time of day," he murmured softly, his lips very close to her ear.

"Christmas shoppers." Her own voice came out on a breathy exhalation.

"Are you okay?"

"Yes, thank you. Just a little overheated." She undid the buttons of her red coat, giving him a glimpse of a necklace that caught the light in the same manner as her earrings.

He talked to her all the way into the city but afterwards Winnie could not remember anything they had said, only the intense physical magnetism that made her want to melt against him every time they accidently touched. The sweat running down between her breasts had surely destroyed her favorite white silk blouse.

"Can you have lunch with me?" he asked as the passengers began filing off the train at Grand Central Station. With a well–practiced gesture, he slipped his hand deftly beneath her elbow and helped her out of her seat.

"No, I'm sorry. I'm meeting the Carnegies for lunch." She indicated the boxed window she was carrying.

He shrugged and did not press the issue. "C'est la vie. Perhaps if I'm in town again, I'll call you. I've got your card." He patted his breast pocket.

She knew this was it, the proverbial end of the line, and as they walked through the station she felt a pang of sorrow at what might have been. At least he had reminded her of how a man could make a woman feel. That in itself had made the brief encounter worthwhile.

She was surprised to see how closely he was watching her when she turned to him suddenly, an unexpected grin lighting up her features once more. "I don't even know your name," she laughed.

7

He smiled at her, displaying his perfectly straight white teeth. With his dark hair, neatly trimmed moustache, and deep chin cleft, he was as handsome as any movie star. "You never asked. It's Monroe. Travis Monroe."

"Well, I've enjoyed talking to you, Mr. Monroe."

"The pleasure was all mine..." Somehow he made even the traditionally gracious phrase sound immoral. In an outdated gesture he lifted her gloved hand to his lips and kissed it. "Till we meet again, Miss Scupper."

Winnie had never expected to see Travis Monroe again. After a few weeks she could not remember exactly what he looked like or whether he reminded her more of Clark Gable or Cary Grant. The memory of how he had excited her lasted long after his image had faded away. She clung to that recollection each time her ever-hopeful mother invited another lackluster bachelor to dine with them, reminding herself that somewhere out there was a man who could actually light her flame.

Then, one warm day in mid-March, she looked up from her workbench to see a broad-shouldered figure filling the open doorway to her studio.

"The door was open..."

"It's such a nice day, I thought the fresh air..." She shook her head in amazement as she realized who the suntanned stranger hesitating in her doorway was. "I can't believe it. I never expected to see you again. How did you find me?"

"Oh, I was in the neighborhood, thought I'd drop in." His light words did not ring true, but Winnie didn't care. "Did you really do all these pieces? This is extraordinarily fine work." He moved confidently around the studio admiring the windows, lamps and mirrors that all featured Winnie's own unique style of glass work. "Sort of three dimensional, isn't it?" He ran his fingers lightly over a Tiffany-style lamp shade that showed a Garden of Eden scene.

Winnie wiped her hands self–consciously on the dirty canvas apron that covered her cotton dress. This was not how they had met in her dreams; this was worse than she could have ever imagined it. He was so well–groomed; beneath his blazer, the spotless white shirt accentuated his bronzed face and hands. She could not remember if she had even brushed her hair that morning before rushing across the green lawn to the gatehouse she had converted to a studio. She was so engrossed in her latest project, that lately she had not paid much attention to her personal appearance.

"I'm sorry, I'm right in the middle of something. If only you'd called..." Her voice drifted off as he reached across the work table and grasped her hand. "You're very tan." Her voice was like a thin piece of wire. "Where have you been?"

"I had some business in Havana. Lovely place, Havana. Ever been there?"

"Cuba, you mean? No. I've been to Bermuda once. Is it anything like that?"

Travis laughed. "Oh, no. Much more exciting and...exotic." He squeezed her hand meaningfully before letting go and walking back to the door. "Do you live in that grande manse up there on the hill?"

"Yes, my mother and I do. When my father lost his fortune in the stock market crash, he told my mother she had to chose one house to live in and that we would have to sell the other properties in order to afford it. So he sold the house in Southampton and the brownstone on Central Park and of course, because it was the Depression, he got almost nothing for them. We still have an old summer home on a lake in northern Vermont that we'd inherited from my mother's mother; I guess he couldn't unload that one. I haven't been there in years."

Winnie had been putting her tools away as she chattered nervously and now she joined him at the door. "Why don't we go up to the house? It's nearly cocktail *hour and I'm sure mother would love to meet you." She was anxious to change her clothes and make herself look attractive. She was determined that Travis was not going to disappear from her life again.*

Despite the fact that Charlotte Scupper disapproved, three weeks later they were engaged, with a wedding planned for early June. Travis did his best to charm Winnie's mother, but Charlotte, although she was desperate to find her daughter a good husband, was not swept away by his dashing looks and perfect manners the way Winnie was. While Winnie found Travis and his mysterious past intriguing, Charlotte was not fooled by his evasive answers about his business and family.

"Who cares who his people are, Mother? He's the most exciting man I've ever met and he loves me. I'm thirty years old and I'm finally getting married. After all these years of thinking it would never happen, I'm not passing this up."

Charlotte could not argue with this line of reasoning, and yet there was something about Travis that she just did not trust.

"He's just too nice to be believed," she remarked one evening to Stella, the elderly housekeeper who had been with the Scuppers since before the Depression. Through the French doors leading to the porch, the two gray–haired women watched the couple cuddling together on the wicker porch swing as they waited for a cab to take Travis back to the train station.

"As I recall, at one time Mr. Scupper was an awfully nice man too," was the soft–spoken servant's reply.

Charlotte sighed, remembering how her husband had changed after the Crash of '29. He had eventually become so depressed and moribund at losing virtually everything that he could no longer face himself, let alone his proud wife and two young daughters. In an attempt to help him regain his self-esteem, Charlotte offered to sell some of her heirloom jewelry to finance a real estate venture he was interested in. Unfortunately her gesture had the opposite effect she had intended. One night he disappeared: his body was found a few days later at the bottom of the trout pond. Tied around his waist was a rope attached to a large cement block. There was no question of anything but suicide as a motive.

"Well, I daresay we'll never have to worry about Mr. Monroe being as idealistic as Mr. Scupper was." Charlotte gave a sarcastic little snort. "I'm sure if he loses his shirt on one race horse, he can always find another to place a bet on."

Travis, on the other side of the glass doors, might have lost some of his suave composure if he could have heard Charlotte's shrewd comment. Instead he appeared to be devoting his undivided attention to Winnie. As usual he was artfully avoiding answering her questions about himself by feigning a greater interest in her own background.

"Forget about Havana. Tell me more about your sister, the missionary in China."

"I told you, she's not in China anymore. It's Malaysia now or wherever Singapore is."

"Do you think she'll come home for the wedding?"

Winnie made a face. "You'd be happier if she didn't. She's not your type, Travis."

Travis knew this was true from all she'd told him about Roberta. Winnie's homely older sister had had her own way of dealing with the family's fading fortune. After she saw what the love of money had done to her father, Roberta had become a zealous fundamentalist, renouncing all her worldly possessions and leaving home to spread the word of God to those less fortunate than herself. Disapproving of how her mother and sister clung to the remains of their wealthy lifestyle, she rarely came home anymore.

11

"One time when she was here she kept criticizing Mother for passing all her old jewelry on to me. Finally Mother gave her an exquisite diamond brooch and Roberta immediately turned around and sold it for her mission in China. We had quite a brawl after that. Mother told her if she wanted money she could have found some other way to get it besides selling what's left of our family heirlooms. Roberta has no appreciation of material beauty or artistic value. After she was gone, Mother gave me nearly all the jewelry she still had."

"Really?" Travis's tone indicated typical male boredom, but beneath this facade he was actually listening intently.

"You know, so Roberta wouldn't be able to get her hands on it in case Mother should die suddenly or something. Because she knew I would love and respect the jewelry the way the women in our family always have." Winnie stood up suddenly. "Your cab is here, darling."

"So it is. Listen, I've got some business to wrap up in Chicago this week, I'll be gone for about ten days. Oh, no you don't." He put a finger over her lips to keep her from asking what it was. When she pouted, he gave her a long, lusty kiss that promised more. "Remember that while I'm gone," he said and then hurried down the porch stairs to the waiting taxi.

"I'm waiting for you, Winnie."

Travis's voice from the bedroom brought Winnie back to the cold tiles of the bathroom floor where she sat freezing in her lacy wedding underwear.

"Put on those shoes and come out here, sweetheart."

Winnie shuddered at a glimpse of herself in the mirror as she went through the door into the honeymoon suite. She had thought she desired Travis but now she wasn't so sure. She'd heard that sex was

12

always scary the first time, but it was better once you got used to it.

Travis was propped up in bed against the satin-covered headboard. His burgundy silk smoking jacket was open, exposing his total nakedness underneath. "My God, Winnie, you take my breath away, you're so beautiful." His voice had a huskiness she did not recognize as he reached out a hand to her.

"Can't – can't we turn out the lights, Travis?" she asked timidly as she came towards him, blushing and trembling.

"Of course not, dear. How can I appreciate how beautiful you are if I can't see you?"

As Winnie stood there, he ran his fingers up and down the bare flesh exposed between the top of her stockings and her underpants, and she swore to herself she would not cry.

She did not really have a chance to reflect on the events of the night until around noon the following day. They would be leaving on their honeymoon trip in an hour, traveling across the country from New York to San Francisco, via Las Vegas, by train, a romantic reminder of how they had first met. Now Winnie was packing up quickly, racing around the room, trying to erase any traces of what she instinctively knew had not been a usual wedding night.

When she discovered the torn remnants of her lace underpants beneath the bed, she crumpled them into a tiny ball and stuffed them into a corner of her suitcase. What would the maid think if she found them? She would probably be as horrified as Winnie had been when Travis had ripped them off her.

But that had been early in the evening. A wave of exhaustion overcame her and she sat down on the bed. It had been hard to believe at first that she would ever enjoy some of the unspeakable things he did to her. She flushed with shame to think of how pleasurable a few of those acts had felt and she cringed inwardly at how he had watched her, persisting until she had clung to the edge of the mattress, begging him to stop. He had carefully prepared her for the moment when he plunged inside of her, and after the initial pain, it didn't hurt her anymore.

Although the blood was throbbing in her brain, she could hear him murmuring unconscious exclamations like,"Oh, God, Winnie, you're so tight! I'd forgotten how a virgin feels." It made her feel cheap, but she kept telling herself that of course a man like Travis would have had other women before her.

Then in the morning...for a moment she buried her face in hands. Then she was frantically searching the room for any stray belongings, trying not to think about what he had made her do to him in the shower. She could not imagine that her mother had ever done that to her father.

Winnie's knees buckled under her and suddenly she found herself face down on the plush carpet, sobbing. Stop it, you're just tired, she admonished herself. But thinking about the long train trip ahead with only Travis for company, she burst into tears again. The glamorous dream of the honeymoon now seemed like a spangled gossamer curtain covering the dark reality of her future married life.

As they travelled west, Winnie began to see the true nature of her marriage to Travis unfolding. By day he was the perfect gentlemen, a loving husband who adored his new wife, proudly leading her on his arm through the dining car, listening attentively as she talked about the changes she wanted to make in the old Vermont vacation house that her mother had given them as a wedding present.

At night, alone in their deluxe sleeper/lounger, he taught Winnie how to take and give sexual pleasure, showing a creativity that he displayed in no other aspect *of his life. Although she found many of his methods perverse, she often became very aroused by what he did to her or asked her to do. Travis kept a mental catalog of what excited her and soon he was leading her through nightly performances that seemed to leave her as spent and satisfied as he was.*

But he always stayed in control by pushing her one step too far, just enough to keep her terrified of what he would think of next. One night he insisted that she accompany him to dinner wearing no bra or underpants beneath a thin, rayon shirtwaist dress that would reveal the hardness of her nipples and the jiggle of her breasts and buttocks as he paraded her through the passenger coaches and club car on their way to the dining car. When she had protested, he had gathered up all her undergarments and to prove that he meant it, he began flinging them one by one out the window until she saw that he was serious and nervously agreed.

Throughout the meal, beneath the white tablecloth covering the narrow table between them, he would slip his hand beneath her skirt and force it between her thighs, stroking and coaxing until finally, flushed and tearful, she fled from the table and back to their compartment only to discover that Travis had the only key to the door.

He was right behind her however, too aroused to finish his meal. As soon as they were inside, he dropped his trousers and lifted her skirt and took her standing up as she braced herself by holding onto an overhead luggage rack.

"That was incredibly exciting, sweetheart," he said as he collapsed afterwards on the plush covered couch.

"That was horribly embarrassing to me, Travis! Why would you want to humiliate me like that?"

"You need to get over your sexual inhibitions, Winnie, so you can truly enjoy our marriage. You should be proud of your beautiful body and what just the sight of it does for me sometimes."

"But everyone was staring at me! All those men—"
Nausea gripped her stomach and she could not continue.

"I know and it made me even more excited because
you're mine, not theirs. You pleased me very much
tonight, darling." Pulling up his pants, he came over
and kissed her lightly on her pouting lips. "You should
want to do things for your husband to make him feel
good. You know, keep the home fires burning..." he
laughed at his own joke. "I love you, dear, but I need a
drink. I'll be back in a while to make you feel as happy
as you made me."

As soon as he left, Winnie ripped off her wrinkled
dress and wrapped up in a chenille bathrobe. Then,
leaning out the train window into the warm rushing air
of the summer evening, she heaved the offensive frock
as far as she could into the prairie grass below.

Sitting alone in the compartment, she tried to
calm herself down by telling herself over and over again
that once they settled down in the quiet house in the
Vermont countryside that everything would be different.
She would do her stained glass work when Travis was
gone on business for a few days at a time and they
would be a normal, happy couple with children and pets
and a lovely home life.

When they arrived in Las Vegas, Winnie finally
discovered what the underlying key to Travis's
character really was.

It had been Travis who had suggested they make
the detour in their direct trip across the country to
include Las Vegas, one of his favorite cities in the world.
He had booked them into a classy hotel above a famous
casino and Winnie was surprised and impressed when
the desk clerk greeted him by name. The desk clerk, in
turn, mirrored Winnie's own reaction back at her with a
raised eyebrow. He murmured a few confidential words
to Travis, who laughed and slipped him some cash.

16

A few minutes after being shown to their room, Travis announced he was going down to the casino for a few hours. "How does dinner at eight sound, dear?" He kissed her and then, without waiting for a reply, was gone.

Winnie had been dressed and waiting impatiently for some time when the phone finally rang. "Mrs. Monroe? Your husband would like you to join him in the casino, if you would please."

"What? Yes, of course. Thank you."

Confused and angry, and more than a little hungry, Winnie took the elevator down to the first floor to look for the casino. She was stunned by how busy and colorful the lobby looked compared with its dark quietude of mid–afternoon. Men in suits, many of them sporting cowboy hats, escorted lavishly dressed women, sometimes one on each arm. Most of the women wore strapless gowns in glossy fabrics and were adorned by flashy jewelry. In her ruffled high–necked blouse, full black skirt, and very proper gloves and hat, Winnie felt more self–conscious and dowdy by the minute as she entered the smoky casino with its red walls, gilt edged mirrors and glittering chandeliers.

Several women looked at her with mild amusement on their very made–up faces and the manager hurried up to her, assuming she was lost on her way to somewhere else. By then she had spotted Travis at a roulette table. He had a large pile of chips in front of him and, as she walked towards him, he raked several more chips in from across the table.

"Travis–"

"Oh, there you are, darling." In a large public gesture, he gave her a long kiss and then quickly let her go, saying, "I couldn't leave. I'm on a streak and I'm winning big."

"Take your lady friend to dinner, Monroe, and give the rest of us break," cracked someone else at the table.

"Not until I win my dough back from him!"

"Are you in or not?"

"I'm in." Travis shoved a stack of chips onto the number nine and the wheel began to spin.

"Ten. Your streak's over, Monroe. Good time for a romantic supper, eh, sweetie?" The stranger pinched Winnie's behind and she jumped and moved closer to Travis.

"Yeah, let's go, Winnie. I'll be back later, Jack," he called over his shoulder. Scooping up his winnings, he headed for the cashier.

Sitting across from him at dinner, Winnie observed a glow in Travis's face she had never seen before. His striking features were more animated than usual, and he made light, lively conversation throughout the meal. He was obviously enjoying himself thoroughly and she began to remember why she had fallen in love with him.

"I feel really lucky tonight," he said as he signed his name and room number to the dinner check. "Do you want to come back to the casino with me?"

She declined his invitation, saying she wanted to write a letter to her mother while they were on solid ground and not in a vibrating railroad car. Gambling was not her sport but she was willing to humor Travis for a few harmless days if it made him happy.

"I'll be waiting for you," she whispered in his ear before she got on the elevator.

It was the first time in a week she had gone to bed alone and she indulged herself with a bath and the white silk wedding nightdress she hadn't worn yet. She awoke at three a.m. to find she was still alone, drenched in sweat, her fancy nightgown wrinkled and deeply creased. As she turned up the air conditioning, she wondered if Travis was all right, but she was unwilling to get dressed and leave the safety of the hotel room at this time of night.

She lay awake in bed, worrying, until he finally staggered in, an hour and half later, reeking of smoke and alcohol. Pretending to be deeply asleep, Winnie murmured, "Everything all right, Travis?"

"Wonderful, dear. Made a grand sweep of the night." His words were slurred and through her half closed lids Winnie could see he was having trouble unbuttoning his shirt. "We're rich. Tomorrow I'm gonna take you shopping. Buy you some fancy dresses, show off those knockers of yours..."

He fell into bed next to her and she turned away from him, overpowered by the disgusting smell of gin and tobacco. "Forgive me, dear. I'm too drunk to get it up tonight. We'll screw in the morning, okay?" And then, almost immediately, he was snoring.

He slept so soundly that he did not hear her when she slipped out to the coffee shop for breakfast a few hours later or when she left again mid–morning for a swim in the outdoor pool. But when she returned, he was sitting up in bed, smoking a cigarette and drinking coffee which he had ordered from room service.

He greeted her by asking her to stop at the door, remove her terry beach robe and her swimsuit, and then walk across the room to him wearing only her cork–soled sandals and straw hat. Winnie was already learning to turn her brain off when he asked her to do disturbing things; she would mechanically go through the motions while dreaming of how right things would be once they set up housekeeping in Vermont.

She was still daydreaming a few hours later when he led her into an expensive dress shop adjacent to the lobby of their hotel. "You're coming to the casino with me tonight," Travis had told her, "and I want you to look sensational."

When the salesgirl led them to a rack of evening dresses, Travis said to Winnie, "Pick out whatever you like." But when she had selected a full skirted gown of iridescent blue taffeta, he shook his head disapprovingly. "Too matronly. Here, try this."

He held out a slinky, stretchy cocktail dress covered in glittering red sequins. It had a low cut heart-shaped neckline and was held up two slender spaghetti straps that left the arms and back completely bare.

Winnie laughed nervously. "That's not me, I couldn't wear that."

She looked to the clerk for support, but the girl just shrugged and commented, "Great dress for a hot summer night. Wish my boyfriend would spend that kind of dough on me."

"We'll take it."

"Wait, Travis—" Winnie grabbed the dress from him and looked inside at the tag. "It's too small – it's not my size. It wouldn't fit right."

"You'll look fabulous in it. It will go perfectly with that old ruby necklace your mother gave you. Wrap it up," he ordered the salesgirl. "Do you have any stockings to match?"

Winnie turned away, her cheeks burning, and pretended to examine the price tag on a bathing suit. She was not going to cause a scene in public but there was no way she was going to wear that dress.

Travis made a few more purchases and then they left the store. "It's fun buying beautiful things for you," he remarked, ignoring her stony silence as they waited for the elevator. "Maybe I'll go out by myself this afternoon and buy some things to surprise you."

"No, please, it's not necessary..."

"Of course not. I'm doing it because I want to, not because I need to." He kissed her lightly on the lips. "I want to splurge a little on my wife on our honeymoon."

Although she no longer totally trusted him, Winnie let herself be fooled by his sweet sentiment because she wanted to believe it was true. While he went shopping she went back to the pool. She spent the rest of the afternoon reading a novel in a lounge chair and refreshing herself with frequent dips.

When she returned to their room, there was a pile of boxes on the bed topped by a note which read, "For my love. Rest up – we have a big night ahead."

But the flood of warm feelings that swept over her initially turned cold when she saw the kind of clothing he had bought for her. Most of it was lingerie; underwear that belonged in a bordello, negligees of sheer black chiffon, fishnet stockings and elbow length lace gloves. A black strapless dress with a boned push up bra built into it; a white fur bolero jacket and matching hat. A tight red angora sweater.

She could not be the person he wanted her to be, didn't he see that? She was too proud to admit that her mother had been right; perhaps they had married too quickly.

Blindly, she pushed the open boxes onto the floor. Then, mindless of her wet bathing suit, she threw herself across the satin bedcover and cried desperately. She could not face failure so soon. Somehow she had to make her marriage work.

Travis found her asleep in the same position three hours later. He had spent those hours playing some lively Black Jack and he was already well liquored up.

"Want to model some of this lovely clothing for me or are you ready to put on that fantastic dress and have some supper with me, my queen?" Travis's mood was as jolly as the previous evening.

Winnie sat up stiffly and stared dully at the damp spot on the bed where she had been sleeping. "I don't want to wear that dress, Travis. It will make me look like a tramp."

"Don't be ridiculous." He laughed a good natured laugh that was not his own. "It will make you look like what you really are, my sexy, luscious lady." He kissed her on the top of the head and tugged at the straps of her bathing suit. "Come on, just try it on. If it looks awful, well, of course you won't wear it."

She was so sure that it wouldn't even fit, that she got up immediately to try the dress on. But as Travis zipped up the short zipper in the back, the fabric just eased and stretched around her body like a second skin, hugging all her curves. The fact that it was a size too small showed only in the way it hung tantalizingly from its taut string straps, straining to cover her high breasts.

"Jesus, you look incredible!" Travis gasped, stepping back to admire her.

"I feel like a whore!"

"You look like a goddess." He rummaged through the pile of underwear on the floor and came up with a red g–string. "Put this on and let's go."

"You're crazy! It's too small. I'm not leaving this room in it. And I'm certainly not wearing THAT." She tossed the g–string he was offering her onto the floor.

Travis took a step toward her and opened his mouth to speak and then checked himself. "Fine," he said after a brief second. "Don't come with me tonight. But come over here right now."

He was unbuttoning his pants as she approached him, trembling. "Now just look at what the sight of you has done to me. I think you better get down on your knees and take care of it." Seeing the defiant look in her eyes, he put his hands firmly on top of her shoulders and pushed her down into a kneeling position in front of him, holding her there until she began to comply with his demand.

"If you won't make me happy by accompanying me to the casino, you can at least please me here in our room," he said to her. She had to agree that she preferred nearly anything to the thought of being seen publicly in the red sequined dress. He ordered room service for their supper and asked her to wear only the sheer negligee and the fishnet stockings while they dined. She agreed readily; anything was better than the red dress in the casino.

She sat primly, with no interest in the food in front of her. She kept her eyes averted over his shoulder, unable to meet his gaze. When he finished eating, he took her to bed and when he had satisfied his ravenous sexual appetite as well, he left for the roulette table.

Winnie felt numb and cold as she folded up the clothes that had been strewn all over the room. She had only to get through another half day of Las Vegas; their train was scheduled to depart for San Francisco the next afternoon.

She did not see Travis again until he found her by the pool late in the morning of the next day. He was still wearing his suit from the previous evening and his face was covered with a fine stubble of beard. He had come to inform her that he had changed their train reservations; he was still on a winning streak and there was no way they could leave yet.

"Just one more night," he promised.

Winnie went to a bookstore to buy another book to read that evening. This was not her idea of how to spend a honeymoon, but it was obviously something Travis had to get out of his system. He was apparently quite good at it. As long as he didn't start losing...

They had an early supper at a club with a floor show that was ongoing from noon until dawn, featuring high-kicking girls in spangled bikinis and feathered headdresses. Afterwards he left her quietly at the door to their room. She settled down with her new book and turned in early.

She was awakened sometime before midnight by the sound of the door slamming shut. Before she had opened her eyes, the covers were yanked rudely away and Travis growled at her, "Get up and get dressed. You're coming downstairs with me."

"What's wrong?" She looked at him, bleary-eyed and bewildered.

"My luck is on a down slide and I need you with me. Here, put this on." He tossed the red sequined dress on to the bed. "And these and this." The sheer red stockings and matching garter belt and g–string followed.

"Travis, I'll come with you but I told you, I'm not wearing that in public." She started to get up but suddenly found herself reeling back against the pillows, her hand on her stinging cheek.

"Put it on."

"But you promised–"

He smacked her again, harder this time, on the other cheek. "Do what I say."

At the tone of his voice, her eyes filled with tears that spilled down over her smarting face. "Please–"

"I don't have time for this, damn it. I can't lose tonight." He pulled her roughly to a standing position. "Now take off your nightgown this minute." When she didn't respond, he took the flimsy material in both of his hands, ripped it down the front and threw it aside. "Now hurry up, goddam you." As she stood there sobbing and hiding her face in her hands, he struck her on the arm, then the hip and then across her naked buttocks. His rage seemed to grow with each blow and he could not seem to stop smacking her until finally her knees buckled under her and she collapsed at his feet.

"I'll do it, I'll do it. Please don't hit me anymore!"

At the sound of her begging voice, his manner changed completely and he knelt beside her and gathered her in his arms. "I'm sorry, baby, I didn't mean to hurt you. It just makes me so mad when you don't listen to me. I'm your husband, to love, cherish and obey until death do us part." He kissed her swollen face. "I love you, you know that. Now get dressed and let's go."

Winnie hesitated only a fraction of a second before reaching for one of the stockings and beginning to work it slowly up her leg. Travis left her, but was back momentarily with her ruby and diamond choker which *he hooked around her neck as she started on the other stocking. He brushed her hair and clipped on the matching earrings as she continued dressing, keeping her gaze downcast, never once looking at herself in the mirror.*

It was no surprise to Winnie when Travis announced the next day that they were staying on so that he could win back some of his losses from the night before. She didn't seem to care anymore. She spent the day flat on her back in bed. Her butt was too sore to sit on and her head throbbed from all the martinis she had consumed to produce the necessary alcoholic haze to blur the faces in the casino.

Her self–esteem was completely gone; it was only a small shred of pride that kept her from admitting defeat and taking the next train back to New York. Travis brought her tomato juice and vodka for her hangover and she drank several glasses until it dulled the pain in head and her body, particularly her aching heart, and left her feeling pleasant and pliable. She protested when Travis tried to truss her into the black strapless sheath. But when he threatened to call her mother and describe to her what Winnie did for him so expertly on her knees, her protests became feeble. After another cocktail, she stumbled into the casino on his arm.

It was a pattern that repeated itself for the next several days. When Travis lost, he raged and beat her; when he won, he showered her with unwanted gifts. Her mornings were spent drinking Bloody Marys in bed, the afternoons were spent asleep by the pool, evenings were spent being displayed in some skimpy, revealing outfit at Travis's side in the casino or passed out in the bedroom from too much drinking. The creative, hardworking stained–glass artisan had disappeared into a frightened, submissive shell of a sex object who consumed numerous cocktails by day and night to keep away the ugly truth of what her life had become.

The crashing climax came finally at a pre–dawn, high–stakes poker game played in the smoky hotel suite of an oil baron from Oklahoma. Having already watched Travis gamble away several hundred dollars that night, Winnie had wanted to just go back to the room and sleep, but Travis insisted she come with him. Fearful of how he would treat her if she didn't do as he said, she let herself be dragged along.

Her feet hurt painfully from standing up in three–inch heels all night. After seating herself in a comfortable wing chair a few feet from the card table, she had kicked off her shoes, tucked her feet up into the folds of her silver lamé sheath and fallen asleep sitting up.

She awoke to a tickling feeling at the back of her neck and found Travis hovering over her, trying to remove her diamond necklace. "Travis, what are you doing?" she asked sleepily. The room was unusually silent and the other men were all watching them.

"I'm out of cash and I've gotta play this hand. Don't worry; you'll get it back in a minute."

"Travis, you can't–"

"That necklace is worth a fortune, Monroe. Your hand must be pretty good."

The diamonds sparkled atop the pile of hundred dollar bills.

"It is."

"You're right. But mine is better."

Cries and whistles of amazement came from the other players as Travis brought his fist down on his cards and cursed loudly.

With a gasp of horror, Winnie ran forward to grab her grandmother's necklace off the table but Travis swung out an arm to stop her. "I'll buy you another tomorrow," he hissed.

"It's an heirloom! It can't be replaced!"

"Then give me the bracelet and I'll win it back for you."

"No!"

"Give it up, Monroe. You're wiped out tonight. Pack it in."

Winnie sobbed all the way back to their room and did not stop even when Travis smacked her hard across the face a few times. He stopped abruptly and walked away from her. "Okay," he said in a dark voice. "We'll leave on the afternoon train. Have our luggage packed and ready to go."

When she threw him an accusing look through her tears, he punched her squarely in the jaw and said, "You might say, 'Thank you, Travis.'"

Fleeing to the bathroom, she locked herself in and waited until she heard no noise from the bedroom. Expecting Travis to be asleep in bed, she was surprised to find he was gone again.

Unable to unwind, she dragged their suitcases out of the closet and began to pack up. Most of the clothes she had begun the honeymoon with were either gone or destroyed. The only thing that was suitable for travel was her gray linen suit, but Travis had thrown away the high collared blouse that she usually wore with it.

It was nearly six a.m. Sighing, she sat down to call the front desk. "This is Mrs. Monroe. Can you tally up our bill for us, please, as we will be checking out this afternoon?"

"As a matter of fact, I was just doing that, Mrs. Monroe."

"You were?"

"Yes, Mr. Monroe has already informed me of your departure. I have the figure right here for you." He quoted an enormous sum of several thousand dollars which included all their meals and services for the ten previous days.

Winnie was stunned but merely said, "Thank you. And also, I'll be down in a few hours to get my jewelry out of the hotel safe."

"Oh, there'll be no need for that, Mrs. Monroe. Your husband has already seen to it."

"What do you mean?"

"He was just here a few minutes ago to retrieve your valuables from safekeeping."

Winnie hung up the phone without saying goodbye. Her head swam at the thought of where Travis was right now with her priceless, inherited jewels.

"I needed some fast cash to pay our bill. And you didn't have enough in your checkbook. Or your personal bank account."

"How do you know so much about my finances?"

"I made it my business to find out. Besides, you're my wife now, so what's yours is mine."

"Couldn't you get it wired from YOUR bank?"

Travis threw back his head and laughed coldly. *"Darling, I thought you realized by now, you ARE my bank."*

"What do you mean by that?" she snapped angrily.

"You're the one with the money in this marriage. I'm just your handsome, adoring husband who loves you to pieces and is going to invest your money wisely for you in the coming years."

If he had expected her to break down again, he was wrong. As the truth of her situation became clear to her, Winnie's eyes became round and glassy and her expression more hollow. *"What exactly did you do with my jewelry?"*

"I pawned some of it and sold the rest. It didn't quite cover it but –" He fumbled through her pocketbook on the dresser until he found her checkbook. *"There should be enough here to cover the rest of it and get us back to New York and on to Vermont. San Francisco will just have to wait for another time."*

"You sold my grandmother's jewelry?"

"Relax, Winnie." He poured her a martini but she shook her head. He sat down behind her and began

massaging her shoulders and neck. "Your mother never has to know. Besides, we had more fun with it than your sister Roberta and the missionaries would have had, now didn't we?"

CHAPTER ONE

OCTOBER 1986 – WEST JORDAN, VERMONT

As Sarah pushed open the door of the West Jordan Inn, she was greeted by the resounding slam of a telephone receiver and someone uttering a string of expletives that ended in, "Well, shit. What am I going to do now?"

Sarah cleared her throat. "Excuse me–"

The man slumping dejectedly over the front desk straightened up, startled at the sound of her voice. His stained white apron indicated he had come out of the kitchen to take the call, but the manner in which he quickly cleaned up the desk suggested that perhaps he was not only the cook. Running his fingers distractedly through his curly gray hair, his eyes focused on her at last. "Sorry. What can I do for you?"

"I'm looking for a – a room for ..." Her voice trailed off as she realized that the man had suddenly paled and was staring at her intently now. "What's the matter?"

"Nothing. I mean–" He passed a hand in front of his eyes as if to clear an image. "For a minute I thought...Never mind. You remind me of someone I used to know, that's all. Ever been here before?"

Sarah laughed a little nervously. "No, never."

"Where're you from?"

"I just drove across country from Arizona. This is my first time in New England actually." As she talked she looked around, noting the exposed wooden beams, the sloping floor of wide, painted pine boards, and the windows with their many panes of old, wavy glass. "Do you have rooms here or is this just a restaurant?"

"Well, now, we do have a few rooms upstairs that get rented out every now and then. Being well off the beaten track, we don't get many tourists out here. Except during foliage season when all the hotels fill up everywhere and they'll send some hardy folks out this way. And sometimes when somebody in town has a not–so–welcome relative come to visit, they'll put 'em up here."

He stared at her curiously again. "There's not much going on here, you know. What made you pick this place anyway?"

Sarah shrugged. "Just looking for an out–of–the–way town with lots of Vermont charm, I guess."

The smell of burning onions drifting out of the kitchen set him in action suddenly. "Holy shit. I forgot what I was doing when the phone rang. I'll be right back." There was the sound of water hissing in a sizzling pan and then he was back, drying his hands on his apron and apologizing. "Sorry, I'm a little bit behind the eight ball today. That was the bartender on the phone just now, quitting. Giving me one hour's notice."

Pulling a ring of keys off a hook behind the desk, he motioned for Sarah to follow him up a worn, wooden staircase. "Where the hell am I going to find a bartender at this hour? Does he expect me to cook and tend bar at the same time? Not to say I haven't done it before. I don't suppose you'd know how to tend bar, would you?" He unlocked the first door they came to at the top of the stairs. "Shit, I knew it, the bed hasn't been made up. Some days you just can't win."

Sarah looked around as he stormed off down the hall to the linen closet. It was a corner room, simply furnished, with a view of some distant mountains through one window, a view of Main Street out the other. She opened a door which turned out to be a closet; the bathroom was obviously down the hall.

"Actually," she said when he returned with the sheets, "I am looking for a job. My car broke down a

31

couple of times on the trip and I'm a little short on money."

He stood still for a second and gave her another inquisitive look, scrutinizing her differently now. She was long–limbed and athletic–looking, probably in her late twenties, with the healthy, naturally tanned appearance of someone who spent a lot of time outdoors. A bandana rolled up and tied as a headband kept her short dark hair out of her eyes. "You ever tended bar?"

"No. But I'm a quick learner."

His gray corkscrew curls shook as he gave a loud belly laugh. "I must be crazy, hiring a stranger, a guest."

"Look, if I had happened to walk in, looking for a job fifteen minutes from now and you didn't know I'd just come into town, you would have hired me, wouldn't you?"

"I AM crazy. Well, if you're going to be working here, I guess you can make your own bed. I'll see you downstairs in half an hour." He turned to go. "Christ, I don't even know your name. I'm Woody Foster." He held out his hand.

"Sarah Scu– Sarah Monroe."

Woody's eyes narrowed suspiciously. "You're not sure of your own last name?"

"I just got divorced and I'm taking my real name back." She turned away from him. It was only half a lie, she told herself. Sarah Monroe was her real name. Her grandmother had changed it when Sarah was a child. "Just trying to put some distance between my past and my present."

"Oh. Sorry."

Alone, Sarah sat on the unmade bed and breathed heavily. She didn't exactly know why she hadn't told him the truth about what she was doing in the tiny village of West Jordan. Maybe she wasn't ready to accept it herself yet.

It was late autumn now and nearly a year and a half had passed since that stroke of luck had given her the job at the West Jordan Inn. But still every time she unlocked the door to the lounge and flicked the light switch, her heart still pounded the same way it had that very first day when she had seen the stained glass window behind the bar.

"And that's why it's called the Night Heron lounge," Woody had informed her when he saw her standing in the doorway, staring at the colorful glass window that was the highlight of the room. She stood speechless, examining the exquisite image of a leafless tree by a river on which roosted a flock of red–eyed birds in varying shades of black, gray and white. The eyes were faceted and always seemed to be watching you wherever you stood.

"That's what those birds are – night herons." He was hurrying around, pulling chairs off tables and setting the bar up.

"It's beautiful."

Woody stood beside her for a moment. "I don't even look at it much anymore, I'm so used to it. But it's really a work of art. Winnie Scupper made it. Ever hear of her?"

Sarah cleared her throat before speaking. "My grandmother, uh, told me about her."

"She was our local celebrity around here for a little while a long time ago. I was away at the time, Korean War, but apparently she owed my father some money and he suggested she make him something he could light up and put behind his bar. He was really blown away when she brought this in. Wanted to pay her for it but she insisted that it was an even exchange. Personally, I think we got the best part of the deal. That window turns a regular old town bar into a somewhat higher class joint. You'll see what I mean. Now, over

33

here is the ice machine and you're gonna want to use this bucket under the sink–"

"Do other places in town have any of her windows?"

"Oh, yeah, a lot of the older buildings do. Once people saw this one, a lot of people in town wanted them. Or maybe we weren't the only ones she owed money to." He laughed a little. "Now, this is a pretty friendly local bar, a lot of people pass through here on a regular basis and they're all gonna know you're new in town. If you don't know how to make a drink, ask them or ask anyone else at the bar; around here chances are someone has been a bartender at one time or another. Most of them drink beer anyway. When it gets crowded, it's hard to keep an eye on the people eating at the tables..."

Taking a last appreciative look at the night herons, Sarah hung up her jacket and began working. She really had never expected to settle down in West Jordan for very long. And yet here she still was, a familiar face and a permanent fixture behind the bar of The Night Heron, the hub of life in that small town. By the end of the first month, her original reasons for visiting had become faded memories as she became readily accepted as "the prettiest bartender in West Jordan."

"I know that's not much of a compliment, considering this is the only bar in town," Woody had admitted, "But everybody likes you and in a town like this, someone who is enjoyable to look at AND talk to means a lot."

As she changed the "CLOSED" sign to "OPEN", she quickly checked her reflection in the mirror on the antique coat–rack chair by the door. Her hair had grown long since she'd left the southwest and her skin was no longer brown year 'round, although her color had come back quickly during the summer. She had hiked in the mountains nearly every day that she wasn't sunbathing at a nearby lake.

Much to her surprise, she had found that a night job suited her, leaving her days free to do whatever she wanted. She had a small amount of guilt, thinking of the money her grandmother had spent on her college education. That last year in the tiny house in Phoenix she had cared for her grandmother as she quietly wasted away, promising her anything that would make her happy. After that year of isolation, the rowdy comraderie she found at the Night Heron filled an empty space that desperately needed filling. Besides, coming to West Jordan had been one of the promises she had made to her grandmother, even if she wasn't carrying through on the reason.

Through the door she saw a car pulling into the parking lot and she quickly retreated to her place behind the bar. "Oh, it's only you. I thought it was some real customers," she joked as her landlord and his wife sat down on stools across from her. "What can I get you, Steve? Tanya?"

"Well, as long as we're here – a couple of gin and tonics. We actually just stopped by to leave off the key to our house. We're leaving tomorrow and probably won't be back up until May, so if anything should happen–"

"Not that anything is going to happen–" Tanya assured her.

"Of course not, but just in case, the plumber and the electrician know you have the key out at the cottage."

It had been love at first sight when Sarah had inquired about the one bedroom cottage that was advertised for rent on the bulletin board at the village grocery store. Up a steep hill and then turning onto first one dirt road and then another, Sarah had first been impressed with the quietness that enveloped her when she had turned off the motor and stepped out of her car. The little bungalow set into the edge of the woods had instantly appealed to her, fulfilling the fantasy she had had upon leaving Arizona about living in the mountains of Vermont.

"Anyway, you have our number in Pennsylvania in case the house should burn down or something–"

"Steve! Don't scare her. The house is not going to burn down! Everything will be shut off. Don't pay any attention to him, Sarah..."

But Sarah had already tuned them out, a useful skill she had cultivated in her year and a half of bartending. She turned her attention to the parking lot, where a couple of logging trucks were pulling in. She grimaced as she recognized the two grimy characters hopping out of their respective cabs.

"Looks like a couple of your boyfriends, Sarah," Steve commented, winking at her.

"Right. That'd be the day. For some reason I can't quite fathom, Lyle hates my guts. He wouldn't come in here at all if there was another bar in town. Maybe if I put on some music I know he can't stand, he won't stay long." She shuffled through the box of tapes under the counter and by the time the door opened, the Grateful Dead was blasting loudly through the speakers.

"Damn it all, Bo, they're playin' that hippie music again. Can't you put on Crystal Gale or Alabama or somethin'? I wish old Richie never quit workin' here. Give us a coupla Buds and a coupla shots of Jack, Sarah." Lyle twisted his greasy cap around backwards and sat down on a stool. His hands and fingers were caked with black dirt that also ran down his arms in long sticky streaks. An oily smudge ran from his ear to his mouth and the end of his nose looked like it had been wiped several times with the back of his filthy hands. Bo was dirty in a similar, but much less offensive, fashion.

"You know, Woody would prefer if you guys would clean up before you came in here. It turns the other customers off to see you two looking like this when some of them have gotten dressed up to come out."

36

"What the hell does he think this is, the fuckin' Holiday Inn? I've been living in this town all my life and no two–bit, flatlander bartender is–"

"We ain't stayin' long, Sarah," Bo assured her. "After all, there ain't no pool table or TV or nothin' here to entertain us like what they got over to the Center Club, is there now, Lyle?" Bo nudged Lyle and the two men guffawed loudly.

Sarah looked over at Steve and Tanya and rolled her eyes. There were only a few customers who came into The Night Heron that made her wish she worked somewhere else and these were two of them. Unfortunately, Lyle's brother was the town cop and Woody had instructed her to be careful how she treated Lyle. "You can't not serve him," he had explained to her, "but you can't let him get too drunk either. And you have to be careful because half the time he's already loaded when he comes in here."

Sometimes dealing with Lyle made it seem worthwhile to have a college degree in Human Psychology.

An hour late, however, the lounge was full and she still hadn't succeeded in getting rid of Lyle and Bo, when a couple of unfamiliar faces walked in the door. The room was quiet for a few seconds as most of the heads at the bar turned to see who was coming in and noted the two strangers in citified clothes. Then the conversation resumed and the newcomers were left to Sarah, who came out from behind the bar to greet them.

"Can I help you with something?"

But the man and the woman were both already staring past her at the night heron window. "Isabel, look, it's one of hers. I can't believe it. The first place we walk into in West Jordan. This is fabulous."

"Well, at least one of us is happy." The woman turned to Sarah and despite the fact that she was at least four inches shorter than Sarah, gave the impression of looking down at her. "I hope you have rooms for the night here."

"We do, but..." Sarah eyed Isabel's expensive–looking pumps, her well–designed suit, gold jewelry, expensive haircut and the way she kept her alligator purse tucked under her arm, New York style, so as not to invite pickpockets. "They're nothing fancy and they don't have private bathrooms."

Isabel's eyes widened a little, and she tugged on the sleeve of her companion who was still staring at the stained glass window. "What– oh, fine. We'll take it."

"Tyler...we at least ought to look at the room first."

"Isabel, we don't have much choice. Pretend you're on safari or something and this is your first night in Nairobi. Relax, this is an adventure!"

Sarah raised an amused eyebrow and Tyler caught her look and shrugged. They were a handsome pair; his sandy brown hair was streaked with gold, impeccably styled and blown dry for an impossibly natural look. He was wearing a brown corduroy blazer that blended well with his coloring and a very contemporary Rolex watch, which flashed in her eyes as he put his arm comfortingly around his petite girlfriend.

"Hey, Sarah, can I get my tab? I'm outta here."

"If you wait a second, I'll get the owner," she called over her shoulder as she went back behind the bar, trying to keep one ear on their conversation to see if she could learn more about them.

"I can't believe I let you talk me into coming on this trip. There aren't any leaves left on the trees up here at all!"

"Well, how was I supposed to know that? It's still fall in New York. Look, I have a feeling this story may come easier than I thought. We'll probably only have to stay here a couple of days."

"And what am I supposed to do the whole time? These people look like– like hicks!" The whispered word came out in an angry hiss.

"Oh, come on, Isabel. Think of how romantic this will sound to your friends in the city. A couple of days in an old country inn in Vermont. Look – they even have a fireplace. We'll eat cheddar cheese and apples and have pancakes with maple syrup..."

"Don't be ridiculous. I can't eat something as fattening as pancakes! I don't understand why you couldn't just get this information from a book at the library instead of tramping all the way up here."

"You still don't get it, do you? I don't want to do articles on material that is easily accessible."

"You're right, I don't get it."

Although Sarah was enjoying eavesdropping on their argument, she knew she'd better get Woody while she had a chance. She would find out later why this guy was doing some kind of story on West Jordan.

It was a busy evening and it was not until much later, when most of the customers had gone home, that she got a chance to chat with the house guests. Tyler and Isabel had finished their "romantic supper" at a little table in front of the fireplace and were now sitting at the bar, sipping Courvoisier from oversized brandy snifters. Isabel was more than a little drunk and in much better spirits than earlier. Tyler had changed into casual clothes, but his plaid shirt, wide wale corduroys and forest green fisherman sweater all matched a little too perfectly to seem truly casual.

"So what brings you two all the way out here to this tiny little hamlet?" Sarah asked over her shoulder as she cleared away the dishes that still remained on their table.

"I'm an investigative reporter –"

Isabel burst into laughter. "Tyler Mackenzie, Investigative Reporter," she said sarcastically in a dramatic voice. "It's really his own fancy title for being a freelance journalist for any magazine that will take his stories."

"So what could you possibly be doing a story on up here? If you're looking for fall foliage, you missed the leaves by about two weeks." Sarah gave a final wipe to the table top and returned to her place behind the bar.

"Winnie Scupper, of course. Some friends of mine in the city have one of her windows and told me a little bit about her tragic story. I thought I would come up here to see if I could find out any more for myself. It hadn't even occurred to me that there would be a gold mine of her glass work up here, but what's his name, Woody? He says this town is full of her windows. They're very valuable in New York right now; sort of a trendy thing to own."

"Really?"

"He says there are older people in town who remember her and what happened. Gave me a few names to talk to. Did you grow up around here? I don't suppose you'd be old enough to remember her anyway."

"I came here from Arizona about a year and a half ago." Sarah's voice was a little faint. She bent down to pick up a knife she had dropped and her face was flushed when she stood up.

"I told you she didn't look like she was local," Isabel said triumphantly, slurring her words a little. "Tyler thought you looked familiar. Didn't you use to work in that club on 59th Street?"

Sarah gave a small smile. "No, I've only been to New York City a couple of times. And this is the first place I ever tended bar." She turned to Tyler. "I don't think we've ever met, I would have remembered you."

Tyler's eyes narrowed as he looked at her. "I guess you remind me of someone..."

"Tyler, I'm falling asleep sitting here. Let's go to bed." Isabel closed her eyes and rested her head possessively on his shoulder.

"Why don't you go up and I'll join you in a few minutes. I'm still kind of revved up from the drive. I think I'd like another one these, if you don't mind, Sarah?"

As Sarah poured another shot of brandy into his snifter, he walked Isabel over to the door of the room and kissed her goodnight. At the same time Woody poked his head in and said, "You all set, Sarah? I'm off to bed."

The only other two customers took this as a cue to drain their beers and put on their coats. Sarah locked the outside door behind them and, leaning against it for a second, closed her eyes and took a deep breath. Should she do it? It was only a matter of time now before someone found out.

"So you must like it here."

Tyler was back on his stool and she squared her shoulders, putting on her professional facade again for another few minutes.

"Yes, I do. It surprised me that I would enjoy this kind of work, but I like the people here and I like this town and –" She poured herself a stiff shot of tequila and knocked it back quickly.

"And?"

Her cheeks flushed again, this time presumably from the tequila. "And, believe it or not, I like never knowing exactly how much money I might make. Every night is different. Usually I make a lot, but sometimes, on a sub–zero night, no one comes in and I make diddly. But that's the fun part about it. You know, kind of like gambling."

"My work is a little bit like that too. The magazine I work for never assigns me anything interesting to do. I usually get the stories on city planning and budget deficits. It's my bread and butter, but the kind of work I like doing is never the kind I'm assigned to do. I never know if I'm going to be able to sell something I do on my own, like this article on Winnie Scupper." He sipped a little of his brandy. "I just hope I can find some people in this town who can remember when she was alive."

He looked up just in time to see Sarah downing another shot of tequila. "It's okay. We're closed now," she said quickly. Leaning across the bar, her next words came out in a husky, confidential tone. "I'd like to help you with your – your – `investigation'."

Misinterpreting her advance, he leaned back on his stool a little. "Uh, thanks. I can use all the help I can get, but I don't see how you– I mean, you aren't from around –"

"My name is Sarah Monroe." As she cut him off, her voice came out unnaturally loud. Taking another deep breath, she spoke quietly again. "But until I came here I was known as Sarah Scupper. Winnie Scupper was my mother."

CHAPTER TWO

"Winnie Scupper was your...mother?"

Sarah nodded as Tyler stared at her in amazement.

"Why didn't you mention this before?"

"Because nobody here knows. You're the first person I've told."

"But, why?" He could not take his eyes off her now.

"I don't know. When I came here a year and a half ago, I'd never planned to stay. And then everything happened so quickly. I didn't know how people would react."

"So it was no accident that you ended up here."

Sarah sighed and looked away. "When my grandmother died, I promised her that I would come to West Jordan and –" she stopped suddenly, before she revealed too much to this stranger who might be ready to publicize every word she uttered. "How much do you know?" she asked abruptly.

"What do you mean,'how much do I know'? About what?"

"Do you know anything about my father?"

Tyler looked uncomfortable. "I know he was a playboy and a professional gambler and that he didn't hang around very long. Why?"

Sarah stared down at her long legs stretched out in front of her. "All I know is what my grandmother Charlotte told me and she hated him more than anyone on earth. She says he ruined us, our family, I mean."

Tyler resisted the urge to pull out a pen and notepad and asked gently, "How did he do that?"

"She told me we used to have a lot of money. She said that because my mother had been so dependable and level–headed and her other daughter, my Aunt Roberta, was a compulsive religious fanatic, that my grandmother had put most of the family stocks and property in my mother's name, just in case she should die suddenly. She wanted to make sure everything stayed in the family. Then my father came along and my mother made the one impulsive move of her life – she married him."

Noting the empty glass in Tyler's hand, Sarah automatically got up and refilled it, pouring one for herself as well.

"I guess after they got married, they didn't visit my grandmother very much and she had no idea what was happening. But after my mother died, it turned out that all the property and bank accounts had been put in both of their names jointly. Not only had my father gambled away all the money, but he owed so much that, to cover his debts, both houses had to be sold, the one in New York and the one here in Vermont."

Tyler whistled softly. "I had no idea..."

"Most people don't. It just about killed my grandmother. I never knew most of this until I was older. I was only an infant at the time and all I ever knew was the two bedroom apartment in an old Victorian house near White Plains where she raised me. She moved to Arizona about ten years ago – she thought it would be good for her health."

There was a silence while Tyler digested the story. "So I still don't understand why you didn't want anyone here to know who you were."

"Do I have to worry that everything I say is going to end up in print somewhere?"

"Well, this is a great story but–" He held up his hand. "You have my word. If there's anything you don't want me to write about, I promise you I won't."

Sarah gazed down into the amber liquid at the bottom of her glass and then back up into Tyler's eyes, distracted momentarily by the fact that his eyes were nearly the same color as the brandy.

"It's funny," she mused half to herself. "The people in this town think I'm not a native but the truth is I was born here. I lived here until I was three months old. That was when my mother died."

"Now that's the part I'm unclear about. How did she die?"

"That's the part everybody's unclear about. My grandmother started telling me all kinds of things during that last year when she knew she was dying and I was caring for her. And one of the things she kept saying was that she always thought there was something fishy about how my mother died, but she never wanted to talk about the specifics. But I know that was one of the reasons she urged me to come here to West Jordan."

"And you thought–" Tyler spoke slowly, choosing his phrases carefully– "that if no one knew who you were, you might be able to get a more objective view."

"That was part of it. And partly I wanted people to accept me for who I was, I didn't want them gawking at me and making wide circles around me just because my last name was Scupper. Grandmother Charlotte had the Monroe dropped off my name before I could even talk. I never even knew about it until I needed my birth certificate so I could register to vote."

"So you mean to tell me that not even this guy here who you work for, Woody, knows that his bartender is the daughter of the artist who made this exquisite piece of glass work?" He made a mental note to get a picture of her working in front of the Night Heron window.

She laughed. "Sometimes I wonder. He knew my mother, and I looked familiar to him – the same way I looked familiar to you."

He snapped his fingers. "Of course! I never would have made the connection if I didn't know why."

"Anyway, after I'd made some friends here and sort of settled into my own life, I just stopped really caring. I decided the past is the past and I'm happy enough in the present. It doesn't really matter to me if I'm ever rich. Money only seems to bring people trouble, anyway."

Tyler frowned, not quite following her train of thought. "What do you mean? How was coming here and finding out how your mother died going to make you rich?"

"Well, I guess I'll have to tell it all to you now, won't I?" Sarah was beginning to feel very relaxed, not only because of the liquor but as a result of unburdening the secrets she'd been keeping for so long. "Like I said, my mother's death was only part of the reason for coming here."

"And what was the other part?" Tyler leaned forward in anticipation of her reply.

Sarah laughed a little. "This is going to sound crazy, but – here goes. During the last few months of her life, my grandmother kept slipping in out of reality and sometimes she ranted incoherently. I didn't always pay close attention. She became obsessed with talking about the family jewels. Apparently her mother, my great–grandmother, had been European aristocracy who had come to America with a dowry of priceless jewelry. Grandmother Charlotte had given most of it to my mother when she married. When my mother died and my grandmother came up here to take me back to New York, she couldn't find any of that jewelry anywhere. When it turned out that my father literally had to sell my grandmother's house out from under her, she questioned him about the heirloom jewelry. He claimed that everything had already been sold in the previous years and–"

Sarah stopped for a moment and laughed softly to herself again, this time wiping a few tears away from her eyes. "I'm sorry. She must have told me about that conversation fifty times, how she slapped him across the face and called him filthy names I cannot even imagine her saying, let alone knowing the meaning of. But she swore over and over again that Winnie would not have let him sell those jewels. She would have hidden them somewhere, or left them with a friend or, I don't know, buried them in the backyard maybe."

There was a moment of silence and then Sarah lifted her eyes to meet Tyler's with an unspoken challenge.

Tyler cleared his throat. "Well, that's a pretty wild story, Ms. Scupper–Monroe. What do you propose to do about it?"

"What can I do about it? Once I got here it seemed like a wild goose chase. What am I going to do? Go dig up somebody's backyard of the old house where she lived? I mean, we're talking about thirty years ago. If somebody gave you a bunch of diamonds for safekeeping and then up and died, what would you do with them?" She stood up abruptly, retrieved a broom from a closet in the corner and began sweeping up around the barstools.

"Well, you could at least talk to some people and find out who she was close to and who might remember her." He followed her around the room, talking to her as she swept. "I can't believe you've lived here a year and a half and haven't pursued this."

"And what would I find out? I know this much, nobody will agree on what happened. In a small town like this, when one old person tells a story about something, two dozen other people will repeat that version as the gospel truth."

"But there are ways–"

"Look, I'm not an `investigative reporter'–"

"But I am."

Sarah turned sharply, about to make a smart, sarcastic remark, but Tyler's expression of sincere interest made her come up short. Before she could say anything he grabbed her by the arm and said, "Let me help you, Sarah."

She snorted and pulling her arm away, continued sweeping. "Who would be helping who here? Somehow, Tyler, when it was all over, I think you would be the rich one, not me."

"I thought you didn't care about being rich."

"I don't."

"But you do care about finding out the truth behind all this, don't you? Don't you want to at least know how your mother died?" Taking her lack of response as affirmative, he went on. "Okay, meet me here tomorrow morning and we'll do some exploring together. You can be my guide to West Jordan and I'll be your guide in your search for the past."

She was put off by his presumptuous attitude, but having just related the whole story to him, she was once again feeling intrigued by the prospect of unraveling her family secrets. "Okay, okay. I'll do it."

They agreed on a time to meet and Tyler said goodnight. "It's so late," he said almost as an afterthought. "Are you sure you'll be all right getting home?"

Sarah burst into loud laughter. "I do this every night I work! Of course, I'll be all right."

"You're not scared to drive home alone at this time of night?"

"Why should I be? This isn't the city. Most people here don't even lock their doors at night." She shook her head. "Now go to bed and don't worry about me."

She was glad when he finally went upstairs. It was true that most nights she locked up and walked across the dark parking lot to her car without a second thought. But every now and then she had the feeling she was being watched; once she was almost sure someone had followed her part of the way home.

She shook herself and put her mind back on closing up. There was no point getting spooked over nothing. She had dealt with all her silly fears during the first few weeks of living alone in the cabin in the woods. She had become ultra–sensible and was able to identify sounds for what they were – a branch scraping on the roof, or the walls shrinking and crackling from dropping temperatures on a subzero night.

If she started getting scared again, she would not be able to survive here. She counted the cash in the register and pocketed her tips. Turning off the lights, she walked directly to her car without once looking over her shoulder.

"Let's start with the library." Tyler fastened the seat belt in the front passenger seat of Sarah's car. "Woody told me there were some great examples of your mother's work in the building there."

"You didn't tell him–"

"I think that's up to you, don't you?"

Sarah breathed a sigh of relief and then chuckled. "We can't start with the library. It's only open on Tuesday and Thursday afternoons and on Saturday."

"Well, all right then. How about the cemetery?"

"The cemetery? You want to see her gravestone?"

Tyler shrugged. "It's a place to start. I bet you don't even know what day she died."

Sarah started up the engine and turned right onto the main road, heading in the direction of the cemetery. "Actually I did go there once, the first week I was here."

Tyler took advantage of being able to take a good look at her as she kept her eyes fixed on the road. Although he could sense her tenseness, she appeared casually at ease with her long body. Her thick, dark hair grazed the padded shoulders of the wool jacket she was wearing open over a red cotton sweater. A snug pair of faded blue jeans accentuated her endless legs. But it was her red Reebok high top sneakers that made him feel uncomfortably overdressed in his white shirt and tie, even if he had substituted a thick wool cardigan for his usual suit jacket.

Sensing that she was getting the once over, Sarah threw him a withering look as she turned the corner and stopped at the iron gate of the West Jordan cemetery. He hid behind his Vuarnet sunglasses as he retrieved his camera case from the back seat.

Sarah was already heading across the grass, dry leaves crunching underfoot as she passed beneath the large oaks that graced the graveyard with their stately presence. Although the sun shone brightly through the bare branches, its warmth hardly took the edge off the brisk and breezy autumn day. When Sarah stopped finally and looked down at a particular headstone, Tyler shot a quick picture of her before she looked up and called him over.

"So – Winifred Amelia Scupper Monroe. Born January 18th, 1920. Died August 27th, 1955. Doesn't tell you much, does it?" Sarah did not look at him as she spoke.

"Well, now we know the exact date she died. If we can get into the archives of the local newspaper, we know which edition to start looking in to find out what was reported on her death at the time. And that newspaper will give me names of local people who may still be around and who may love to talk about a long dead local celebrity."

Sarah regarded him with increasing interest. Maybe he did know what he was doing. She was glad that Isabel had opted to take their rental car and drive to Montpelier for some shopping. She did not feel particularly comfortable around Tyler's girlfriend or wife or whatever she was.

They drove down the road about five miles to Jordan Center, where the weekly newspaper, The Jordan Ledger, had its office building. Tyler asked Sarah lots of questions about her family and recorded their conversation on a small, voice–activated tape recorder that fit into the pocket of his sweater.

"The truth is, I know almost nothing about her life after she married my father and moved up here. Apparently, she almost never called my grandmother after that and the letters and holiday cards she wrote were very generic, dutiful messages about things like the weather and her health and small town gossip."

"You said they used to vacation here when Winnie was a child. Probably she would have looked up some old family friends when she moved up here, don't you think? Did your grandmother mention any names of people she knew from back then?"

"We're talking about the late 1920's! Anyone who was alive back then would be in a nursing home by now."

"Precisely. And that's a great place to look for some of these people. Woody mentioned a couple of old timers that still have sharp memories. But let's see, if Winnie was alive today she would be sixty–five."

"That's not so old. There must be lots of people who remember her."

"And she was thirty when she got married, a fairly ripe old age for those days, if you don't mind my saying so. You would think she would have gotten started on having children right away. But no – she was thirty–five when she gave birth to you and then three months later she died."

"Maybe she had trouble getting pregnant," Sarah snapped at him. "But I don't see why that should matter to any of your readers."

That ended the conversation until they were in the basement of the Jordan Ledger building, looking through a stack of newspapers from the file drawer marked 1955–56.

"I can't believe they don't have this stuff on microfiche," Tyler complained after the secretary had left them alone. "It's criminal. These papers will disintegrate if too many people look at them."

"It's a tiny operation. I'm sure they can't afford it. Oh, my God, look. Here it is." They both looked at the headline of the old newspaper Sarah held in her hand. "Freak Accident May Claim Life of Local Artist." Suddenly overcome by new emotions at the realization that her mother did not die an instant death, Sarah thrust the paper at Tyler. "You read it to me."

She sat down on a wooden folding chair and faced slightly away from him. Tyler cleared his throat and began to read.

"A local woman lies in critical condition at the Jordan Center hospital after a near fatal accident on Tuesday night in West Jordan. Winifred Scupper Monroe, 35, was found early Wednesday morning on the banks of the Sugartree River just below the highway bridge on Route 73. West Jordan patrolman, Earl Dewers, says he was alerted by a call from Dora Evans, the Monroe's housekeeper, who claimed that Mrs. Monroe was missing from home at dawn on Wednesday. Mrs. Monroe, known to most people by her professional name of Winnie Scupper, had apparently taken her dog for a walk around 11 p.m. the night before as was her usual custom, according to Evans. It is believe she lost her footing while crossing the bridge and plunged over the railing to the rocky riverbed, 53 feet below. The dog, a German shepherd, was sitting patiently beside her when she was found unconscious and bleeding. Rushed to the hospital, she was diagnosed as having several broken bones and a fractured skull. 'It was a freak accident,' was Patrolman Dewers comment. 'Unless she regains consciousness we'll never know what really happened.'

"Winnie Scupper is well–known for her stained glass windows that can be seen in many buildings throughout the town of West Jordan and that grace many of the finer homes of New York City. She is a native of Bedford Hills, New York, and has made her home for the past five years in West Jordan. Her husband, Mr. Travis Monroe is out of town and could not be reached for comment. Mrs. Evans is caring for their three month old daughter until relatives can be notified."

"Anything else?"

"Situation in Argentina Worsens Under Dictator Juan Peron." Tyler flipped quickly through the remainder of the eight page paper. "Look at this! They list the names of people who got tickets for speeding and traffic violations."

"They still do that. And their ages and addresses. Not usually much other news in a small town." Sarah stood up and looked over Tyler's shoulder at the picture of Winnie Scupper beneath the front page article. "She must have died the next day."

"If you did your hair like that you would look just like her." Tyler handed the paper to Sarah and looked back in the file. "This next paper would be a week later and would probably have the obituary."

"No wonder my grandmother would never tell me the details. How gruesome it must have been for her." Sarah looked at the article. "The Route 73 bridge. How many times have I driven over that and never even known..."

"I wonder if that Dora Evans is still alive. She would be an interesting person to talk to." Tyler was so swept along in the thrill of discovery that he was not aware of Sarah's mood. "And you must know where the old house is. I think we ought to make a visit there too, talk to the current owners."

"It's been turned into apartments. I don't think the owner lives around here."

The tone of her voice made Tyler look up. "Listen, Sarah, you shouldn't let this depress you. If you don't want to come around with me, you don't have to. But like you said yourself, this all happened a long time ago and in the end, it might not even have any effect on your life."

"It's too late – it's already having an effect on me." She passed the back of her hand across her eyes and then squared her shoulders. "So let's get on with it."

They had lunch at the only restaurant still open on Main Street in Jordan Center. "Almost everything closes October 15th, as soon as foliage season is over," Sarah explained, "and doesn't open again until Christmas."

By the time they returned to West Jordan, the library was due to open, so they waited on the steps of the small square brick building for the librarian to arrive and unlock the door.

"The only brick building in town," Sarah commented. "Less likely to burn down that way, I guess."

The morning's invigorating breeze had grown into a cold, sharp wind that whipped Sarah's hair around her face as she talked and gave her cheeks a healthy glow. She looked up to see the crystal blue sky being quickly obscured by dark, foreboding clouds. "I hate to say it, but it feels like snow."

"Snow!" Tyler laughed heartily. "This early?"

"It's been known to happen."

"Isabel will throw a fit if it snows while we're here! Oh, look, this must be the librarian."

A stooped, gray–haired woman carrying an armful of books was making her way up the path, bent double against the threatening wind. "Winter's here early this year," she remarked breathlessly to them as she rummaged in her purse for the key. Muttering to herself, she unbuttoned her coat and put on a pair of glasses that hung from a chain around her neck. "Aha, there's the little bugger. Now we can go in. Oh, it's you, Sarah. Can't see up close worth a darn these days."

"Hello, Mrs. Winslow. Let me help you there." Sarah relieved the older woman of her heavy load, but Tyler pulled her back to let Mrs. Winslow go in alone.

"She's old enough to remember your mother!" he hissed in her ear. "Is she lucid?"

"You'll have to judge that for yourself!" Sarah dumped the books into his arms. "There. Go make conversation with her." She stepped aside to let him pass.

"Hey, what's going on?" He turned to her, puzzled. "Did I say something wrong?"

"I don't know. I guess I'm still afraid of this whole thing, of ruining my peaceful existence here with ugly truths from the past."

"Don't be ridiculous. Look, you just go in and pretend to look for a book and listen to how I do it. You don't have to say a word and if you don't like what you hear you can just step outside and then I'll know it's time to go." Without waiting for a reply, he entered the library. Sulking, Sarah followed behind him. She still had a feeling she was a pawn in Tyler's game, but her own curiosity was getting the better of her.

She listened as Tyler smoothly introduced himself and his project, flashing his credentials. Mrs. Winslow was already dazzled by the idea of someone doing research right here in West Jordan on Winnie Scupper's windows. She and Tyler admired what she called "The Blackberry Borders" and "The Green Mountain Valances" that surrounded the four large windows of the library's only room.

"You can see that each of the valances depicts a different season. The winter one is the most beautiful – a night time scene. See how the stars actually seem to sparkle in the sky!"

Sarah had to admit that Tyler was incredibly polite and attentive to Mrs. Winslow, who was well known for her gushing descriptions, which could be excruciating at times. "Did you know Winnie Scupper when she lived here?" he asked. The genuine interest was so obvious in his voice that Sarah felt guilt at having distrusted him.

"Of course, we all knew her! I mean, not as a close friend. She didn't seem to socialize much but she did read a lot, at least at first." Mrs. Winslow frowned and rubbed her forehead, thinking.

"So you were the librarian back then?" Tyler could not conceal his excitement. "Thirty years ago?"

"Oh, it was more than thirty years ago, young man. Yes, I was the town librarian when Winnie made these windows for us. There is a little story behind them if I can get it straight."

Sarah saw Tyler's hand slip into his pocket and flick the switch of his tape recorder. Sleazy, she thought. That must be illegal. But then Tyler said, "You don't mind if I record our conversation, do you?"

Deep in her own recollections, Mrs. Winslow just stared at the winter sky window and did not answer.

"What do you mean by `she read a lot at first'?"

"Well, I'm trying to recall now just exactly what the circumstances were that blessed us with these windows." Lost in thought, she sat down automatically in the chair that Tyler pulled out for her. "Well, I remember that she lived up there in that old house all by herself most of the time. I guess her husband did a lot of traveling, he was almost never home. I always knew when he was around because she never came down to the library then."

"I don't suppose you remember what kind of books she used to take out."

Sarah started with indignation that Tyler should expect the old librarian to remember such trivia. She was surprised when Mrs. Winslow answered him.

"Well, she didn't take novels or bestsellers much. It was mostly art books and field identification guides and books on birds and flowers and sometimes the reference books. It was my fault really. I should never have let her take them."

"Take what?"

"The reference books. They're not supposed to leave the library. They're so expensive, you know. When she didn't bring them back right away, I figured nobody would notice. Most people don't do research in this library, they go into Jordan Center or into St. Johnsbury. But she was always on foot."

"She walked to the library."

"It was only a couple of miles. If people saw her walking they'd offer her a ride. Her husband always had the car with him on his business trips."

Tyler glanced meaningfully at Sarah. "And what did he do for a living?"

"Oh, I don't remember. Can't say if I ever knew. I doubt that I ever met the man. Anyway, it was the record player that finally did it." She chuckled to herself and then continued. "We had one of those old portable record players, hardly portable by today's standards mind you, it was a big, square box and occasionally I would lend it out to some civic organization or to the grammar school. Anyway, one day Winnie came in begging to borrow it for the weekend."

"She walked home with the record player?"

The wrinkles around Mrs. Winslow's faded blue eyes creased with thought. "No, I believe she had the car that day. Her husband must've have been home. Anyway, she came back in the next time the library was open, must have been a Tuesday afternoon, and she was crying and said the record player had gotten ruined and she didn't know what to do. Well, I quickly assured her that it could probably be repaired for a few dollars and then she said," she paused here, shaking her head. "Funny how I can remember this part clear as a bell. She said that it had been destroyed beyond repair. I still find that hard to believe. How could a phonograph be

57

`destroyed beyond repair' unless someone took a sledge hammer to it?"

Once again Tyler's eyes met Sarah's across the room. Delighted with her rapt audience, Mrs. Winslow took no notice and continued.

"Now this is the other part that I have a hard time believing. When I told her she would just have to buy the library a replacement, she started crying even harder and she said she didn't have the money. Now there she was, wiping her eyes on a lace–trimmed handkerchief that she pulled out of the pocket of her cashmere coat. Now how is it that a lady like that wouldn't have enough money to buy a portable phonograph?"

There was a loud clatter as the book Sarah had been absentmindedly holding in front of her slid to the floor. "Sorry," she apologized. "Don't let me interrupt you."

"Oh, I forgot you were here, Sarah. You let me know when you're ready to check your books out." As she looked over her shoulder at Sarah, Tyler was shaking his head vigorously and frantically mouthing the word, "No."

"I'm not done looking yet. Don't mind me, Mrs. Winslow."

"So, anyway, Mr. Mackenzie, to make a long story short, I was going to lose my job for lending out the record player unless she and I came up with some great idea. That was when she suggested making the windows as payment for the record player and the reference books. It took a little bit of fast talking with the library trustees who were certainly a crusty old lot in those days. But in the end it saved her skin and mine. We did a little fundraiser, supposedly to pay for the windows, and raised enough to buy a brand new record player and replace the lost books. I never did understand how she lost those big books."

"Well, that is certainly quite a story, Mrs. Winslow. Would you mind if I took a few pictures of your 'valances'?"

"Of course not." Mrs. Winslow got up rather stiffly. "I don't suppose what I've told you is very useful."

"On the contrary. Can you think of anybody else who might remember some stories about Winnie Scupper?" Tyler began setting up a collapsible tripod for his camera.

"Oh, I don't know. It's so long ago. Probably anyone over fifty who lived here back then would have something to tell you." She gave a furtive glance at Sarah and lowered her voice. "But there's so many newcomers these days. It's hard to remember who's native and who's not sometimes."

"What about the woman who was her housekeeper at the time of the accident? Dora somebody." He shuffled in his bag for his notes.

"Oh, Dora Evans? You won't get much out of her. She's got kind of a chip on her shoulder, won't talk to most people. Lives over on the back side of Darby Mountain. I've even heard tell she's a little cuckoo. At the time people said that Winnie's accident really upset her, but she's always been a bit loony since then."

They talked for a little longer, ascertaining which of the local business people had been around long enough to have known Winnie Scupper. By the time Sarah and Tyler left the library, they had been given a wonderful synopsis of local history. The old postmaster was dead; the general store had gone out of business and the owner retired to Florida; they'd closed the one room schoolhouse in the sixties and bussed the children to Jordan Center now; the gas station must've changed hands a dozen times since the fifties. Of course, Woody's father, old Elwood senior, must have known Winnie pretty well since she made that fancy stained glass window for his bar.

59

"What a find! She was fabulous." Tyler could not stop talking about Mrs. Winslow as they walked back to the car.

"Shit. Look at the time." Sarah cut him off suddenly as she noticed the clock on the dashboard. "I barely have time to drop you off and race home and change my clothes. I'm supposed to be at work in twenty minutes."

"Sorry about that. I just lost all track of time. I forgot you had to work tonight." He fastened his seat belt as, with a squeal of the tires, Sarah took off back in the direction of the inn.

They had not gone more than half a mile when Sarah once again said, "Shit." This time her eyes were glued to the rear view mirror which reflected the flashing blue lights of the police car behind them.

"Just what I need, a speeding ticket," she grumbled as she pulled off to the side of the road.

"It's my fault. If I hadn't stayed so long at the library, you wouldn't have been speeding. If he gives you a ticket, I'll pay it," Tyler offered apologetically.

"It's Lyle's brother, Brian," Sarah said, recognizing the square, solid figure that came towards them.

"Is that good or bad?"

"Guess we'll find out soon enough." Sarah rolled down the car window.

"Well, Sarah, I didn't recognize you, speeding by like a bat out of hell." Brian peered into the car to get a good look at Tyler. "This is a thirty–mile–an–hour zone through town here. I clocked you going fifty–five."

"Really? That doesn't seem possible. I couldn't have been going that fast." Sarah batted her dark eyelashes at him in a gesture that was just short of mockery.

"Can I see your license and registration please." It was more of a statement than a question.

"Tyler, would you get the registration out of the glove com–" Sarah stopped in mid–sentence as she stared at the license that she had just pulled out of her wallet. Swallowing hard, she handed the two requested items over to Brian.

"What's this? An Arizona driver's license? How long have you lived in Vermont, Miss ...Scupper?" His voice rose as he read the last name on the driver's license. "I didn't know that was your last name, Sarah."

"Well, it's not real–, it's not–" Sarah stammered, flustered.

"Hold on a second. This car is registered to Sarah S. Monroe. That you too?"

"Well, yes. The S is for Scupper."

"Oh, I get it. Right, you were just divorced when you came here..." Brian scratched his brow thoughtfully. Something did not add up, but he couldn't figure exactly what it was. Besides the fact that those two last names reminded him of something from when he was a kid. "Are you related to that artist woman who used to live around here? Her last name was Scupper too."

"Yes, I am." Sarah looked at Tyler helplessly.

Tyler leaned across her and said through the window. "Look, Sarah's late for work and we're kind of in a hurry, Officer..." he squinted at Brian's badge...Evans." He sat back and murmured aloud to himself, "Evans?"

"I noticed you were in a hurry. About twenty five miles over the speed limit in a hurry. That's too much to give you just a warning, Sarah. I'm going to have to write you a ticket." As he walked back to his cruiser Tyler touched Sarah's sleeve excitedly.

"His last name is Evans. That's the same–"

"It's a common name around here, Tyler. Can't you just let the whole thing rest for now?" she said crossly. "It's bad enough he knows my last name is Scupper now. What's even worse is that it will be printed in the Jordan Ledger next week along with my age and address."

"Can't we bribe him or something to keep it out?"

"Don't even try! You can go home to your big city anonymity, but I live here, Tyler. Shit, if I'd only kept my mouth shut last night, I wouldn't be here with you now and this wouldn't even be happening."

"Oh, come on, Sarah. What difference can it really make now? Despite what your grandmother led you to believe, you should be proud of your talented mother. From what we've found so far today, there doesn't seem to be any reason not to admit that you're the daughter of Winnie Scupper and Travis Monroe. Is there?"

"Oh, I don't know. He'll probably come back here and hand me some thirty–year–old parking ticket that my mother never paid and that now, with compounded interest, comes to $30,000." She gave Tyler another sour look and then they both burst out laughing.

Brian was put off by their laughter when he returned. People were not supposed to be enjoying themselves when they were being ticketed for speeding. He tore the pink carbon copy out of his metal clipboard and it rippled violently in the wind as he passed it to Sarah through the window.

"You have thirty days to get a Vermont driver's license, Ms. Scupper Monroe. If you change your name again, you are required by law to let the Department of Motor Vehicles know. And next time allow yourself more time to get to work. I don't want to have to stop you again."

"I'll take that." Tyler took the speeding ticket out of Sarah's hand and tucked it in his shirt pocket. "Evans..."

"Don't."

Tyler settled back into his seat and closed his eyes for a moment. Despite the fact Sarah was so nervous about his story, they already had the kind of comfortable, open rapport it sometimes took weeks to establish with a co–worker, let alone a subject. He wondered how Isabel had enjoyed her day.

CHAPTER THREE

The evening was busier than usual and Sarah was grateful that Isabel had insisted that Tyler take her out to dinner at a posh little restaurant she had discovered about twenty miles down the road towards Montpelier. Still in a bad mood, she was not up to setting up another romantic fireplace supper for them.

A rowdy crowd of highway workers were her first customers of the night and a few of them settled in, setting the tone for the rest of the evening. When Tyler and Isabel returned around ten for a nightcap, there were several people shouting loudly and clapping while an enormously fat man stood in the middle of the floor, shaking his flabby belly to "Whole Lot of Shaking Going On."

Isabel paled and wrinkled her nose disdainfully as Tyler led her past the spectacle to the far end of the bar. He ordered two B and B's. "To put a little color back into your face," he said to Isabel when Sarah brought them a couple of brandy snifters. "Maybe you should take a hike tomorrow, get yourself some natural, healthy color like Sarah has."

Sarah flushed and busied herself washing glasses, pretending that she hadn't heard him. It was true that Isabel did have a pasty, inner–city complexion which was accentuated even more tonight by the black turtleneck dress she was wearing.

"I'm not going hiking alone! There are bear and moose up here, not to mention what kind of crazy, inbred mountain man I might meet."

Tyler rolled his eyes and with a finger to his lips, indicated Lyle sitting to the right of him. Lyle had his back to them and hadn't heard a thing. "You probably have gone hiking alone lots of times, haven't you, Sarah?"

"Well, not lots of times. But it's not a good idea for someone who doesn't do much hiking to go off alone the first time."

"See? Tyler's told me a lot about you this evening, Sarah." Isabel deftly changed the subject. "It's a fascinating story. I'm glad it was worth our while to come all the way up here." She patted Tyler's hand possessively.

"And what do you do in New York?" Sarah tossed the ball back again. "Are you a journalist also?"

"No, not me. I–"

"The income wouldn't be steady enough for Isabel," Tyler interrupted jokingly.

"You seem to enjoy my steady income between jobs, Tyler. I work for a brokerage firm as an investment counselor."

"Oh." Sarah had very little idea what that entailed but there was something about Isabel's superiority that seemed to say, if you have to ask, it means you're not as smart as me.

"Tyler tells me you studied psychology in college."

What hadn't Tyler told her? "That's right."

"It seems funny, you know." Isabel's brandy was almost gone already.

"What does?"

"You know, you have a college degree, but you're a bartender." Isabel said the word with such obvious distaste that Sarah burst out laughing and Tyler's jaw dropped in embarrassment.

"Isabel!"

"Well, anybody can be a bartender, but if you have enough brains to graduate with a degree–"

"Why don't you just be quiet before you swallow your foot whole?" Tyler said in a low insistent voice.

Sarah laughed again. She did not really care what Isabel thought, so her rude comments did not bother her the way they did Tyler. "It's all right. I actually like this work, Isabel. You never know who you're going to meet or what's going to happen."

"I bet it's not as easy as it looks either," Tyler put in hastily. "I'd like to see you back there, Isabel."

Other customers needed attention and Sarah left them to their personal arguing. She avoided their end of the bar, but every now and then she caught Tyler looking at her with an apologetic expression in his eyes.

Eventually the crowd thinned out and Isabel and Tyler retired to their room, after arranging to meet Sarah again in the morning. She was extremely tired after staying late the night before to talk to Tyler. She could barely wait to get home to the quiet solitude of her cottage and the cozy comfort of her bed.

A heavy, wet snow had begun to fall and Sarah shivered as she carried the garbage out to the dumpster behind the kitchen. A cracking sound in the bushes near the road made her heart leap. But as she hurried back into the building, she assured herself, in her ever-practical way, that the kind of weighty snow that fell at warmer winter temperatures always made branches snap and break.

The road surfaces were still too warm for the snow to stick, but everything else was covered with the glistening white coat of the first snowfall of the season. Clusters of large wet flakes stuck to her hair and coat as she fumbled for her car keys at the door to her car. There would be slick places tonight, especially the bridges, and she would have to concentrate on her driving. It was a short and easy four miles; she could do it with her eyes closed, and sometimes she wondered if she did.

The windshield wipers had a hard time cleaning the heavy snow off the windshield and it took a while before the rear defroster began working. Consequently, she was surprised when she discovered that a car was following her up the hill on the road out of town.

She wondered idly who it could be; almost nobody was out at this time of night in West Jordan. But when she turned off the main highway onto the dirt and gravel road, the car behind her also made the turn. There was almost no one who lived on this road at this time of year and she began to seriously consider that someone was following her. When she passed the crossroad that led to South Jordan one way and was a treacherous, muddy track back to Jordan Center in the opposite direction, the headlights were still reflected in her rearview mirror, although some distance behind her now.

Looking over her shoulder nervously, she was surprised to see the headlights go dark suddenly. Probably it was someone who realized they were lost and had decided to turn around and go back. She drove a little farther before she realized that there was no easy place to turn around back where the lights had gone out. Rolling down her window, she stuck her head out and looked quickly behind her, but the swirling snow made visibility close to impossible.

Shrugging her shoulders, she made a right turn into her own driveway, skidding out of control slightly. The snow was sticking to the driveway at this higher elevation and Sarah put the car into first gear for the final run up the last steep slope. Several times last winter the driveway had been too icy to drive up. The car would slide helplessly back to the bottom and Sarah would have to walk in to her cabin.

She made it fine this time, the tires only spinning once or twice. The yellow porch light she always left on was a welcome sight. She ran the few yards from the car to the house and then stopped suddenly on the tiny porch, listening intently.

There was no mistaking the sound – somebody's tires were spinning on the patch of ice at the bottom of the driveway. Sarah stood frozen with her hand on the doorknob, not sure what to do. But then came the clear sound of an engine driving back down the road into the valley. Soon all was starkly silent again except for the soft slushing sound of the wet snow hitting the warm hood of her car.

Sarah let out her breath and, picking up an armload of firewood, went inside. She had not had time to make a fire in the wood stove before she left for work and the house was cold and damp. Without removing her jacket, she began to split kindling with a small ax. But after a moment she stopped and walked back to the door with the ax still in her hand. The deadbolt was stiff from disuse, but after a few hefty tugs it shot into place.

The persistent sound of the telephone ringing jarred Sarah into wakefulness. She had no idea what time it was; she was still sitting up in bed, propped against two pillows with a book in her lap. The bed lamp was on and the sun made a broad streak across the patchwork quilt on the bed.

She ran barefoot across the cold floor to answer the phone in the other room.

"Did you forget we were supposed to meet at ten?" Tyler's voice on the other end jolted her memory into focus.

"Shit. What time is it? I overslept. Sorry. Be right down." Sarah spoke thickly in short sentences, the second sleepless night beginning to take its toll on her. She had been awake until nearly four a.m.

"Listen, Isabel is coming with us today if that's okay with you."

"Why should I care?" But she knew it would make a difference.

A quick glance outside told her that last night's snow was already this morning's mud. She pulled on a black turtleneck over a pair of black jeans, stepped into a pair of high rubber boots and brushed her hair on the way out the door. Woody would have a pot of coffee going at the inn.

Tyler was waiting for her outside, leaning against their powder blue rental car. "I wondered if you'd talked to Woody yet about who you really are."

She stared at him crossly. "Tyler, I haven't even had a cup of coffee–"

"He knows a lot about your mother and I think he'd be more inclined to tell us the things we need to know if he knows who you are." Tyler was his usual fast–talking, high–strung city journalist self this morning. "He's in there right now, in the little breakfast room. It's a great opportunity."

Sarah took a deep breath and was about to tell Tyler to go fuck himself and his stupid story, but he had already opened the door and was announcing her arrival to Woody. "I'll be out here in the lounge if you need me," he said with a smile. She gave him a sour look and went inside.

Woody was her oldest and closest friend in West Jordan, and the hardest part was going to be admitting that she had deceived him all this time. He had looked out for her from the first with a fatherly affection that sometimes was a little more than fatherly. Sarah was unaware of how deep his feelings for her were; she knew he had a girlfriend who came by to see him once a month or so and she figured that was how he liked it. Besides, he was the nearest thing she had to family here and she treasured him for that.

It turned out to be easier than she had expected. "You didn't fool me for very long," Woody confessed with a laugh that made her blush. "I suspected it the first day you walked in here but with your short hair it was hard to be sure. But one day when your hair was longer, I guess it was Thanksgiving, when you got dressed up in that old black velvet dress and you had curled your hair and put on makeup...." His words drifted off and Sarah wondered who he was seeing in his mind, her or her mother. "Well, it was almost as if you wanted me to know without having to say it."

"Maybe subconsciously I did."

"It finally came back to me also that Travis's last name was Monroe. My father was good friends with Winnie and Travis both. When Travis was home they used to come down here a lot, drink, play cards–"

Sarah flinched slightly. "I never knew him." She forced the words from her mouth. "What was he like?"

"Good looking guy, real city slicker, didn't try to hide it like your friend in there." Woody jerked a thumb towards Tyler. "Flashy dresser, good tipper. Winnie was a knockout too. Sometimes she would come in with him dressed up in some slinky sequined thing like she was going to the opera instead of to the local bar. They didn't really mix with the locals. Winnie never seemed like she enjoyed herself when she was out with him."

"Did– did she wear a lot of expensive jewelry when she was dressed up like that?" Sarah asked nervously.

Woody looked at her oddly. "I don't remember, but probably she did. Now if my mother were alive she would be able to tell you the answer to that one right off. Why?"

Sarah could see Tyler pacing restlessly in the next room. "Tyler and Isabel are waiting for me. I have to go. But we'll talk tonight, okay?" She gave him a quick hug. "Thanks for being so understanding. I would like to have been honest with you sooner, but it seemed harder and harder to admit I had been deceiving you all this time."

"He's cool?" Tyler asked her as she walked past him with a funny smile on her face.

"Yeah, he's real cool." She fumbled in a drawer behind the bar. He was surprised when she lit a cigarette and took a deep puff.

"I didn't know you smoked."

"I don't usually. I just needed one right now." She inhaled again. "So where are we off to?"

69

"I thought we would visit the actual scenes of the crime. So to speak," he added hastily. "The house and the bridge."

"The house and the bridge..." Sarah repeated thoughtfully, stubbing out the cigarette. "And what do you expect to find?"

"Can't know unless we go." Isabel appeared in the doorway as if on cue and the three of them headed out to the parking lot. "We can take our car today."

Sarah got into the back seat, thinking about her conversation with Woody. In a certain way it bothered her that he had let her get away with her deception for so long. Did that mean he felt she had good reason?

"Isabel and I have been discussing this," Tyler was saying in the front seat. "Isabel has a very logical way of looking at things and—"

"Well, I asked myself if I were a woman without a car and a husband who kept taking my jewelry and selling it, what would I do? The only thing I could probably do would be to hide it somewhere in my house or around my house. Right?" Isabel sounded so smug with her deduction that Sarah felt slightly nauseated.

"It makes sense, doesn't it, Sarah? This is where I turn, right?" The car began to climb up the Darby Mountain road.

"So what are we going to do? Knock on the doors of the apartments and ask if we can tear the walls down or dig in their cellar because thirty years ago a woman may have hidden some jewelry there?" Sarah gave a derisive snort. "Don't you think I thought of that right away, when I first came here? Ask yourself this one, Isabel. If you found out that there might be valuables hidden somewhere in your apartment house, would you hesitate to search for them and claim them for your own? Why do you think my grandmother never told anybody what she suspected until she was dying?"

There was an awkward silence in the car and then Tyler slowed the car down and said, "This must be the

70

place." He held up an old photograph of the house that Woody had given him and compared it to the building in front of them. Some changes had taken place; the black and white photo showed a rambling three story summer "cottage" painted a dark green or brown with a wrap-around porch full of wicker furniture. In the corner of the snapshot someone had written in ink that had faded to sepia, "Safe Haven, 1930, Scupper summer home." The house had since been painted white and the porch closed in and turned into separate entrances for the three or four apartments, but it was still recognizable as the same building.

"It's nice the way they always named houses in those days," Isabel commented taking the old picture from Tyler and studying it.

Sarah looked at the yard where a rusty Chevy Nova rested on cinder blocks because it was missing a tire. There was also a large black dog chained to a dilapidated dog house. He stood at attention, anticipating the moment they would get out of the car so he could begin barking. "Let's go," she said abruptly.

Tyler laughed. "We just got here! At least I have to find out who owns the place now. And I'll bet you anything there are some fabulous examples of Winnie's windows here."

He swung open the car door. The black dog began howling and straining to break loose from its chain. If Isabel hadn't said, "I'll wait here," so promptly, Sarah probably wouldn't have had the courage to follow Tyler.

A door on the side of the building opened almost immediately and a young woman with a baby on her hip yelled, "Major! Quit that yapping this instant or I'll bash you one!" Then she saw Tyler and Sarah approaching and she shouted at them, "I told you goddam Jehovah's Witnesses to leave us alone!"

The two of them looked at each other and burst into laughter. By then the woman had time to realize they weren't dressed like Jehovah's Witnesses or carrying bibles and she hastily apologized.

But that was where the good luck ended. She had never heard of Winnie Scupper, said there weren't any stained glass windows in any of the apartments as far as she knew, and it was a damned good thing because the rent would probably be higher if there were. Her place was a mess or she would invite them in. No, she didn't know who owned the building, she sent her rent to some rental agency in New York who kept a local plumber and electrician on call in case of problems and took care of stuff like mowing the lawn and plowing the driveway. Tyler wrote down the name of the agency and thanked her anyway. They walked back to the car.

"Well, at least I got this," he said pocketing the address of the agency in New York.

"You know they won't give you the owner's name," Isabel remarked informatively. "It violates the privacy of their client."

"Probably true, but it's worth a try."

What a pair, Sarah thought to herself and said aloud, "The town hall has property maps that are open for public inspection. I'm sure they would have the name of the owner."

Tyler flashed Isabel a triumphant look. "Okay, now for the bridge. It must be this way." He made a right turn out of the driveway and continued up the winding road. Soon they could see a rocky stream bed below them at the bottom of the steep hillside. Within half a mile they came to a place where the road passed above a narrow gorge through which the stream flowed.

"This is it."

"Right here?" Isabel looked out the window in disbelief as Tyler slowed down and parked on the shoulder of the road. "But it doesn't look like anything."

Tyler laughed. "Not all bridges are as big as the Brooklyn Bridge, Isabel."

"There's actually a really nice view from here. We're up pretty high." Sarah's nonchalant comment disguised the fact that beneath her turtleneck sweater, she was sweating and shivering at the same time.

Opening the door, she stepped out and her rubber boots immediately sank a few inches into the earth. The melted snow had turned the side of the road into soft mud. She turned around to warn Isabel who was already gingerly sticking one foot out, apparently wondering whether to risk ruining her expensive, handmade Italian boots.

"I think I'll wait in the car again," she announced. Sarah and Tyler tromped back to the bridge.

For the first few moments they stood by the railing, looking down at the rocky stream far below and saying nothing, as if they were observing a silent memorial to the tragedy some thirty years ago. It was hard to imagine it on a sunlit day so clear that the snow–capped White Mountains could be seen in the distance.

"That's New Hampshire over there, where those mountains are," Sarah said at last.

"I guess that would be where the moon would rise. Must be beautiful here on a full moon night. I can see why she would walk by here."

Sarah put one foot up on the railing and perched on the bar at the top. Tyler automatically reached out a hand to steady her. "Careful." He laughed nervously. "We don't want history to repeat itself."

"I'm all right," she replied, looking down at his long, slender fingers gripping the black wool of her sweater sleeve, silently willing him to let her go before Isabel looked out the back window of the car and decided to join them.

Reading her thoughts, he turned his body so it blocked the view from the car. "I'm not letting go of you until you get down." Sarah didn't move. With his other hand, Tyler ran his fingers over the cold metal of the railing. "I wonder if this was how the bridge looked back then."

"Does it matter?" She tossed her head and looked at the horizon. Tyler found himself watching the silver hoops she wore in her ears as they flashed in bright contrast to her dark hair.

"Well, it just seems like it would be pretty hard to accidentally fall over the edge. I had this idea that maybe her dog had seen something and jumped at it and pulled her along on the leash, perhaps tripping and..."

"Plunging to her death on the rocks below?" she finished dramatically for him. "It's possible. Maybe there was no railing at all in those days."

"Or maybe she stopped and sat...just where you are now...to admire the view lit by the harvest moon..." He felt her tremble a little beneath his grip. Gently but firmly he pulled her down to stand beside him. She turned away, leaning forward over the waist–high railing once more.

"There is one more possibility."

"What's that?"

"That she did it on purpose."

"You mean, committed suicide?"

Sarah nodded. "My grandfather did it after the stock market crash. He was such a proud man, he couldn't stand that he had lost everything. My grandmother said that, unfortunately, my mother had inherited his sense of pride. She couldn't admit she had made a mistake when she married my father, so she lived with her error and hid her unhappiness from everyone. Maybe she was just so miserable she couldn't take it anymore."

Tyler nodded his head thoughtfully. "Well, it's an interesting theory, however–"

Laughing ruefully, she turned her back on the view to face him. "Tyler, sometimes I just can't stand your analytical talk! We're talking about my mother's suicide, not an `interesting theory'."

"How can you be so sure–"

"I just am." She started to walk back to the car.

"Then answer me this one!" He was shouting at her from the bridge now. Through the back window of the car, he saw Isabel's face staring at him curiously.

Sarah stopped and turned. "What?"

"Why did she bring the dog with her then?"

"Maybe she didn't. Maybe he just followed her after she left her three–month–old daughter alone in the house in the middle of the night to go jump off a fucking bridge. Isn't that sensational enough for your stupid story?" She was shouting now and hot tears were running down her face. "Tyler, I've had enough. I don't want to do this anymore. Take me back to my car."

He was at her side in two long strides, ignoring Isabel's blatant "I told you so" look. "I'm sorry, Sarah. I didn't think it would upset you so much. You seemed so objective about it, always saying that it's in the past and that it doesn't matter."

She looked down at the ground where her rubber boots met his expensive running shoes; both were caked with mud now. "You're right, I'm sorry," she said flatly. "I never even knew her and it doesn't matter. I'm acting ridiculous." She sniffed a little and wiped her nose on the back of her hand. "I guess I'm not really very much like her. I could never do it."

"Do what?"

"Kill myself."

"Of course not. You enjoy life too much." But he was frowning as he led her back to the car and opened the door for her. Misinterpreting his expression, she gave a tiny smile and patted him reassuringly on the arm as she got in.

"Don't worry. I'll still help you with your research."

Down in a hollow on the other side of Darby Mountain, the same tiny stream became wide enough to be called a river. Beside it there was a settlement of three or four rundown houses, numerous ramshackle outbuildings and enough broken down trucks and cars and scrap metal to be considered a small junkyard. Beside one house was a huge pile of ten foot log lengths waiting to be cut and split for firewood.

"Well, this matches the description Woody gave me of where Dora Evans lives." Tyler peered through the windshield dubiously. "Did we cross a train track back there? Because this is certainly the other side of it. I wonder which house it is."

"This place gives me the willies," shuddered Isabel, looking at the side of an old garage where a deerskin, which appeared to have been tacked up to dry several centuries ago, hung next to a bear skin equally as old if not older.

"Well, you haven't got out of the car yet today. Why break a perfect record?" Tyler slipped the little tape recorder into the pocket of his sweater. "Let's go, Sarah."

Sarah was surveying their surroundings with curiosity. "You're broadening my horizons, Tyler. This is the first time I've ever been down this way."

Tyler was already knocking on the door of the nearest house. It was eventually answered by an ancient and gnarled man who pointed with a crooked finger to another house up on the hill behind him. "You from the IRS or something?" he asked suspiciously.

"No, nothing like that," Tyler assured him.

"Must be that boy of hers is in some kind of scrape again then." The old man nodded to himself, satisfied with his own answer. Tyler thanked him and they started up the hill.

There was a familiar red pickup in the dooryard of Dora's house. Sarah was sure she had seen it more than once in the parking lot at the inn but she couldn't put an owner's face to it. She thought that perhaps she already knew Dora and didn't realize it, but the woman who answered the door was not someone she recognized.

Dora's hair was the first thing that caught a person's eye. It was an unnatural and startling red, teased and hair–sprayed into a stiff style that had lost its popularity at least fifteen years before. Her shapeless and overweight body was zipped into an ill–fitting housedress that made it hard to tell where her breasts ended and her plump torso began. On her feet she wore a pair of brown men's socks that were full of holes.

"Who are you? What do you want?"

Sarah hung back, waiting to see how Tyler would attempt to charm the pants off this one.

"Hi, I'm Tyler Mackenzie. You must be Dora Evans?"

"What do you want?"

"I was told you could probably help me with a project I'm working on." Tyler fumbled for the right way to approach this stalwart mountain of red hair and flesh in front of him.

"What project? Who told you to come here?" She moved forward, her body filling the doorway, just in case he was thinking of sneaking past her into the house.

"Well, a number of years ago you worked for a woman named Winnie Scupper, or maybe you knew her as Mrs. Travis Monroe. I'm sure you remember – it was a tragic accident." Tyler noticed that Dora's grip on the doorknob had tightened and as she opened her mouth to speak, he quickly plunged into his speech again. "Anyway, as you probably know, Winnie Scupper was a superb artisan in the craft of stained glass window–making and I'm researching a story on her life for a magazine in New York City. Oh, by the way, this is her daughter, Sarah Scup–"

77

As Tyler stepped aside to introduce Sarah, Dora's ruddy face suddenly went several shades whiter and then almost immediately filled with a color that rivaled her hair. "Get out!" she bellowed. "What do you mean by coming here after all these years? If you think I'm going to tell one of you reporters something you don't already know—

"But Mrs. Evans –"

"I'm telling you, my son is a cop and I'll have him arrest you if you ever even set your big toe on my property again! Now get out, get out, GET OUT!" She effectively pushed Tyler off her door jamb and slammed the door in his face.

"Well, that was interesting," Tyler remarked in a calm voice, clicking off the tape recorder in his pocket. "I wonder what she was so worked up about."

Sarah shivered a little, thinking about herself as a tiny baby being cared for by such a woman. "Do you think she was like that thirty years ago?"

"Probably not." In a protective, masculine gesture, Tyler put a hand on Sarah's back and turned her away from the house. "She could have been a real beauty when she was young. A hard life can do amazing things to a person."

"But wouldn't you think she would be excited to see me, grown up after all these years?" Sarah shook her head at the thought which was inconceivable to her.

"We don't know how well she got along with your mother. Maybe she was just the housekeeper, and when you were born it meant extra work for her that she hadn't bargained for. Maybe she hates kids." His face lit up in a boyish grin suddenly. "Now tell me, was I right or what? That cop who ticketed you wasn't just related to her – he's her son!"

Exhausted emotionally from the events of the last few days and exhausted physically from lack of sleep, Sarah left Tyler and Isabel for the rest of the afternoon.

They went on planning to track down stained glass windows that could be photographed for Tyler's story; Sarah went home to nap for a while before work.

She had been sleeping soundly for an hour when she was awakened once again by the shrill bell of the telephone. She rolled off the couch and reached out stiffly to grab the phone with the least amount of effort and croaked a surly, "Hello," into the receiver.

"Sarah? Did I wake you?"

"Yes." Recognizing Tyler's voice, she closed her eyes and wearily rested her head on the rug.

"I'm sorry but it's important."

"So important it couldn't wait until I came into work in an hour?"

"We won't be here; we have to leave right away."

Sarah opened her eyes and stared at the ceiling above her head. A spider was weaving a web across one corner of the room. "I thought you weren't leaving until tomorrow."

"Isabel called her office and there was some emergency – she's got to be back in the morning. It was a mistake to bring her along on this trip. It could have been so much more... productive without her. I decided that after I wrap up some work in the city, I'm going to come back up alone and keep working on this project."

"Sounds like a good idea." The spider was descending to the floor from its web on the finest of gossamer strings.

"But that's not the real reason I called. I found out something this afternoon that I think you should know."

"What's that?" The spider landed on the rug, inches from Sarah's face and scurried away.

"Isabel and I went to the town hall this afternoon to look at those property maps like you suggested. We found out the name of the owner of your mother's house."

"So does it help you any?"

"Not really, but it may help you. Apparently the name of the property owner only changed once in the last eighty years. And that was in 1951."

"What do you mean? I thought the house was sold in 1955–"

"Well, just to make sure, we took a quick drive over to the county courthouse and did a title search to see if the person who owns the property and the person who has paid the taxes on it for the last thirty–five years were one and the same. And sure enough–"

Sarah broke in impatiently. "So who does own it?"

"Your father, Travis Monroe."

CHAPTER FOUR

Sarah was glad that the bar was busy that night. The news that Tyler had given her over the phone had more implications than she had ever imagined and she didn't want to think about what it meant just yet. She put her mind on her work and made mindless conversation with the customers. She accepted an invitation to dinner on her night off from a soft–spoken building contractor named Ron whom she'd gone out with a couple of times. She let herself get caught up in the speculative gossip that had the room buzzing about what had caused an emergency room doctor to drive off the road and into the river.

But when she was cleaning up after hours, Woody appeared, wearing a plaid flannel bathrobe and carrying a cardboard box under one arm.

"Thought you might like to look at a few of these," he said, opening the box and spreading some photographs out on the bar. Sarah put down her sponge and came around to look at the pictures.

In the corner of the first one was written "Thanksgiving, 1953." Seated around a table that held a half carved turkey, was a woman with curly gray hair not unlike Woody's, a very young, slim Woody with crew cut and dress uniform, an older man with glasses, obviously Woody's father, and a beautiful, dark–haired woman with sparkly eyes whose mouth was open with laughter as she mugged for the camera.

"I've never seen a picture of her laughing before," Sarah said slowly, noticing also that Woody's father had his arm around the back of Winnie's chair and that Winnie was wearing some sort of gaudy choker around her neck, inlaid with large stones.

"She looked so much prettier when she was happy. I think my father was half in love with her. But this is how she looked more often."

He pointed to a picture of Winnie sitting on a barstool with her back to the bar. She was dressed in a strapless black dress; a lacy shawl covered her shoulders. Her hair was pinned up and back to display the flashing gems in her ear lobes that seemed to match that same choker that she wore around her neck. Strangely enough, she wore dark sunglasses.

"Was this taken during the day? Why is she wearing sunglasses?" Sarah noticed now the handsome profile of the man sitting next to Winnie, slightly out of focus as he turned to the camera just as the picture was snapped. "Oh, that's him, isn't it?"

She flipped the picture over. In the same spidery handwriting that had identified the photo of the Scupper house was written, "Mr. & Mrs. Travis Monroe in the taproom, 1952."

"Oh, this is before the Night Heron window, isn't it?" She looked back, recognizing the very seats they were occupying right now." She looks so – mysterious, doesn't she?"

There were a couple of other pictures where Winnie could be picked out in a crowd of people, both times with a sorrowful, faraway expression on her face. "And here's the best one – I was saving it for last." Woody put down a faded Polaroid snapshot.

Winnie sat in an old–fashioned wooden swing in the middle of a beautiful garden full of peonies in bloom. She was wearing a faded, loose fitting summer dress and her hair looked uncombed. A peaceful smile played on her lips as she gazed down at the tiny baby asleep in her arms.

"Guess who?" Woody teased.

Sarah did not hear him. Frowning, she stared at the picture, thinking hard. This was a woman so in love with her infant that she no longer cared about her own appearance. Could this woman possibly have abandoned her baby and thrown herself off a bridge?

"Do you think she was emotionally unbalanced?"

Woody gave her an odd look. "Why would you ask that?"

Sarah shrugged her shoulders and shivered a little. "You know, after giving birth, some women suffer severe hormonal depressions that they have no control over. I just wondered if..."

"I wasn't around when the accident happened." Woody did not look at her as he replaced the pictures in the box. "My father must have taken this picture. When she was pregnant, and after the baby was born, I mean, you were born, he used to help her out some, bring her groceries when she couldn't get out, cut the lawn. She didn't have many friends. Finally he arranged for Dora Evans to live up there with her and help out."

Sarah told him about their visit to Dora that afternoon. Woody shook his head. "Dora carries a long–standing grudge against just about everyone in town. Unwed mothers weren't too popular in the fifties and Dora kept getting into trouble. She already had one small boy when Dad set her up at Winnie's. He thought it would be a great arrangement that would work out for both of them. Guess it didn't change much of anything. After Winnie died, Dora got knocked up again as soon as she moved back home. Nobody had much patience with her after that."

"Woody–" Sarah paused, about to alter her question to something less significant, but changed her mind and went on. "Did you know that my father still owns that house?"

Woody let out a low whistle of surprise. "Is that right? I wonder why he never sold it. I remember the contents being auctioned off. Everyone talked about that for weeks because Travis had the stained–glass windows removed from the house and sold along with everything else. Even her works in progress were sold."

"I never really even thought about him being still alive." Her words came slowly and sadly. Woody was not used to hearing Sarah speak like this. She was usually tough, cheerful and diplomatic, hiding her true feelings well. He watched her light a cigarette, something she did only at moments of intense stress. Then collecting herself once more, she said, "So. Who else around here would remember my mother?"

"You know, I gave that journalist some names to look up but I purposely left out someone who knew your mother pretty well."

"Who was that?"

"The doctor, Dr. Wilder. He's retired now, but he was the town physician for years. I didn't think it was appropriate for someone to be poking around in Winnie's personal health problems but I think the doctor would be happy to talk you. Christ, he delivered you! And he's got a couple of beautiful examples of your mother's glass work."

"Payment for services rendered?" Sarah knew the pattern by now.

Woody nodded.

They talked for a few more minutes while Sarah finished cleaning up. Then Woody said goodnight to her and watched from the door as Sarah walked across the parking lot to her car. She knew she should let the engine warm up but she was always too tired at night to wait. She pulled out of her parking spot and the windshield immediately fogged up with her breath. She stopped the car to search between the seats for the ice scraper when a sudden pounding on the passenger window made her heart jump and her throat tighten.

It was only Woody, yelling something to her frantically. She leaned over and rolled down the window. "You have a flat tire," he panted, hopping up and down as he spoke. She remembered he had been barefoot went he came down to the bar. "I didn't want you to drive a mile down the road and then discover it."

"Shit." Sarah got out and slammed the door. The tires on the driver's side looked fine, and angrily she stomped around to the other side of the car. The rear tire on the passenger side was almost completely out of air. "Damn it. I don't get it. That's a brand new snow tire. It's just not fair."

She threw open the trunk to look for the jack and the spare.

"Sarah, why don't you just spend the night here and we'll deal with this in the morning?" Woody's gentle suggestion sounded like a good idea and he turned off the engine as she shut the trunk.

"I'm sorry I yelled at you," she apologized as they walked back to the inn. "I must have backed up too far into the bushes, maybe I ran over a nail. I never would have seen that tire on my own. I mean, who walks around their car looking at their tires before they drive home at night?"

Woody had the tire fixed before Sarah even woke up the next morning. "I hate to say it, but unless there's a slow leak that the garage couldn't find, it looks like someone let the air out of this tire on purpose. The valve stem was broken clean off."

"Must have been a high school prank," was Sarah's response to his report. But she was thinking about the car that had followed her home the night before. She didn't like to admit it, but she had a sickening feeling that the flat tire was no coincidence. Something creepy was definitely going on.

Nearly two weeks went by before Tyler returned to West Jordan. Except for a few disturbing bouts of insomnia, Sarah's life had almost returned to its previous peaceful cycle of work and relaxation. She decided she had learned enough about her past to know it was better to leave some stones unturned. She did not visit the retired doctor; instead she stacked firewood, took long walks during the crisp, short November days, and spent the evenings socializing with the regulars in the Night Heron.

When her real name was printed in the paper in the list of speeders ticketed in West Jordan, she was surprised at what little fuss was made. Most people made comments like, "I didn't know you were a Scupper!" as though it was their own lack of perception that was responsible, and that possibly they were the only ones in town who been ignorant of who Sarah was. She realized she had been foolish not be straight about her identity in the first place, yet how could she have known?

She had not thought about Tyler Mackenzie in several days when he finally blew through the door of the lounge on a Friday night a few minutes before closing. She did not even recognize him at first. He had two weeks growth of beard on his jaw and was wearing a faded denim jacket and worn blue jeans. The few patrons of the bar gave him only a cursory glance and satisfied with the response, he strode right to the bar and asked for a Budweiser.

Sarah laughed merrily. "Not bad, Tyler. But wouldn't you rather have this?" She poured him a shot of top shelf brandy.

"Well, all right, just this once, but I'm on a budget this time around. I'm going to have to develop a taste for Budweiser whether I like it or not." He sipped his brandy and then stretched his arms, stiff from the ride. "So how've you been?"

"Fine. And you? How long are you here for this time?"

"As long as it takes."

Her eyes met his over the brandy snifter. "Really? No time limit?" Her response was not as casual-sounding as she tried to make it.

"No, I'm on my own with this one. No one's supporting me on this story anymore." His eyes watched as she moved around the bar, admiring her graceful figure.

"Not even Isabel?"

He laughed. "Especially not Isabel. No, I'm here until we've exhausted the possibilities or until the money runs out and the credit cards reach their limit. Whichever comes first." He swallowed the rest of the brandy in one gulp, shivering a little from the hot rush it gave him. He pushed the glass across the bar to Sarah. "Now, I'll have a Budweiser, if you don't mind, miss." He leaned forward, suddenly his old excited, confidential self again. "I've got all kinds of things to tell you, Sarah. I've been doing a lot of investigating in New York in the last few weeks. How about you? Find anything out?"

"No, I haven't." She pretended to concentrate on washing dirty glasses. It was something she could have done with her eyes closed by now and Tyler knew it.

"Nothing? Then what have you been doing?"

"Just living my life and having a good time, Tyler. I was really pretty happy here until you came along."

"What, living a lie?"

"I'm not living a lie anymore, everybody knows who I am and guess what? It doesn't matter, I'm still happy. So maybe you ought to go back to the city and just leave this be. You must have enough material for a nice, lightweight article with lovely color illustrations of Winnie's Scupper stained glass."

"Good God, do we have to start this all over again? I thought we'd already covered this territory." Tyler sat back in his seat and shook his head, muttering to himself.

They did not speak again until the other customers had gone home and they were alone. Tyler was on his third beer by then and was scribbling notes on the back of a cocktail napkin with a thoughtful expression on his face. He looked up as Sarah dumped an armful of bed sheets into his lap.

"You should have called to say you were coming. Woody's gone to bed and making beds is not part of my job description."

"Sarah – "He grabbed her by the arm as she turned away from him. "You've got to face it."

"No, I don't. I don't care."

"Well, I do!"

She whirled on him angrily. "Why should you care?"

A red flush spread across his face suddenly and he dropped her arm as if it were on fire. "Fine. If you don't want to help me, I'll finish it up myself and good riddance to you and your damn suicide and your damn heirloom jewels!"

Sarah stood staring at him for a moment. Then she went back behind the bar and poured herself a shot of tequila. With the safety of the bar between them, she relaxed a little. "Tyler–" she hesitated for a second. "What got you so interested in my mother?"

He looked up in surprise, the hurt and anger fading from his expression as he launched into his favorite subject once more. "My parents had one of her windows in our house in the city. I grew up with it and it was one of my fondest childhood memories. I used to play games in the colored patches of light it made on the floor. There was one beveled piece of clear glass that made rainbows at a certain time of the day when the sun hit it just right. But when you grow up with something beautiful and you see it every day, you tend to forget how special it is."

He had been looking above her head at the Night Heron window as he spoke and glanced at her face now to see if she was still with him. Reassured, he went on.

"So one day I returned home as an adult and was struck once again by the unique style and beauty of the window. I asked my parents about it and they said it was a "Winnie Scupper window" that they had purchased at a gallery in Soho in the early fifties. I decided I wanted to buy one for my own apartment and it didn't take long to find out the rest of the story. None of the private owners I tracked down wanted to sell; her work is very valuable now, you know. The more I found out, the more interested I became. I decided if I couldn't afford to own a window, I could at least pay my respects with a magazine article."

"Or at least pay your bills with it." A ghost of a grin flitted across Sarah's face, her amusement disappearing as, through the window, she saw the lights of a pickup truck circling in the dark parking lot outside. Every few nights she became aware of the fact that someone was still following her home when she left work, usually turning off at the intersection before her driveway. It was such a scary thought that she had to push it to the farthest reaches of her mind or she would not be able to continue working such late hours.

Tyler's eyes followed hers, wondering why she looked so serious. "Someone you know?" he asked.

Her "no" was little too emphatic. "Just a customer who's a little too late, that's all." Turning off some of the inside lights, she changed the subject quickly. "So. What is this great new info that your investigating has turned up?"

"Well, I found out where your father lives."

His words had the effect he had expected. Her frightened eyes met his own for a brief second and then she moved about the room straightening this and that, avoiding his gaze. "And?"

"And I think we ought to pay him a visit."

Sarah laughed harshly. "Who, you and me? What the hell for?"

"You're awfully bitter towards your own flesh and blood whom you've never even met."

"You're damn right I am! What am I supposed to do – walk in and say, `Hi, I'm your daughter and now you can try and ruin my life the way you ruined my mother's'?"

"No, that wasn't exactly what I had in mind. I just thought you might want to reclaim some of what might be rightfully yours."

Sarah had a distant look in her eyes. "Where does he live?" she asked.

"Atlantic City."

Sarah shook her head and closed her eyes, suddenly very tired. "Of course, where else?"

"Listen, you must be as tired as I am." Tyler yawned. "Why don't you meet me here in the morning and we'll talk some more. I'd like to go over to the nursing home and chat with some of the gray hairs there." He stood up with his armful of sheets. "Same room?"

Driving home she was lost in thought about Tyler and how much he knew about her and her life. She did not notice the lights of the car until it was almost on top of her. It was tailing her so close this time that she searched for a place to pull off and let it pass, but the shoulderless dirt road offered nothing. And if the driver wanted to pass her; there was certainly plenty of room in the other lane for that.

She jolted forward in the seat as a crunching noise told her that she had been rammed from behind by the other car. "That's it," she said aloud and slammed on her brakes, skidding a distance on the gravel before she stopped.

The driver of the other car turned off his lights and whizzed past her, a shapeless shadow in the dark. Through the trees Sarah could see the lights go on again as the car safely rounded the next bend.

She sat there for a long time with the engine running and her heart pounding. After a while she got out and looked at the damage to her back bumper. She could not go on being harassed like this. Something would have to be done.

"Hey, what happened to your car?" Tyler's sharp eyes immediately noticed the dent in Sarah's rear bumper. "Back into something last night?"

"No, hit–and–run on the way home. Some drunk was tailgating me, rammed my car from behind and then took off. I've only got liability insurance, so it looks like I'll be driving it this way for a while." Sarah got into the driver's seat, indicating the conversation was over.

"You don't sound very upset," Tyler remarked, getting in beside her. "Isabel would be steaming over something like that for days."

Sarah shrugged as she started the car. "There's nothing I can do about it. And obviously I don't care about appearances as much as Isabel." The unkind thought had slipped out before she could stop it. "Sorry, I didn't mean that to sound insulting."

Tyler laughed. "I don't know anybody who cares about appearances as much as Isabel. She drives me crazy sometimes."

"How long have you been married?"

"We're not. We just live together."

"Oh, sorry, I thought–"

"That's what Isabel would like everyone to think. It started out as a matter of convenience – it was stupid to pay rent on two places when we spent most of our nights together. That was before she got this high–powered job. Now that she makes all this money, all she can think of is bigger and better and more expensive."

"Oh." Sarah concentrated on her driving, knowing that Tyler would keep on talking if she didn't.

"To tell you the truth, it's been really refreshing coming up here, driving around in a beat–up car with a beautiful woman who enjoys rubbing elbows with the salt of the earth. No, I mean that as a compliment! I'm three hundred miles from home so I can say this –" He lowered his voice conspiratorily – "But I'm sick to death of Isabel telling me what to wear and deciding who we should party with and which restaurant is the right one to be seen in."

"Really?" By the time they reached Sunny Hills Nursing Home on the outskirts of Jordan Center, Sarah had learned all she needed to about Tyler's personal life and had neatly avoided having to talk about her own.

"You know, Tyler, even in the country people do dress up a little when they come to places like this," she told him as they walked up the path to the building. "Your old jean jacket and scruffy face might not win over the old ladies the way you usually do."

"Then you'll just have to help me win them over, darlin'." He gave her his most dazzling smile and Sarah knew that there would be no problem once he turned on the charm. It was sickening how easily it came to him.

Despite the homey appearance of the lobby with its overstuffed chairs and sofas covered in cheerful flowered prints, the antiseptic smell of a place of sickness pervaded the atmosphere and gave Sarah a feeling of overwhelming and instant depression. A nurse pushed a shriveled and tiny birdlike woman in a wheelchair through the room. Two bald old men watched a TV game show in the corner, loudly shouting the answers to no one in particular.

She sat down in a chair and thumbed through a copy of Modern Maturity, while Tyler talked to a receptionist who couldn't have been older than twenty. Although eager to please the handsomest hunk of manhood she'd seen in weeks, she still looked at him blankly and finally left her desk to return with a middle aged supervisor who might know what he was talking about.

Before long Tyler was surrounded by a group of chattering nurses and volunteers arguing among themselves as to which one of the patients would be a likely candidate for having known Winnie Scupper. Eventually Tyler motioned to Sarah to join him and they followed a nurse down one of the several corridors that led out of the main lobby.

"She's taking us to see Mrs. Alfred who used to own an antique store in West Jordan," he whispered to Sarah as they walked down the dimly lit hallway. "They say that her mind's still sharp as a bell even though her body stopped functioning years ago."

"Mrs. Alfred, you have company!" The nurse called brightly as she knocked on the door to announce their arrival.

Through the open doorway they could see the old woman's thin face light up at the prospect of visitors. She was propped up on several pillows and around her shoulders she wore a bed shawl crocheted in alternating squares of turquoise and yellow. She gave a feeble pat to her soft, wispy white hair and then said in a quavering voice, "Well, come right in."

Tyler automatically stepped back to let Sarah enter first. Mrs. Alfred peered inquisitively at the guests she had not been expecting. Then suddenly her face became a mass of wrinkles as she broke into a smile.

"Why, Winnie Scupper, I knew some day you'd come back for that lamp you left with me!"

CHAPTER FIVE

Stunned by Mrs. Alfred's words, Sarah backed up a few steps, bumping into Tyler. He pushed her forward again and whispered reassuringly, "Just go along with it for a few minutes and see what happens."

But before Sarah could reply, the old woman rubbed her forehead and reprimanded herself aloud. "I'm sorry, I don't know what is wrong with my brain sometimes. You can't be Winnie Scupper, she's been dead for years. Seems like sometimes I just get all mixed up these days, can't remember what year it is and whether I'm old or middle–aged or just graduated from high school. But I have to tell you, young woman, that you remind me a lot of someone I used to know, many years ago."

Sarah cleared her throat and came forward to sit down in the wooden chair beside Mrs. Alfred's bed. "It's all right, Mrs. Alfred. Your memory served you well this time. I do look like Winnie Scupper because I'm her daughter, Sarah."

"Is that right?" Mrs. Alfred oohed and aahed over Sarah for some minutes, in the way they had expected Dora Evans might. Finally she said, "So, I guess you probably have come about that old lamp, haven't you? Well, I'm sorry to say that I don't have it anymore. It's at my daughter's house, over in Burlington. She said it matched the Victorian furniture in her living room and it certainly would look silly in here, wouldn't it?"

Sarah looked helplessly at Tyler, who made a gesture that seemed to say, "Keep her talking."

"Well, actually, Mrs. Alfred–"

"Now, don't be so formal, dearie. My friends call me Maude. I know, it's a funny, old–fashioned sounding name but you can say it." She reached over and patted Sarah's hand. "You don't hear about anybody naming their new babies Maude these days, now do you?"

"Okay, Maude." Sarah laughed a little. "This is my friend, Tyler Mackenzie, and he's writing a magazine article about my mother. And we'd like you to tell us the story of the lamp."

"Well, there's not much to tell, really." Maude sniffed a little and picked at a loose thread in her bed jacket. "I mean, it's rather sad in a way, and he probably doesn't want to make his readers sad, does he?"

"Oh, he knows how to write things so they sound good even if they're not so good." Sarah looked to Tyler for help again, but he looked at the ceiling and drummed his fingers on his notebook. "Why don't you just tell us about it?"

"Well, let's see..." The old woman's high, thin voice trailed off as she searched her failing memory. "It was back when my shop used to do a crackerjack business during the tourist seasons, summer and fall. I knew Winnie because she had come in a few times to sell me some pieces of Depression glass that she had found up in that old summer house. Quite valuable they were, I tried to convince her to keep them, but she said they were of no use to her and she'd rather have the money. One of them was a very rare orange juice squeezer –" she stopped suddenly and cackled. "Oh, you kids probably don't even know what I'm talking about."

"When did she bring you the lamp?" Tyler had moved over to stand at Sarah's shoulder, so that his tape recorder could pick up Maude's voice more clearly.

"I think it was just about this time of year, maybe a little closer to Christmas. I remember because it was a bad time to sell anything, no business to speak of, and I wasn't too keen on increasing my inventory if I was just going to sit on it for another six months. But there was poor Winnie with her broken arm–"

"She had a broken arm?"

95

"Yes, well, that was the whole point, you see. She'd had a nasty fall or something and had broken her arm and couldn't do any of her glass work. That was her livelihood, you know. She did such beautiful work." Maude sighed and then went on. "Anyway, she'd made herself one of those Tiffany lampshades for an old parlor lamp. What a lovely piece of work it was! I wish you could have seen it. I told her I couldn't afford to buy it from her but I would put it in my shop until it sold. Then – I'll never forget what she said –" Maude's voice drifted off and she closed her eyes.

Sarah and Tyler looked at each other in alarm. "What did she say, Mrs. Alfred, I mean, Maude?" Sarah asked loudly.

Without opening her eyes, Maude continued her story. "She said she had actually brought the lamp as collateral, that she wanted me to loan her some money. She said she would repay me within a year and that if she didn't, that the lamp would be mine and that I would be able to sell it for a profit. You see, the lamp was worth far more than she wanted me to lend her. I told her I would lend her the money, to take the lamp home, that she could pay me back when she could work again. But she insisted. She said, `Please. It's safer here than at home.' Now what could she have meant by that?"

There was no obvious answer to her question and nobody said anything for a moment. "Well, you probably know the rest of the story," Maude said finally.

"Tell us," Tyler urged.

"She died before the year was up. And there I was, stuck with a lamp and a promise to a dead woman. I never could bring myself to sell it after that. Took it home and put it in my sitting room. Now Betsy's got it."

"Would Betsy mind if we visited her and took a look at it?" Tyler asked hesitantly.

"Certainly not! Besides, it's rightfully yours, missy, you know."

"Uh, I don't think so...I mean, a deal's a deal, Maude," Sarah said nervously. "You lent her the money. Now it's your lamp."

"But I told you, I was going to lend it to her without the lamp. She insisted on leaving it. I was just holding onto it for her until she was ready to take it back."

"But it matches your daughter's Victorian decor!"

Maude leaned forward one more time and grasped Sarah's hand firmly in her own. "Listen, Winnie's daughter, I've forgotten your name already, for twenty some years, or however many it is now, I've felt guilty that your mother died and I still had her lamp. I thought her husband would come by and get it when he settled up the estate, but he never did. So I say screw Betsy and her damn decor! If you want that lamp it's yours. Now maybe I can die in peace."

Tyler leaned against the car, laughing uncontrollably. "I'm sorry but when she said, 'screw Betsy and her damn decor'...What a ticket!" With the back of his hand, he wiped away the tears streaming down his face. "Is Burlington too far for this afternoon?"

"Afraid so." Shivering in the cold November air, Sarah climbed into the car. Out of the wind, she felt like talking a little. "What do you make of it, the broken arm and all? We've never heard anything about that before."

"Maybe Travis wanted to sell the lamp and Winnie wanted to get it out of the house so he couldn't. Maybe they had a fight and he broke her arm." Tyler pressed the rewind button on his tape recorder.

"Tyler! She had to have been pregnant with me by then. It must have been an accident."

"Well, the only person who might know differently is the doctor who set the bone." He popped the cassette out and flipped it over.

Sarah pursed her lips, thinking hard for a moment. "Tyler, why don't you go back inside and ask that superintendent if she knows where Dr. Wilder lives."

"Maybe we should have called first."

Sarah looked dubiously at the imposing, three story house. Its perfectly painted white clapboards contrasted with the wooden shutters in colonial blue that framed every white–curtained window. The gardens had all been neatly turned under for the winter, the perennials clipped back and mulch hay spread over the strawberry beds. Everything was orderly and immaculate. Sarah had a feeling that, even in retirement, the doctor probably kept to a strict schedule.

"There's only one way to find out." In high gear as always, Tyler started to bounce out of the car, but Sarah grabbed him suddenly by the sleeve.

"Tyler – wait." He looked at her expectantly, impatient not to lose his momentum. "When Woody told me about Dr. Wilder, he also said he had specifically not mentioned his name to you. He didn't think it was right for you to pry into my mother's personal health problems. I don't what he meant but..."

"Hmmm. Sounds like Woody knows something he doesn't want to tell you about. Something he'd rather a doctor told you." He sat back in his seat. "Do you want to go in alone?"

Sarah looked at the massive front door with its heavy brass knocker. "No. I'd rather have you with me. But don't tell Woody you came here, okay?"

"Maybe he won't talk to you if I'm here," Tyler said as they approached the house.

"Maybe he's not even home," remarked Sarah.

Sarah's supposition turned out to be true. Mrs. Wilder, an apple–cheeked butterball of a woman, let them in and gave them tea and homemade gingerbread in a tidy kitchen with polished butcher block countertops and calico cushions on the ladder back chairs.

"The doctor should be back any minute," she told them. "He just drove down to the hardware store to match some paint for our guest bedroom. I'm sure he wouldn't want to miss you. He always enjoys seeing how the babies he delivered turned out."

Having skipped lunch, both of their mouths were full of gingerbread at that moment, so Mrs. Wilder continued talking. "When you finish eating, I can show you the windows your mother made for us. One is on the landing of our stairwell and the other is in the piano alcove. She told us they weren't quite finished, that she would be back when she had time to change a few pieces and make them right. She was such a perfectionist! The windows looked perfectly fine to me. But, of course, she never did get a chance to come back."

There was an uncomfortable pause, which Tyler broke by standing up quickly. "Let's go take a look."

Rueful of Tyler's endless energy, Sarah left her half–eaten gingerbread and followed him and Mrs. Wilder to the staircase. "Look at how different it is from her other work, Sarah," Tyler whispered. "It's so geometric and traditional."

Triangles and rectangles formed a pattern radiating out from a square piece of faceted green glass. Four other similar but smaller pieces of glass marked each corner and repeated the motif on a lesser scale.

"That was what I wanted," Mrs. Wilder told him. "She made it to my specifications."

Sarah could tell from Tyler's expression that he had finally found a piece of Winnie Scupper's art work that he did not like. The sound of the front door slamming, however, relieved him from further comments.

"That must be the doctor now." Mrs. Wilder descended the stairs to inform her husband of the unexpected visitors. Before long, they had been ushered into a spotless living room by the tall, distinguished, white–haired doctor and his round little wife.

For a while they made small talk about Sarah — where she had grown up, what she had studied in college, and how she had come back to West Jordan. Then they talked about Tyler and his work. Finally, at a discreet signal from the doctor, Mrs. Wilder left the room and Dr. Wilder said, "Now what can I do for you?"

"Woody Foster suggested we talk to you." Sarah felt suddenly timid, confronted with the true purpose of the visit. "He thought you might be able to tell us some things about my mother and the last few years of her life."

Dr. Wilder took a pouch of cherry tobacco from his pocket and filled a wooden pipe that sat in an ashtray on the end table next to his easy chair. "I know a doctor shouldn't smoke," he apologized. "But even doctors aren't perfect and old habits die hard." He sucked deeply on the pipe before he spoke again. "Are you in contact with your father at all, Sarah?"

She swallowed hard. "No. Why?"

He blew a smoke ring and squinted at her through his wire–rimmed glasses. "It's not a pretty story, you know. I'm not sure you'd want your boyfriend here to hear it."

"Do you want me to leave, Sarah?"

"Actually, I think I'd like to talk to Sarah alone, Mr. Mackenzie. Then she can decide what she thinks is appropriate for you to know. Why don't we go into my office, Sarah? If you don't mind, Mr. Mackenzie?"

With her round gray eyes full of dread, Sarah turned to Tyler seated on the couch next to her. "Go for it," he said quietly. "This part is more for you than me, anyway." He picked up a copy of National Geographic from the coffee table and settled back against the cushions to read.

Sarah followed the doctor into a dark room, paneled in wood and lined with bookshelves and file cabinets. Medical charts and diplomas covered whatever wall space was available. Dr. Wilder sat down behind an enormous mahogany desk and indicated that Sarah should sit across from him in an uncomfortable chair upholstered in stiff green leather. The professional attitude he was assuming began to make her feel even more uneasy than before.

"Now what exactly is it you are trying to find out, young lady?" He lit his pipe again and peered at her over the top of his glasses.

Sarah bit her tongue to keep from making a snide remark about not being young or a lady. "Do you think my mother committed suicide?" The question came out bluntly and without preface.

"As I recall, your mother was a rather unhappy woman. It is entirely possible." He rose abruptly and crossed to the file cabinets, returning in seconds with a manila folder. "It probably would be prudent for you to know what health problems she had if any, in case she might have passed some hereditary condition on to you."

"You mean like mental illness."

The doctor took off his glasses in a classic gesture and looked squarely at her. "All right, Sarah. I can see it would be useless to beat around the bush with you. Your mother was not mentally ill. Nor was she manic depressive. She coped with her situation the best she knew how. In those days it was not a topic to be discussed openly, the way it is now. People were ashamed of it and hid it at home the best they could."

"What are we talking about?"

He looked down at the open file on his desk, putting his glasses back on to read. A slow minute ticked by. Sarah twisted the sleeve of her sweater back and forth nervously, waiting for him to say something. Finally he removed his glasses again and began speaking.

"The first time I saw your mother was a few months after she'd moved up here, in the fall of 1950. That was back in the days of house calls. She was in the midst of a painful miscarriage, cramping and hemorrhaging. Upon examination I discovered that she also had two broken ribs. She insisted that she had fallen down the stairs and I didn't argue with her although it was obviously not true. We both knew she wasn't fooling anybody, but we didn't talk about it. I've patched up too many drunks after barroom brawls not to recognize the damage done by a right upper punch to the stomach."

"You mean someone hit her in the stomach and caused her to lose the baby?" Sarah's head was still reeling from the revelation that she was not her mother's first pregnancy.

"I think we both know who that someone was. I doubt if the loss of the baby was intentional." He cleared his throat. "I assured her that her reproductive organs were not damaged and that she would be able to conceive again. But she asked for the most foolproof method of birth control I could provide her with." His gaze left Sarah's and wandered to the hammered tin ceiling. "We didn't have birth control pills for distribution back then, so the diaphragm was the most trusted form and generally worked when used properly. Are you emotional about all this or can I talk to you absolutely frankly?"

Hanging on his every word, she was startled by the sudden question. "I– I– never knew her. And I want to know everything. I don't care how ugly it is. I want to know the truth."

"Okay. Well, then." He cleared his throat. "When I told her she would have no problem giving birth to other children, she said she didn't ever want to get pregnant again. I consoled her, of course, telling her women always felt like that after a miscarriage but eventually they usually got over it. But she swore she would never have 'that man's child.' Those were her words."

As much as she had wanted to hear it, the truth stung sharply. "But in the end she did."

102

The doctor's stern expression softened for a minute. "I believe the only time I ever saw her happy was in those months after you were born. She loved you very much. She had seemed so frightened about it until then. She–" he hesitated and then threw up his hands in a helpless gesture. "I'm sure if she had lived she would have eventually told you everything I'm telling you. She cried when she found out she was pregnant with you. It had been an accident.

"But I'm getting ahead of myself. I did some blood work on her that first time and discovered she also had gonorrhea so it was probably just as well that she lost that fetus."

"Gonorrhea!" Sarah sat up straight in disbelief.

"She had caught it from her husband, of course. That was the only time I ever met him, when he came in for his penicillin shots. I guess he was gone most of the time, thank God. I didn't seen Winnie again for three years, except occasionally at church or the post office. The next time I saw her she came to my office, nursing a fractured arm, a split lip, a black eye and multiple bruises."

"He– he beat her up again?" Sarah's words were not much louder than a whisper.

"Wife abuse is a terrible thing, Sarah. I don't mean to upset you, but I'm sure this was not the first time he had battered her, just the only time it had been severe enough for her to come see me about it. She told me she'd slipped on a patch of ice walking the dog at night. She knew she wasn't fooling me but she stuck to her story. I asked her if her husband was home and she told me he would be away for at least six months on business. I thought perhaps she was lying to protect him."

Sarah shook her head. It was hard to comprehend what kind of woman her mother must have been. "I've never understood why she couldn't admit she made a mistake and just divorce him."

103

"Fear, pride, any number of reasons. We'll never know. When she returned to have the cast removed six weeks later, she asked me to do a pregnancy test on her. And sure enough...I suggested to her that she continue to have Dora Evans live with her until the baby was born. She had hired Dora as a live–in companion while her arm was broken and I thought that it might be a certain amount of `protection', so to speak, to have someone else around the house all the time. I couldn't figure out why Winnie was so hesitant about the idea until finally I realized that she was financially strapped. So I commissioned her to make me those two windows; one as payment for my services, the other I paid her for on the condition that she use the money to keep Dora around."

"Was he there when I was born?"

"Your father? I should think not, but I don't recall actually. "

"Were you her doctor when she died? I mean, before she died, when she fell."

"No, I didn't see her then. They took her to the hospital in Jordan Center and treated her there. I believe she was comatose for a day or so before she passed away. What was the name of that old ER nurse..." Dr. Wilder frowned and scratched the end of his nose. "She finally married some rich old geezer in a wheelchair and moved to Florida with him, what was her name? She's the one who took care of her in the hospital. Damn it all." He slammed his fist on the desk. "I hate when I forget people's names. Maybe Mrs. Wilder would remember."

"I guess it's not that important." Feeling rather dazed, Sarah rose stiffly from her chair. "Well, thank you for telling me all this, Dr. Wilder. I appreciate you taking the time."

"Not at all." He rose to see her to the door. "And you understand now why I thought perhaps your journalist friend shouldn't hear all of this. Pretty personal stuff, wouldn't you say?"

Very personal, Sarah thought as they stepped back into the living room and Tyler's eager face came into view. It would take some sorting out in her mind before she could decide what, if anything, she should share with him.

"Everything okay?" he asked anxiously. "You look a little pale. Mrs. Wilder showed me the hummingbird window over the piano. It's really a beauty, you ought to take a look at it before we go."

But Sarah was already heading for the front door, as though she had not heard him. Hastily he gathered up his paraphernalia and followed her outside. Halfway down the walk they stopped as Dr. Wilder hailed them from the porch.

"Clara Dobrinsky!" he shouted. "The old man she married was named Dunbar! I told you Mrs. Wilder would know."

"What's he talking about?" Tyler looked at Sarah in bewilderment.

"Oh, nothing." He watched her swallow hard and then shout, "Thanks!" to the doctor, before getting into the car. She did not notice Tyler whipping out his notebook and jotting down the name of Clara Dobrinsky Dunbar, just in case it meant something.

The large raindrops that smacked against the windshield as they drove back to West Jordan had turned into wet sloppy snow by the time Sarah opened the bar at the inn. Customers came in, drank or ate quickly, and left early, anxious to be home before the roads became any worse.

Irritated because Sarah had revealed nothing to him about her conversation with the doctor, Tyler circulated through the lounge, talking to everyone. He interviewed them casually, making small talk and appearing equally indifferent to most of the answers he received. Nobody seemed to remember anybody named Clara Dobrinsky, although an older woman who worked in accounting at the hospital and who was on her fourth martini seemed to think she could recall someone with that name. But everyone had something to say about Dora Evans.

"She used to be quite a beauty although you wouldn't guess it to look at her now," remarked a grizzled welder named Pete, as he sipped the draft beer Tyler had bought for him. "Homecoming queen one year even. Ain't that right, Lyle?"

"What's that?" Hunched over his beer, Lyle lifted his dark eyes to see who'd called him.

"Wasn't your mama homecoming queen once at the old high school?"

"Dora Evans is your mother?" Tyler looked over at Sarah, but her back was to him so he tried to put the pieces together for himself. He had figured out that the cop who had ticketed Sarah was Dora's son but he had forgotten that Sarah had mentioned that Brian Evans was Lyle's brother.

"What about it, city boy?" The winter weather meant Lyle would not be able to work with his log skidder in the morning and he was in one of his surlier moods.

"This here reporter is doin' research on Winnie Scupper, that woman your mama used to work for, before you was born. Gonna put this stuff in some magazine or somethin'. Your mama could be famous!" Pete gave a wheeze that passed for a laugh and sucked the foam off the beer in his mug.

Lyle's deep set eyes seemed to sink further into his face as he slammed his bottle on the counter and approached Tyler. "Don't you put nothin' about my mother in that article of yours, you understand me?"

The room became quite still, awaiting Tyler's response. "Why's that?" he asked nonchalantly, not backing away from Lyle's menacing presence.

"Because I said so, that's why. Because there's a great big axe in the back of my truck that could take off your pecker, that's why too. And if you don't believe me, just try it and see what happens."

"Lyle." Sarah did not shout, but her voice was firm and commanding. "Either sit down and finish your beer quietly or leave right now. You understand me?"

Tyler was surprised that, without a word of protest, Lyle went back to his barstool and returned to his previous hunched–over position. A hum of conversation resumed and when it seemed safely loud enough, Tyler spoke to Pete in a low voice.

"Why is he so touchy about his mother?"

Pete shrugged and stared down into his beer so that Lyle wouldn't know he was talking about him. "Maybe because all her kids are bastards. Lit'rally, that is. I don't think she was really a whore. Just stupid. Never could find anybody who'd marry her. Her beauty was the only thing she had goin' for herself. The family's sort of protective of her now that she's a fat old cow." He gave a few wheezing chuckles and then looked furtively at Lyle from beneath the brim of his cap.

"Does she work anywhere?"

"Not for as long as I can remember. Doesn't go out much anymore. I think she wants people to remember her the way she used to be. When she was a juicy piece of ass."

"Sounds like you speak from experience." Tyler threw out the bait, hoping he was not off the mark.

Pete hesitated before replying. At the end of the bar, Lyle was paying his bill and throwing a quarter onto the counter for Sarah. "Cheap tipper," Bo teased him from the next seat.

"Shut up, Bo." Lyle skulked out into the snow storm without bothering to button up his red checked woolen jacket.

"Yeah, old Dora and me, we had our good times," Pete answered when Lyle was out the door. "But that was back in those days before she worked for that stained glass woman. Then she got kinda uppity; said she couldn't see me no more, she had to behave herself." He snorted and then spit into a napkin. "Well, sir, Lyle's the living proof that she couldn't do that for long."

Another old–timer had joined them at the bar. Beneath his green woolen cap, his pale blue eyes twinkled. He sported a long white Santa Claus beard that hung down over his patched overalls. He ordered a shot of whiskey and introduced himself to Tyler as Red. "Hard to believe now, but red used to be the color of my hair," he explained.

"Red used to know Dora way back when too," Pete said with a wink.

"I guess all the men in town were pretty friendly with Dora back then," Red responded, a slight flush of embarrassment coloring his cheeks. "She was not what you call high–class merchandise."

"She thought she was when she got that job at the Scupper place, remember?"

"How could I forget? Old Elwood used to pay me to plow that driveway in the winter. Don't ask me what for – didn't look like they even had a car up there. Oh, I guess the Scupper woman was pregnant, wasn't she? Dora wasn't supposed to have any male visitors up there, that was part of the deal I guess. But she used to come out and climb into the truck with me while I was plowing. Oooh–weee!" Red chuckled to himself. "Queen of the quickies, that's what we called her."

Tyler was beginning to understand why Lyle didn't like people to get started talking about his mother.

"I always thought that Scupper woman could've taken some lessons from her. Now that was one tight–assed woman! You couldn't even flirt with her joking–like."

Behind the bar, Tyler could see Sarah's lips forming a thin line and the color draining out of her cheeks. Much as he wanted them to keep talking, he knew he had pushed the conversation out of bounds in Sarah's estimation.

"Quite a storm," he said, so suddenly that both men looked up at him, startled. "How much snow do you think we'll get?"

By ten o'clock the Night Heron lounge was empty and the snow was piling up outside. Sarah decided to close down early, so she could get home before the driving was any worse. As she cleaned up she could hear Tyler talking in the living room with Woody. He had disappeared up to his room for a while and she thought he had gone to bed. But now they were looking through Woody's old high school yearbooks for pictures of Dora Evans.

She wished he was not so driven. It seemed as though he couldn't let the subject rest, even for an hour or two. He'd only been back one day and she was already emotionally worn out again. She knew he was mad because she hadn't told him anything that Dr. Wilder had said about her mother. But Woody had been right. It was really none of his business.

In fact, the whole thing was none of his business.

Without saying goodnight, Sarah locked the door and slogged through the snow to her car. It was snowing quite heavily now, and covering the road fast enough to fill in the tracks of any cars that might have traveled the same way in the last hour. It gave the road a false appearance of untouched virgin snow, an illusion that continued right to the end of her driveway, where, after a few unsuccessful tries, she abandoned the car, and trudged up the hill to her cabin.

She stomped the snow off her boots on the porch, under the welcome yellow glow of her porch light. She did not notice anything was amiss until she flicked the switch inside the door.

From where she stood, it appeared as though every piece of furniture had been overturned or pulled apart. Couch cushions were on the floor; kitchen chairs lay on their sides. Through the door to the bedroom she could see the covers had been ripped off the mattress which hung over the edge of the bed, half on the floor. Every drawer had been opened, some dumped out, some rifled through. Boxes had been pulled from the storage closet and emptied unceremoniously.

She had not been home since mid–morning to stoke the woodstove and a wintry chill had settled into the cottage. But it was not the air temperature that gripped at Sarah's heart with an icy hand.

Out the open door behind her, the whiteness of the driveway extended into the night, covering any trace of whoever had come and gone. Perhaps they had come during the day and beneath the snow lay a perfect tire track or footprint that would never be found.

This nightly harassment had gone one step too far. It could no longer be ignored. She crossed to the phone and with shaking fingers dialed the operator. "Put me through to the West Jordan police department, please. I'd like to report a break in."

CHAPTER SIX

From the time she made the telephone call, it took at least three hours before Brian Evans rapped on the door of the cabin. With the night being as stormy as it was, Sarah had figured it might take him an hour to drive from the center of West Jordan and then walk the length of the driveway, but three hours seemed excessive. Ignoring instructions not to touch anything, she had built a fire in the stove and huddled next to it with a blanket around her shoulders, trying to get warm as she surveyed the damage.

The truth was that nothing had been destroyed. A couple of hundred dollars in cash was missing from a jar on top of the dresser where she usually kept her tips until she had a chance to deposit them in the bank. The box she kept her earrings in had been dumped on the dresser and without touching anything she could see that a pair of antique gold hoops was missing. Her few personal treasures had been swept off the mantelpiece into a pile on the floor but did not appear to be broken. Pains had obviously been taken to rough the place up enough to scare her but not enough to actually destroy anything.

"Sorry to take so long but the weather held me up," Brian apologized as he brushed the snow off his overcoat. "I couldn't get anybody to come out with me so I brought a camera myself. I'll have someone come by in the morning and dust for fingerprints." He looked around. "Boy, somebody really did a number on this place. Anything missing?"

"It seems the burglar had a conscience." Sarah explained to him all that she had noticed during her long three hour wait.

"Is there anybody who might be out to get you for some reason? You know, a revenge motive, perhaps?"

She shook her head. "But I've noticed a car that follows me home sometimes after work." She told him about the hit–and–run of the night before.

He looked at her oddly. "Why didn't you call me about that last night?"

She shrugged and pulled the blanket closer around her shoulders. "What could you have done?"

After a few more questions he made some notes on a legal pad, then insisted that she lock the cabin and spend the night at the inn. He would drive her there himself and come back for her in the morning. After a few feeble protests, she decided he was right, pulled a change of clothes out of the heap on the floor, damped down the stove, and followed him down the driveway, walking behind him in his tracks. The snowfall seemed to be easing up and by the time they got to town it had stopped entirely.

Too tired to make up one of the beds in the guest rooms, Sarah collapsed on the sofa in the downstairs living room. Covering herself with the crocheted afghan that hung over the back of the well–worn cushions, she fell into a fitful sleep at last.

It seemed like only minutes later that she was awakened by voices in the next room. She squinted at her watch, blinded by the brilliance of the morning sun reflecting off the snow outside. 7:30. She sunk back against the throw pillows and closed her eyes again, unable to keep from listening to what had now become apparent as only one voice, Tyler's, talking on the telephone at the front desk.

"No, I won't be back by this weekend, I told you that when I left...Do I have to answer that now? Thanksgiving is a whole week away...Your mother could care less if I didn't come...Oh, give me a break, Isabel, you're the one who has a problem dealing with your family, not me...My brother said I could keep the car indefinitely. His company gave him a car to drive...I know, I know. Listen, I hate to say this when you sound so stressed out, but I told you that I was staying here until I was satisfied that I had done all I could no matter how long it takes...Will you stop saying that? You sound like some jealous schoolgirl...no, I haven't shaved off my beard yet. Look, I've got to go. I'll call you in a few days, okay?...All right, all right, how about Sunday at 11?...Right. You too. Bye."

Tyler slammed the receiver down, muttering expletives that Sarah could not hear. "Holy Mother of God, you scared me half to death!" he exclaimed suddenly from the open doorway of the living room, coffee sloshing onto his shirt from the cup he held in one hand. "What are you doing here? Did your car break down on the way home or something?"

Sarah groaned and turned her back on him, not feeling awake enough to chat. "My house got burglarized last night. Brian asked me to sleep here until they could get it fingerprinted this morning."

"Are you okay?" She could sense him hovering over her in concern.

"I'm fine. It was my house that got ransacked and ripped apart, not me." Although she had her eyes shut and the afghan pulled tight up around her neck, he did not seem to get the message. He sat down on the edge of the couch by her feet, and she knew without looking that he was quietly watching her as he sipped his coffee.

"Sarah, do you think that I'm responsible for all this sudden harassment you've been experiencing?"

"What?" She rolled onto her back so suddenly that his coffee spilled again, this time all over his jeans.

"Oww! No, I meant indirectly responsible. Do you think it has anything to do with all the questions I've been asking people about your mother?"

She contemplated him silently for a moment from beneath eyelids heavy with sleep. "I don't know," she answered at last. "Maybe. Would you stop if you thought it would make a difference?"

"Are you asking me to?"

"Maybe." She could feel the tension mounting between them now. "Actually, Tyler, I've never told anyone this, but I've had a feeling for months now that someone has been watching me and following me. Long before you ever showed up. So I doubt if you're the cause of it."

He relaxed visibly. "If you'd like, I'll come up to your house today and help you clean it up."

"Thanks, but I think I'd like to be alone today. Don't you have some work you can do without me?"

"Of course, but–" he fumbled for words, in an uncharacteristic way. "Do you think you'll be safe? Up there in the woods by yourself?"

Sarah closed her eyes and breathed deeply, trying to swallow the fears that seemed to be filling her throat, choking her. When she finally spoke, it was the tough, ever–practical Sarah speaking. "Of course I'll be safe. Whoever went through my house took what little they could find of value already. They won't be back. And I'm sure the police will be cruising the road for the next few days on the lookout as well. But you're right. I probably could use some – help." She had been about to say "company". "I'll give you a call later, okay?"

Tyler watched her roll over and hide her face in the couch again. He was glad she had accepted his offer of help. It gave him a good excuse to see where she lived without seeming sleazy and intrusive.

It was nearly noon by the time she was finally able to set one of the kitchen chairs on its feet and sit down in it to call him. The cabin had been thoroughly dusted for fingerprints, her own had been taken, and she had been questioned at least twice, in detail, about how she'd spent the previous day.

114

Upon hearing of the burglary, Woody had promptly told her to take the night off. Initially numbed by the course of events, she now felt a bit shaken as she sat alone in the disorderly cottage. Her privacy had been invaded and violated. Despite the brave, sensible front she put up for others, she was nervous and afraid. Although she couldn't see it, she could hear the clock ticking somewhere nearby beneath some displaced piece of furniture. Its quiet insistence of the continuous passage of time made the hairs on the back of her neck prickle.

She had told Tyler to give her an hour or so to shower and change her clothes, but now she found a greater need to use the time to set as many things as possible back to their proper positions. She felt a little better once the couch was right side up again and the table was set in front of the kitchen window with its chairs pushed in neatly around it. An hour had nearly passed by the time she stripped off her clothes and jumped in the shower.

Sarah was already out of the tub and toweling her hair dry when she realized that Tyler was standing in her living room with his back to her, looking at the family pictures she had haphazardly replaced on the mantelpiece above the fireplace.

"Shit." She grabbed her robe off a hook and had barely tied the belt when he turned around.

"Hi," he greeted her. "I knocked but nobody answered so I poked my head in the door and then realized you were in the shower. I made myself at home, I hope you don't mind."

She gave him a look that said all as she knelt in front of the woodstove to comb her wet hair. Tyler bit his lip to keep from exclaiming aloud at how beautifully sensual she looked, her damp dark hair in contrast with the fluffy white robe. Droplets of water dripped onto the exposed vee of her chest from the ends of the wet strands that framed her face.

"Nice place you have here," he said instead. "I mean, it looks like it must be nice when it's –" he gestured at the mess– "fixed up. You heat with this thing?" He indicated the woodstove that sat in the fireplace opening. "I guess it makes sense up here with all this wood around. But it seems like a lot of work to me."

Sarah was glad that Tyler had no problem keeping up a one way conversation. She looked at him standing there, leaning against the mantelpiece, and felt a little annoyed that, even with his half–grown beard and his worn out "country" clothes, he was still so painfully handsome.

She sat cross–legged on a pillow in front of the stove, drinking coffee and drying her hair, answering his questions about cords of wood and creosote build–up and chimney fires. Eventually they exhausted the topic of wood heat and an awkward silence settled like fine ash over the two of them.

Standing up stiffly, Sarah said, "I'll feel a lot better when this place is picked up. Let me get dressed and then we can get going here." She went into the bedroom and tried to close the door, but an overturned drawer blocked the way. It was hard to tell where things were; when she finally found her underwear drawer, it gave her the creeps to think that somebody she didn't know had probably touched all her underpants and bras. She threw them all into a pile to be washed, grabbing a pair of sweatpants instead. As she pulled these on beneath her robe, the telephone rang.

"Would you mind getting that?" she called but Tyler had already answered it.

"Hello?...Sarah's here but she's in the other room getting dressed right now. Who's calling?..." He put his hand over the receiver and poked his head cautiously through the bedroom door as Sarah's face popped through the top of an old sweatshirt. "Some guy named Ron?"

Sarah blushed, knowing what Ron must be thinking about a strange man answering the phone and telling him she was getting dressed. "Hi, Ron...No, it was just Tyler. You know, the journalist from New York...You heard about it already?...No, they don't have any idea who might have done it...Well, thanks, but Tyler's going to help me clean up. It shouldn't take too long...Dinner?" She was suddenly aware of Tyler waving at her and shaking his head vehemently. "Why not?" she hissed at him.

For an answer he opened the refrigerator door. Inside, on the top shelf, she saw a bottle of wine and pile of groceries that had not been there before. "Because I'm going to cook dinner for you."

"Oh." As she apologized to Ron and thanked him, declining the invitation, her mind was whirring as to how to react to Tyler's generous presumptuousness.

"Who's Ron?" he asked as soon as she hung up.

"Just a friend. We go out sometimes on my nights off." She crossed to the refrigerator and opened the door. She looked at a smoked trout, a wedge of brie, red leaf lettuce and a large ripe avocado, before turning to him for an explanation.

He shrugged. "I went into town this morning. I thought it would be nice. I guess it was a good idea," he added, indicating the contents spilling out of the kitchen cabinets and onto the floor.

"You didn't have to—"

"Of course I didn't have to. I wanted to. Now where do we start?" He picked up a pair of salt and pepper shakers in the shape of black and white dairy cows and placed them on the kitchen table. "Very Vermont," he commented.

"The place came furnished," Sarah explained. "I'm glad the burglar didn't break anything because most of it isn't mine."

For the next two hours they worked together, methodically picking up, cleaning and sweeping. The task broke the tension between them and by the end of the afternoon Sarah found herself chatting and laughing in a natural, relaxed way, even able to make a few burglar jokes. She was perfectly content to stretch out on the couch with a glass of wine and watch Tyler bustle around her little kitchen preparing dinner. With freshly swept and mopped floors, vacuumed rugs and washed windows (Tyler had insisted on doing them), the little cottage glowed once again as her cozy retreat.

"This place needed a good cleaning," Sarah remarked. "Maybe my landlord paid someone to do this so that I would have to clean the place up."

"Do you mind if I ask you a couple of questions?" Tyler had his back to her as he chopped vegetables for a salad, but she knew by his tone of voice what he was referring to.

"Depends. What about it?"

He put down the kitchen knife and picked up the open bottle of wine, refilling her glass and then his own. "I was just wondering about a couple of these keepsakes on your mantel."

Tyler had used the afternoon to carefully examine as many of Sarah's material possessions as possible. She had not brought much with her from Arizona; she had explained to him that after her grandmother had died, she had put most of their things in storage, not knowing how long her travels would last. When she had settled in West Jordan, a friend had mailed a box of requested items to her, but that was the extent of her worldliness. Tyler, living in a world that included such indispensable necessities like personal computers, VCRs, cordless telephones and sound systems with the best and largest speakers, could not imagine leaving these essentials behind in a major move. Although, in a brief moment of self–reflection, he realized he was perfectly content here without his expensive toys.

Now he picked up a polished wooden cylinder that had caught his attention earlier. It rattled as he held it

118

to one eye; he had recognized it immediately as a kaleidoscope, the broken bits of bright glass inside making an intricate and colorful pattern when held towards the light.

"You certainly zero right in on things, Tyler." Sarah laughed a little. "My mother made that when she lived up here. She sent it to my grandmother for her birthday one year. My grandmother thought it was a dumb present to give an elderly woman. She used the kaleidoscope as physical evidence that my mother had gotten a little crazy during her years of marriage. Of course, as a little girl I thought the kaleidoscope was great so Grandmother Charlotte gave it to me."

Tyler could tell from her expression that she had drifted away from him for an instant to some point in her distant past. He wished he could be inside her memory for a moment, to record the picture he imagined of a little girl with stiff pigtails standing by a window in a darkened room with her back to a stern, unsmiling old woman. The kaleidoscope, poked between two slats of Venetian blinds to catch the daylight, was pressed eagerly to her eye.

Imagining her past made him feel intrusive, so he handed Sarah the kaleidoscope and turned back to the mantel where he had placed the other object he wanted to ask her about. It was a tiny silver plated comb and brush set for a baby, the soft yellowed bristles of the brush indicating its age. What intrigued him was the inscription on the handle. "Potters Falls Savings & Loan," he read aloud. "Why would a baby's hairbrush have the name of a bank engraved on it? Rather odd place to advertise, don't you think?"

Sarah responded to his question with peals of merriment. "Oh, Tyler, why pretend to be a journalist when what you really want to be is a private investigator! Why don't you just admit it and go for it?"

Tyler's face flushed as he reached for his wine glass. "All right, I admit it. It's what I've always wanted to be, but the problem is I hate the thought of carrying a gun and it's nearly mandatory in a dangerous line of work like that."

"Couldn't you learn some deadly martial art that might take its place as protection?" Sarah was regarding him with an interested look he had never seen before.

"A lot of good a karate chop would do if someone was pointing a loaded pistol at me from twenty feet away. I'm just not into the violence that seems to go along with the job. It's okay – I keep myself happy doing 2000 piece jigsaw puzzles and solving the New York Times Sunday crossword." But his downcast eyes and the set of his lips said otherwise.

Sarah cleared her throat. "About that comb and brush...I'm not like you. I have wondered but never really cared. It was one of those things that have been around for so long that you never question it. That comb and brush set was always on my dresser for as long as I can remember. I guess someone gave it to my mother when I was born and it got packed along with my diapers and came with me to New York."

"What makes you think you didn't acquire it down there?"

"Well, I had always assumed it had been a gift from one of my grandmother's senile friends until I discovered that Potters Falls is the name of a town about 35 miles north of here."

"Really? Have you been there?"

"Nah. It's on the way to nowhere. You wouldn't go there unless you were headed for the Canadian border."

Sarah got up from the couch, leaving a deep indentation in the cushion she had been so comfortably settled on, and opened the door of the woodstove. They had let the fire burn low during all their afternoon activity and only a few small coals glowed among the ashes. "Clear night. Temperature's dropping outside,"

120

she commented with Yankee abruptness. "Guess I better stoke this thing up."

While Sarah got the fire going, Tyler returned to the kitchen. Before long they were seated at the table across from each other, savoring the delicious eclectic flavor of what Sarah would have called "yuppie food" if she hadn't been afraid of offending Tyler. He had certainly done his best to create an atmosphere of – she hesitated to even think the word – "intimacy." He had even brought candles, and having found no candleholders, had melted the bottoms and stuck them onto saucers instead.

"What will you do for Thanksgiving?" he asked her, as he scooped another helping of tortellini vinaigrette onto her plate.

"Woody always has a Thanksgiving dinner for the wayward singles of the neighborhood. It was fun last year. And you?" She concentrated on her plate, thinking about the telephone conversation she had overheard that morning and not wanting to give away that she had been eavesdropping.

"Oh, I usually go with Isabel to her parents' house. But I may still be here."

"Well, I'm sure you'd be welcome at Woody's."

"He thinks a lot of you, doesn't he?"

The sudden change of focus in the question startled her, and she looked up at him with round eyes full of puzzlement. "What do you mean?"

"You know, he seems to care about you. The way he watches you when you work and the way he talks about you." His fork was poised in the air on the way to his mouth as he carefully observed her reaction to his words.

Sarah looked a little flushed and embarrassed, but all she said was, "We're just good friends. I can count on him to be there if I need him."

"I guess he was good friends with your mother too."

Something in his tone of voice seemed to insinuate more than just the simple face value of the words. Sarah's fork clattered to the plate and her jaw sagged for a second at this new and rather shocking idea. "Woody told me she was a friend of his father's," she replied slowly, and then the unanswered questions behind that statement seemed to shout aloud as well.

"Sarah, I didn't mean –" The usually glib Tyler seemed at a loss for words and instead reached for her hand across the table. "I'm sorry."

She looked at his outstretched hand waiting for her own, feeling powerful but not quite understanding why. The candle flames lit his face from below, distorting his expression, throwing an eerie shadow across his cheeks. His eyes glinted golden like a cat's. It reminded her that, as pleasant and personal as he was, she still was not sure how much she trusted him.

A white beam of light flashed across the table and then moved upwards onto the wall. Both of them gasped; it was Sarah who realized first that it was the headlights of a car coming up the driveway which was now smoothly plowed.

Leaping out of her chair, she hurried to the window in the front door for a better view. Until this moment she had not realized how nervous she still was; her legs felt suddenly jelly–like and buckled under her. She grabbed at the window sill to steady herself but Tyler was right behind her. With one hand he caught her against his chest before she fell, with the other hand he reached over and flicked the light switch next to the door.

The glow of the yellow porch light spilled over the edge of the front steps and across the snow. The headlights hesitated momentarily and then began backing down the driveway until they disappeared behind the curve of the hill. Sarah breathed deeply and tried to stop trembling, thankful for Tyler's warm presence and the steadiness of his arms around her as they stood there together, staring out into the night.

"Should we call the police?" He spoke in a whisper, his mouth to her ear.

"No, it– it could have been anyone," she murmured half to herself. "Sometimes people miss the turn at the crossroads and drive up here by mistake. But I bet it was probably just Ron, coming to see if I'd changed my mind, and when you turned the light on he saw your car and decided to beat a hasty retreat. It would be even more embarrassing if the police stopped him for coming up here."

Tyler seemed to recognize the pattern she used to reassure herself that she was alone but safe. He tightened his grip around her waist, pulling her backwards even closer. With her eyes still on the driveway, Sarah leaned back against him, giving into the sheltering embrace.

"After all, a thief would have to be pretty stupid to return to the scene of the crime the next night." She was still reasoning herself out of danger. "In fact, I would say that now that I've been robbed, the odds of my number coming up again should be nearly zero." She gave a half–hearted giggle that stuck in her throat as she felt Tyler's breath on the back of her neck, followed by the moist warmth of his lips.

"Tyler–" She shivered involuntarily, not from fear but from the electricity that seemed to be passing from his body into her own. "Stop–"

"I can't." He was kissing her earlobe now and the soft hairs at the edge of her forehead.

"You can."

"I don't want to." With a swift and dexterous shift of position, he was in front of her, holding her face between his hands, gazing down at her with a shining look that betrayed all that he had been keeping hidden.

"Tyler, you're as good as married." But as she spoke, she found herself reaching up to touch his cheek, the wave in his hair, his bristly new beard.

"I'm not. It's over."

"Since when?"

"Since now." Their lips met with such a heated intensity they both felt consumed by the hungry, searching kiss which followed. Sarah pulled away from him finally in a ragged gesture, and sat down hard on the couch.

"You're taking advantage of my condition, Tyler." Her voice was uneven and breathless.

"What? What are you talking about?"

"I'm feeling scared and vulnerable and you're turning my need for comfort and security into something sexual."

"You and your damn psychological analysis!" Angrily he reached for the bottle of wine on the table. Finding it was empty, he tossed it into the garbage and then rummaged in the grocery bag as he talked. "You felt what happened between us just now, I know you did. And you want it as much as I do, admit it!" Triumphantly he pulled an expensive bottle of brandy from the paper bag.

"Okay, okay, I felt it. But it's stupid to get involved with you. You don't live here, we don't even like the same things, the only thing we have in common is your article about my mother!"

"So what?" Before she knew what was happening, he was next to her on the couch, kissing her so forcefully that she fell over backwards with him on top of her, straddling her hips in a way that made her aware of everything he was feeling. And then, just as abruptly, he rose and went back into the kitchen, returning momentarily with two juice glasses and the bottle of brandy.

Sarah was still lying on the couch, her arms crooked up behind her head, watching him with a funny smile. He sat down on the floor next to her and poured them each a couple fingers worth of brandy. "To us," he said offering her a glass and clinking it against his own at the same time. Sarah made a face as she sipped at the brandy, never taking her eyes off him, wondering what he would do next.

"Will you be embarrassed if I tell you that all I thought about was you after I left here last time?"

"Yes."

"I tried to pretend that it was the article that was drawing me back, the unsolved mysteries of Winnie Scupper. I could fool everyone else, but I couldn't fool myself. I mean, technically it is Winnie Scupper that's brought me back here, but mostly because she's your mother. It's you and everything about you that I'm interested in."

Sarah tipped up her glass and drained the brandy in one gulp. It made her eyes water, her throat hurt and the blood rush to her head, and it distracted her from the reality of Tyler's confession. After the initial reaction, she felt warm and pleasantly dizzy as she held her glass out for a refill.

"So what do you think? About you and me, I mean."

She laughed loudly and took another swallow of the brandy, feeling it burn its way down to her stomach. "The truth is, Tyler, I never considered it. I don't let myself entertain thoughts about married men or men with steady girlfriends. In my line of work it would be emotional suicide if I let myself follow up an attraction to a man with an attachment to another woman. I can't tell you how many times I was approached when I first came to town." She shook her head despairingly. "So many people, so bored with their relationships, ready to have a fling. It was downright depressing. So even if I did find you interesting and attractive, I wasn't going to do anything about it."

"So you admit that you did find me interesting and attractive?" He twisted her arm teasingly.

"Compared to guys like Lyle and Bo...incredibly so." She knocked back the remainder of the brandy in her glass. Tyler was beginning to appear blurred and distant and the couch felt as though it were spinning. She closed her eyes and held out her glass. "One more, please, bartender. I don't have far to drive."

The next brandy washed over her in an ocean of sleep. She was aware of Tyler pulling her to her feet and she had a vague awareness of sinking into a soft pillow and covers being drawn up. She tried to mumble, "We're not ready to have sex yet, Tyler," but her tongue was thick and wouldn't move. The warm darkness overcame her.

She awoke several hours later with a mouth that felt horribly dry and full of sandpaper. Staggering out to the kitchen for a drink of water, she was surprised to see that the outdoor light was still on and Tyler was asleep on the couch, curled up beneath a heavy Mexican woven blanket. He had not shut the damper on the stove and the fire was nearly out. She shook her head, unable to fathom why he would choose to sleep uncomfortably on her couch in a cold cabin rather than go back to his bed at the inn. But when she returned to her own bed after quenching her thirst, she decided she was glad he was there. She had spent many sleepless early morning hours alone in the cabin. Just knowing she was not alone helped her to relax. As she drifted back to sleep she wondered if maybe Tyler was right about it not mattering how different the two of them were.

Sometime after daybreak she heard his car start up and then drive off into the distance. Rolling over on her stomach she went back to sleep, not waking again until midmorning. Although the cabin felt icy, sunshine streamed in the windows and she could hear the sound of water dripping off the eaves and she knew that the temperature outdoors was above freezing.

With the Mexican blanket around her shoulders, she settled herself with a cup of coffee in front of the woodstove, leaving the door open so that she could feel the direct instant heat of the flames. Within seconds the telephone rang. Grumbling, she grabbed for it; as usual it was just out of arm's reach on the floor.

She was not surprised when Tyler's voice greeted her cheerfully. "What are you up to?"

"Waking up. And you?"

"You're just getting up now? Well, while you slept the day away I've been busting my ass working on a hunch I had and it's paid off." His voice could not conceal his excitement.

"What are you talking about?"

"I borrowed that little baby brush set this morning, I didn't think you'd mind. It occurred to me last night who might know something about it." He waited eagerly for her obligatory response.

She stared at the empty place on the mantel where the comb and brush had sat. "Well, who?"

"Maude Alfred, of course. She deals in all those local antiquities. So I hustled over to visit her at the nursing home first thing after breakfast and sure enough she knew right away what the story was."

Sarah noticed now that there was a lot of resounding background noise behind Tyler, indicating that he was not calling from the front desk at the inn.

"It turns out that it was a promotional thing that this bank in Potters Falls did for a while back in the early fifties, during the original baby boom. Apparently it was some sort of incentive program; when somebody opened a savings account for a new baby, they got this silver-backed comb and brush set."

"Really? Tyler, where are you?" The sounds in the background were unfamiliar to her. It sounded like he was calling from a cavernous, high–ceilinged railroad terminal somewhere.

"I'm in Potters Falls. At the bank. I think you ought to get dressed and drive up here right away."

"You're up in Potters Falls?"

"I told them I was your lawyer, but they said I couldn't have access to anything without you present or without written, notarized permission."

"What?"

"Sarah, there's not only a bank account here in your name, but a safe deposit box as well."

WINNIE

West Jordan, November, 1954

Winnie sat stiffly in a straight–backed chair in the front hall, watching for Elwood Foster's car to pull into the drive. She hated having to call him and ask for a ride to Dr. Wilder's office, but he had insisted, and really, there was no other way. Besides, they could stop for groceries on the way back and it would save her the walk to town. She had been so tired lately and the journey up the hill, dragging the two–wheeled shopping cart behind her, seemed endless.

Life had fallen into a pattern, and unpleasant as it was at times, there was still a small amount of security in the fact that it was a pattern that repeated itself over and over again, year after year. Winnie spent weeks, sometimes months, alone in the big empty summer house, working on her glass projects and trying to enjoy the peace and solitude of the beautiful surroundings. But no matter how many days went by, she was never totally able to relax, knowing that Travis might come home at any moment and shatter the even, predictable pace of her life without him.

Sometimes she shook with fear at the first sound of his voice calling her name up the stairwell and then her fears would prove groundless. He would sweep up the stairs with an enormous bouquet of pink roses and kiss her tenderly, telling her how much he had missed her. But the next time he returned, she might be greeted with an insult and a slap across the face because she had not run eagerly to meet him at the door like a wife was supposed to. Then she would be marched immediately up to the bedroom to gratify his sexual needs which, as the years progressed, had become increasingly bizarre.

The only way she got through those visits was the knowledge that he never stayed very long. A few days, a few dollars in his pocket, and he would be on his way again. She was surprised at first by how little money she was able to live on. Usually she was so glad to see him leave that she didn't care if he drained their small savings account. But when there was no money he would always slip away with some of her jewelry, a ring or a pair of earrings, something that wouldn't be missed for days or months. In fact, it was several months into the marriage, after one visit in which he had been particularly abusive verbally and physically, that she had opened her jewelry box and realized that several expensive heirloom pieces were missing. She didn't wear much jewelry in Vermont, she almost never went anywhere, and she had no idea how long ago he had taken the pieces, but she suspected they had been gone for quite a while. She sobbed openly; even if she was completely destitute she would never sell her grandmother's jewelry. Travis had no respect for anything.

They fought about it the next time he was home and she shuddered even now to remember what he had done to her to prove he was the master of the household. She was glad they lived so far from town with no neighboring houses nearby. Nobody would ever know what went on between this husband and wife. "Safe Haven," her family's name for the house, had become a sad irony in Winnie's life.

She did not know how he would react the next time he came home and found Dora Evans and her little boy living in the house. It was his own fault, she thought angrily, looking down at the plaster cast on her right arm. Why did he always have to show his power over her with physical violence? But what he did to her physically did not compare with the mental degradation

130

she experienced as a result of his abuse. The worst of it was, not able to stand up to him, she had lost all respect for herself.

She would not ever forgive him for the way he had humiliated her in front of his friends the last time he had been home. He had never brought anyone with him before and she was shaken to see a strange car following his up the driveway. Two beefy men with red faces and saggy jowls unloaded a case of liquor from the trunk and hauled it up to the front door, where Travis was telling a speechless Winnie to make up a couple of the spare rooms because they were having company for a few days.

The stale smell of gin and cigars assailed her nostrils as Travis showed the men where the bar was in the dining room. For a few minutes she thought that maybe this would relieve her of the stress of Travis's attentions. But he followed her up the stairs to one of the guest bedrooms and told her they would be expecting hors d'oeuvres in half an hour, after which she would serve them dinner and to wear something appropriate. He stood watching her from the doorway as she made up the bed and then said abruptly, "I'd better lay out the clothes I want you to wear," and disappeared down the hall in the direction of their bedroom.

A card game was already in progress on the dining room table when she descended to the kitchen to hastily arrange some cheese and olives on crackers. There was barely enough food on hand to feed three hungry men, but she could go without and tomorrow Travis could take her to the supermarket in Jordan Center.

As she entered the dining room bearing the requested hors d'oeuvres, she caught Travis's stern expression and realized she was still wearing the woolen skirt and sweater she'd had on when he'd arrived. She backed through the swinging doors, dropped the tray on the kitchen table and darted up the back stairs. Her

131

heart sank when she saw what he had placed on the bed for her to wear.

Awaiting her was a pair of tight black pants that fit so snugly they required a zipper up both sides. There was also a white silk blouse with peasant sleeves that was worn off both shoulders and showed several inches of skin above the waist. There was no possibility of wearing a bra with such a blouse, and the thought of those fat men leering at her made her nauseous. Tossed to one side of the outfit was a pair of open–toed black shoes, the four inch heels gaudily decorated with rhinestones.

Winnie knew he had picked this outfit on purpose because of the memories it would evoke. The last time she had worn it there had been a sordid scene of sexual domination that had left her sickened and fearful of the man who called himself her loving husband. Travis had become angry with the mechanical way in which Winnie accommodated his demands, never showing any pleasure in the act herself. When she told him she was too afraid of him to relax enough to achieve orgasm, he had smacked her hard and told her he'd change that. Before she realized what was happening he had lashed her arms above her head to the headboard with a belt and when she squirmed, he lashed each foot to a bedpost as well so that she was helplessly spread eagled on the bed. He had then calmly used his years of experience with countless women and the power of his well–experienced fingers and tongue to force her to climax again and again between her sobbing pleas to stop. She had finally passed out from exhaustion and when she awoke she was untied and alone, naked and freezing on top of the damp sheets.

Now, biting her lip, she assured herself that she was safer if there were other people in the house. She dropped her skirt to the floor and, with trembling hands, prepared herself for the evening.

132

The atmosphere of the dining room fairly sizzled from the moment she walked through the doorway with the tray. She had forgotten how much Travis enjoyed watching other men admire her; it had been years since the opportunity had occurred. It seemed harmless enough until one of the men accidentally knocked over his martini, splattering gin across the floor as the delicate glass shattered into tiny pieces.

"Clean that up, will you, Winnie?" Travis did not even look up from his cards as he spoke and his command stung even more for its casual delivery.

She had trouble kneeling down in her tight pants, and she ended up having to crawl around on her hands and knees in order to mop up the liquid and pick up the bits of broken glass. Realizing that the neck of her peasant blouse gaped revealingly in this position, she looked up to find one of the puffy–faced men staring boldly down her shirt at the spectacle of her uncovered breasts.

"Nice view from this end too," commented Travis, running his finger up the seam of the shiny black fabric stretched taut across her backside. All three men chuckled.

Horrified at being the source of their vulgar humor, Winnie got to her feet as quickly as she could and ran from the room carrying a dish full of broken glass. There was a tinkling sound from the next room and then Travis's voice called, "Better come back out again, dear. Looks like we've broken another one," followed by more low rumbles of masculine laughter.

She stood frozen in the kitchen until he called again, adding, "Don't make me come in there after you!" Then slowly she returned to the dining room, teetering on her sparkling high heels. With one hand she held her blouse to her chest as she got down on her knees, feeling the little stitches that held her pants together straining against her thighs as she tried to clean up this purposeful mess in a decorous manner.

In the kitchen she dashed away the hot tears running down her face, swearing she would not let him do this to her. But she knew what the consequences would be after the guests left if she did not comply and so she tried to make light of it. Throughout the meal Travis commanded her to do various things that put her into impossible, suggestive positions, from standing on a chair to pull the chandelier down a little closer to the table to adjusting the heating vent on the floor next to his foot.

Finally he followed her as she carried a tray of dishes into the kitchen and came up hard against her back, whispering in her ear, "Can you feel what you've done to me, you little tramp? I feel as though I'm about to explode."

She began putting the dirty plates into the hot sudsy dish water and when he realized she was ignoring him, he grabbed the tabs of the two zippers on her pants and pulled them both down in one motion. The seat of her pants fell down as easily as a union suit.

"No, Travis," she gasped, clutching at the flaps of cloth with soapy hands. "What are you thinking?"

"On the floor, right here, right now," was his answer as he unzipped his pants.

"Not with those men right out there. I won't." As she backed away from him, he came after her, grasping her by the arm and dragging her into the adjacent laundry room, shutting the door behind them.

"Get down on the floor," he ordered. As she looked dubiously at the cold cement under foot, he added, "On your hands and knees." When she stared at him with open disgust, he turned her around bodily and pushed her so that she fell forward into the position he wanted.

Down on all fours like the animal he wanted her to be, she thought, as she tried to sniff back the tears that ran down the side of her nose and splashed onto the floor. He pumped himself into her and then groaned in relief, sitting back on his haunches to rest for a moment before playfully spanking her behind and saying, "That was great, Winnie. I really needed that. Now zip yourself up and get back in the kitchen. I think we're ready for some coffee."

When he left her she sat down heavily on the dirty floor and leaned her head back against the old soapstone laundry sink. The cold cement felt like ice against her bare buttocks as his semen trickled out of her and ran a sticky trail down one leg. Reaching for a dirty towel from a nearby laundry basket, she buried her face in it and sobbed brokenly for the lost remnants of her self–esteem.

She had no idea how long she sat there when she realized Travis was yelling something to her that sounded like "Doorbell." She raised her head and caught the end of a shouted sentence,"–one's at the door, Winnie. Answer it!"

Wiping her face on the towel, she zipped up her pants and walked as quickly as she could back through the kitchen and into the front hall. Catching a glimpse of her lurid, disheveled appearance in the hall mirror, she knew she could not answer the door in her present condition. She hastily opened the hall closet and pulled her long winter coat off its hanger and took the dog's leash off its hook. The German shepherd, Greta, hearing the jingle, ran down the stairs eagerly just as she opened the door.

Elwood Foster stood there, hat in hand, looking rather sheepish. The appearance of someone sane and normal from the real world seemed so incongruous to Winnie that for a minute she just stood there staring at him with the wild eyes of someone has just awakened from a nightmare.

"I apologize for coming so late, but I was driving by and noticed Travis's car in the yard and just thought I would stop and say hello. If this is a bad time... I mean it looks like you were just on your way out..."His words drifted off, his eyes fixed on his feet.

"Not at all, come on in, Travis is in the dining room playing cards, I was just going out to walk Greta." She heard her own cheerful voice as though it was far away, being played on a distant radio. As she stepped back to let him in his gaze shifted, and Winnie realized he was looking at her feet now in their gaudy, ridiculously high heeled shoes, inappropriate for walking anywhere in the dark.

She heard herself give a giggle and say, "I guess I better change my shoes before I go." While he watched, she kicked off the rhinestone studded heels and could not stifle a gasp at the deep red creases and blisters they had left across her instep. Afraid that Elwood would see how painful these disfiguring marks really were, she quickly slipped her bare feet into the first suitable thing she saw in the hall closet, a pair of fur-lined winter boots.

Greta was already waiting eagerly on the doorstep for her romp in the cool, fresh air of the September evening. As Travis bellowed from the next room, "Winnie, where's the coffee?" she bolted out the door. Clamping Greta's leash onto her collar, Winnie let herself be led at a fast clip up the Darby Mountain road, away from the horrors of "Safe Haven."

The last time Elwood Foster had stopped by had been to inform her, in his kindly manner, that Travis owed him a rather large sum of money. Apparently Travis had not paid the bill the previous two times they had eaten at the West Jordan Inn and on one of those occasions had bought round after round of drinks for the entire bar, running up an enormous tab. Winnie had burst into uncontrollable tears, not only because of the sizable figure Elwood had presented her with, but because Travis had misused the generosity of this nice local man. There was only one way she could think of paying their bill and when she showed Elwood some examples of her stained glass work, he readily agreed,

136

returning the next day with the dimensions of a window he wanted behind the bar in his lounge.

It was while she was working on the Night Heron window that the idea had come to her, the way that she could hide her valuable jewelry and eventually get free of Travis.

He had never openly asked her to give him any of her jewelry to sell, but when he did not find enough cash in her purse to suit him, something would always disappear, a ring or a bracelet or a pin. He always denied it when she accused him of taking something, instead twisting the facts so it appeared that she herself had lost the item in question through her own carelessness, and even beating her for it on occasion to teach her a lesson. He seemed to find it amusing that she found her grandmother's treasures more sacred than her own flesh.

But it had come to her how she could do it, little by little, so that he would not notice and she was pleased with her work. She did not know how she would get free of him, but when that day finally came she would be able to retrieve the hidden jewels that were the link to her past and probably the key to her future.

Her heart had stopped one night when he pawed through the jewelry, looking for something for her to wear and complained about not being able to find the bracelet that matched her ruby and diamond choker. Nervously she told him the catch must have been broken the last time she had worn it for him because in the morning it was gone. She had been afraid to tell him for fear he would hurt her and call her neglectful. He had fulfilled her fears by beating her black and blue so that she would not forget and be so careless ever again.

It did teach her a lesson; she had to be more careful in covering her tracks.

Greta had stopped obediently at the bridge where they usually looped around on their walks and returned home. Sometimes on a particularly bright night, Winnie would sit for a minute on the metal railing and drink in the beauty of the moonlit mountains. This time she wanted to sit there just to mark time, to pass some of the night safely in the dark solitude before returning to the smoke and noise of her home. When she raised her foot to hoist herself onto the railing, however, the strained seams of the tight pants gave way, ripping wide open down the back. In a way she was relieved; now she wouldn't have to wear them again.

Her long coat covered the damage on the walk back. Elwood was still visiting and the noise from the dining room told her they had talked him into playing a few hands of cards with them. She took the opportunity to slip upstairs unnoticed. She might as well try and get some sleep before Travis came to bed.

She slipped naked between the sheets, having learned long before that it was pointless to wear a nightgown to bed when Travis was home unless she wanted it destroyed. As she drifted off to sleep she remembered the unwashed dishes in the sink and the coffee she had never served. She would have to be very submissive when he joined her in bed; if he thought she was going along with him, everything might go smooth and fast.

It was the coolness of his fingers tracing the curve of her hip that awoke her. The room was not entirely dark, illuminated by a stripe of yellow light that came from the half–closed door to the hall. She had been sleeping on her side with her back to the door, and when he pulled the covers away she stayed in that position with her eyes closed.

He slipped first one finger then another inside her, moving them slowly in and out in a motion that surprised her for its gentleness. He had not been that way with her for a long time. When he rolled her onto her back, she flung one arm protectively across her face, covering her eyes. If she didn't see him, if she could pretend he was someone else, maybe she could come for real this time. He spread her legs wide and using both hands to massage and expose her, peeling her open, layer by layer, probing, rubbing, and exploring her. If only she still loved him, this would have felt erotic and lovely. She moaned and panted a little to please him, made a crescendo of noises in her throat as if she were climaxing and arched her back, at which point he slid his wet fingers out of her and pushed himself inside.

He glided in and out of her slowly, time and again pulling nearly all the way out before plunging in so deeply that she could not keep from gasping. He rocked back on his knees and grabbed hold of her breasts to steady himself as he slid in and out. He nibbled and bit her nipples so hard that she cried out and had to take her arm away from her face to use both hands to push him away.

It was then that she noticed the shadows in the shaft of light across the bed. Startled, she looked up to see the two broad forms filling the doorway, two pairs of eyes watching the performance taking place before them.

"Travis," she gasped. "Those men – shut the door – they're watching us –" She struggled to get out from beneath him but he held her down, moving at a faster rhythm now.

"I know," he replied. "I told them they could."

"You what?" Her voice was a shrieking squeak. "I lost the game. They said we could call it even if they could take turns fucking you but I said no, I would fuck you and they could watch. I thought it would be better this way. Don't you agree?"

For an answer, Winnie began to scream hysterically, louder and louder. Somewhere in the house, Greta began barking at the sound of Winnie's screams. Travis pounded away faster and faster until at last he was done, but still she would not stop screaming and thrashing and kicking. In vain he struck her across the face several times, finally bashing her in the mouth with his fist. The taste of blood in her mouth quieted her down to a run of jerky, hiccuping sobs.

She heard Travis mutter something and then the sound of the door shutting, leaving her alone in the darkness. Shivering uncontrollably, she groped for the covers and then curled up in the fetal position beneath them, wiping the blood from her lips with the bed sheet.

He had gone too far this time, he had pushed her over the edge. She felt as limp and soiled as a used handkerchief, as worthless as a crumpled candy bar wrapper stuck to the bottom of a garbage can. Life was not worth living when you were treated like trash, there was no point in even trying anymore.

When morning came, she did not get up. Travis burst angrily into the room to see what was keeping her from preparing breakfast, but she did not respond to his threats. She just lay there on her back with the blood-spattered sheet up around her neck, her bloodshot eyes staring past him out of a puffy face with swollen lips. She stayed there all day and into the evening. By then Travis began to seem a little worried.

After trying several times to get a reaction out of her with kind, endearing words, he finally attempted to rouse her by shoving her arms into a negligee and pulling her roughly to her feet. When she crumpled to the floor he grabbed her beneath the arms and stood her up again.

"Enough of this little game," he scolded. "Now get into the bathroom and wash up, and then come down stairs and fix something to eat."

Beneath his grasp he could feel her begin to tremble violently and then suddenly she ripped away from him, turning to face him unsteadily, her eyes flashing with pure revulsion and hate.

"Don't touch me." Her words were a dry whisper.

"Then go clean yourself up, you're a mess." His words smacked of the satisfaction of bringing her back to life.

"I don't care." The fire left her eyes and she slumped back onto the bed, pulling the sheer negligee protectively around her thin body.

"Get up."

When she did not respond, he struck out at her, landing a heavy blow to her thigh but she did not cry out. He hit her again, this time in the eye and she gave a shivering sigh but she did not cower from him.

Angry and desperate, he hauled her to her feet again and then half–dragged and half–pushed her down the hall to the top of the stairs. *"Walk,"* he commanded, still holding tight to her arm, and dreamlike, she put one foot down onto the first step and then another. Dizzy and weak, her legs gave way about four steps from the bottom. Furious, Travis shoved her and she tumbled face first to the floor below, her right arm slamming hard into a cast–iron umbrella stand at the foot of the stairs.

A searing pain shot up her arm almost instantly. Lying there on the polished parquet floor of the front hall, Winnie howled at last, clutching the injured arm to chest. She knew it was broken and her thoughts went immediately to her glass work, to the cutting, piecing and soldering that required the skill of her right hand. He had even managed to take away her one pleasure, the only outlet she had in her miserable married life.

The thought of her unfinished work brought a hot rush of blood to her brain, melting the coldness that had numbed her will to go on, reminding her of a reason for her existence.

"You bastard." The words were out of her mouth before she had even considered them. Travis looked astounded; she had never spoken to him like that before. *"You son of a bitch, you broke my arm."*

The gleam of the gold cufflinks in his starched white cuffs flashed in her eyes as he hovered uncertainly above her. She felt resentful that he could still look as impeccably cool and handsome as ever while she sprawled at his feet, disheveled and frowsy in a blue nylon negligee which had fallen open to expose her aching and battered body.

"You might as well not come around again for a while," she said as she struggled to her feet. "There won't be any money coming in until this arm heals." She started painfully to climb back up the stairs.

"It doesn't matter. I'm leaving tomorrow anyway and won't be back until spring. I'm going to spend the winter in Havana." As she turned in amazement at his words, he continued, "The Samson brothers, those two men who were here, are going to set me up down there. All I need is plane fare and I'm sure we can round that up somehow."

He would be gone until spring, nearly six months. She could not believe her good fortune. Despite an ankle that felt slight sprained, she nearly floated up the stairs to the bathroom. It was difficult removing the robe, her right arm was already useless, and she gave herself a clumsy sponge bath in the sink. After a while Travis rapped on the door.

"Do you need help?" he asked.

She did but she would not admit it to him. Unable to even wrap a towel around herself, she patted herself dry. When she opened the door he was still standing there. "I'm sorry I did this to you." He spoke in a contrite tone she had not heard since the early days of their marriage. Tucking the loose towel around her torso, he said, "Let me help you get dressed."

It was impossible to put the injured arm into a sleeve and he ended up helping her step into a full skirted, strapless dress of his choosing, lilac colored, with a skimpy fitted lace bodice that he zipped up the left side for her. Although she didn't trust his kindness, she agreed that it would be easier to use the bathroom if she didn't wear underpants. He fashioned a sling for her arm from a silk scarf and then brushed her hair for her and pinned it up at the back of her neck. It didn't

142

surprise her that he would do this; there was a strange part of him that loved to dress her up and decorate her, as much as he loved decking himself out in fancy clothes. He clipped some dangling emerald earrings onto her ears and put a matching bracelet around her wrist and as he searched for the emerald pendant that completed the set she spoke up suddenly.

"I'm ravenous. Can you –" she faltered at the thought of asking him to help her.

"What would you like? There's not much food here." He was already whisking her downstairs.

"Probably a bowl of oatmeal would be fine."

He settled her onto a Victorian settee with her feet up and her arm on a pillow, switching on the Tiffany lamp that stood on the end table next to it. "This is a lovely piece of work." He stopped to admire the design she had worked into the glass lampshade. "You could probably sell it for quite a lot of money in the city."

Alarmed by his thoughtful expression, she said, "I'm keeping this one. I like how it looks here."

He shrugged and left the room, returning shortly with a couple of painkillers that he insisted she wash down with a stiff gin and tonic he had made for her. "This will help you sleep tonight. Tomorrow you can go to the doctor."

She was already beginning to nod off when he brought her the oatmeal she had asked for. She had trouble eating with her left hand but she managed to devour it hungrily, as he held an ice pack on her left eye which was beginning to swell shut. The painkillers taken on an empty stomach were starting to work and a few minutes later she began drifting in and out of consciousness. Every now and then she would struggle to open her eyes and the last clear image she had of that night was of Travis sitting in a wing chair opposite her, drinking martinis and smoking the Cuban cigars left by the Samson brothers.

"Walk Greta, will you?" she mumbled and was asleep before he answered.

She barely stirred a few hours later when, having finished the last of the gin, Travis lifted her full skirt and pushed it carefully up around her waist. She winced a little in her sleep when he bumped her bad arm as he tried to mount her unyielding body. When he finally managed to get inside of her, her round eyes flew open suddenly and stared at him in unseeing terror.

"Humor me," he whispered. "It's the last time I'll get to screw you for months."

Her eyes closed slowly and he wasn't sure she'd heard him. Her mouth moved as though she were trying to speak but all he could catch was "can't...my diaphragm..." Thinking she meant she couldn't breathe because of the boned bodice of her dress, he unzipped it for her and pulled it away from her chest without skipping a beat in his rhythmic plunging.

She awoke late the next morning feeling groggy and dehydrated. She knew instinctively by the silence of the house that she was alone. The side of her head throbbed to a different beat than the pain of her arm. She had dreamed delirious nightmares of Travis forcing her to have sex with him while the Samson brothers watched, waking in a cold sweat once when the nightmare had changed to the Samson brothers forcing her to have sex while Travis watched.

Only one eye would open. She sat up and discovered she had spent the night on the settee in the living room. The bodice of her dress fell down loosely and she held it up against herself, wondering how it had come undone. She half remembered Travis unzipping it but she had thought that was in one of her dreams. Looking down she could see a white sticky stain on the inside of the skirt where it showed between her legs.

He must have taken her in her sleep. Drugged soundly by the painkillers and overshadowed by her dreams, she had almost no recollection of it.

144

A note was propped up against the lamp on the table next to her. "Elwood Foster will pick you up at 12:30 to take you to the doctor."

That was it. No goodbyes or endearments.

She stood up, swaying a little. Somehow she had to get dressed on her own in the next hour. She did not know how she was going to manage the next few weeks alone. As she grasped the table for balance she noticed the emerald bracelet was gone from her wrist.

The sound of a car horn tooting brought her back to the present time.

"Your ride's here!" Dora called from the living room. "Don't forget my cigarettes when you stop at the store!"

It was a blessing that Dora was there to do the housework and the cooking, but her brassy personality irritated Winnie most of the time. She played the radio loud and complained that there was no television set. Usually she kept her red hair in rollers, except on Saturday nights when she went out with greasy–looking young men on dates that lasted nearly till dawn. She was very proud of her figure, heavy busted and slim hipped, and had been nearly out of her mind with excitement when Winnie told her she could wear whatever fit her of the sleazy evening wear she found in Winnie's closet. She could spend hours admiring herself in the mirror in a sequined cocktail dress, all the while asking endless questions about Travis. Winnie spent more time with Brian, Dora's four year old, than she did with Dora.

"Oh, it's young Woody! I don't want him to see me like this!" Dora scampered into the kitchen to hide her curlers as the front door opened and Elwood's son peeked his head in.

"Mrs. Monroe? I hope you don't mind– my father sent me– he was busy–" For some reason he blushed to

145

the roots of his serviceman's crewcut and Winnie felt sorry for him.

"Of course, it's fine." His youthfulness made her feel rather old and fussy. "I hope you don't mind if I stop to pick up some groceries on the way home, though. It will only take a minute."

"Of course, it's all right. I have all afternoon. I mean, I don't have to be back until supper." He held the door open for her, looking away. "It should be nice for you to get that plaster cast off your arm finally."

Driving up and down the hills on the way to Dr. Wilder's office, Winnie was overcome by a wave of nausea similar to those she had been experiencing the last few days along with bouts of intense fatigue. She would have to ask the doctor to examine her and hoped that he would not charge her extra for the visit. She had already promised him a stained glass window for his stairwell in exchange for his services as soon as the cast came off.

"When was your last period?" he asked her, pulling out her file.

"I–I don't remember," she confessed and suddenly she knew what the nausea and fatigue and the soreness in her breasts was all about. "Oh, no, it can't be." She covered her mouth, horrified at the idea that was growing bigger and more unavoidable by the second. "Oh, my God. No."

She could not imagine Travis coming home to find her enormously pregnant with his child or how he would behave with an infant or toddler or growing young girl...

"I can't have his baby, I just can't!"

Dr. Wilder let her sit in his office, crying and ranting for close to half an hour, until she calmed down at last. "Maybe you ought to stay with her for a little while," he advised young Woody as he saw her out the door. "She's a bit upset and could probably use some company."

And Woody beamed as he led the beautiful, sad–eyed lady back to his father's car.

CHAPTER SEVEN

Although a green plastic sign with white lettering proclaimed the big, square granite building to be a branch of the "Green Mountain State Bank," the letters carved into the stone above the front door would always say, "Potters Falls Savings & Loan, Est. 1895." Sarah's footsteps echoed sharply as she crossed the tiled floor of the cavernous interior designed during an era when a bank was meant to be opulent and impressive, not space and heat efficient.

Across the room, she saw Tyler rise from an orange molded–plastic chair that contrasted crudely with the dark wooden paneling and gray granite of the walls. He was dressed for the occasion, wearing a white shirt and a tie that seemed custom–designed to match his bulky sweater with the large, tape–recorder–concealing pockets.

"You look nice in a skirt," he said as way of a greeting. He admired the ease with which she had given a casual sophistication to her customary turtleneck sweater and high boots by replacing her jeans with a corduroy skirt in a velvety shade of brown. He could not keep from comparing her style with Isabel's and the hours Isabel spent each day preparing herself to appear in public, making sure every hair was in place and that her outfit was properly accessorized. "Did you bring your proof of identity?" he asked, forcing the comparison from his mind.

"Right here." Sarah patted the pocket of her jacket that held passport, birth certificate and driver's license.

"Okay, let's go." He took her elbow and steered her towards the partitioned cubicle which held the branch manager's desk.

"The way this was apparently set up," Mrs. Mary Foley explained as she led the way to the tiny room where depositors were allowed to view the contents of their safe deposit boxes, "was to have the annual fee for the box automatically taken from the trust account unless otherwise specified. Back in the 50's there were no charges for an unused account, but a few years ago GMSB started charging a yearly fee if an account was not active for more than two years. You're lucky you came by now, because in a few years the account would have been drained between the two annual charges and the bank would have repossessed the contents of the safe deposit box."

Sarah's head was whirling from all the information Mrs. Foley had given her in the last few minutes. Only one deposit had ever been made in the account set up in July of 1955 by Winifred Scupper in trust for Sarah Scupper Monroe. At the same time she had rented the safe deposit box, which had never been opened since. It was painfully obvious to Sarah why Winnie had gone to the trouble of opening an account for her newborn infant in a town some thirty back–road miles from home. She wondered how Winnie had managed the trip with no car and a two–month–old baby.

"I imagine you must be pretty anxious to see what's inside so I'll leave you two alone now. When you're done in here, one of you just signal me, okay?" Mary Foley's plump, gray–suited figure disappeared behind a closing door.

Sarah stared at the box on the table in front of her, not knowing what to feel. Tyler, however, was as jumpy as a small boy on Christmas morning.

"This is so exciting, Sarah! Open it up, what are you waiting for?"

She had thought the sweat on her brow was from nerves, but as she watched Tyler strip off his sweater and loosen his tie, she realized the air in the windowless cubbyhole of a room was already stifling and warm. She felt little relief, however, when she had removed her wool jacket and pushed up the sleeves of her sweater.

"I'm scared," she admitted finally. "Who knows what might be in there?"

"There's only one way to find out. Come on, any live animals would have been dead for years." He reached over and squeezed her hand reassuringly. "Go ahead, just open it."

Sarah lifted the lid of the metal drawer–like box. Heads close together, they peered inside.

The contents took up only one side of the interior; there was a red velvet bag and some small square boxes covered in embroidered Chinese silk. "It must be the jewelry," Sarah whispered, and with shaking fingers removed one of the boxes. Flipping it open, she let out a cry of dismay.

Inside the box, resting in a slot amid plush black velvet, was an antique platinum engagement ring. Unfortunately, the prongs of its lovely filigree setting gaped empty. "The stone is gone!" she cried and then uttered the first solution that came to mind, "Somebody here at the bank must have stolen it."

"It's more likely that Travis took the stone and sold it for quick cash." Tyler's soothing words held a trace of disgust as he took the box from Sarah and inspected the ring.

Sarah was already onto the next box, another ring, a gold one with two tiny diamond chips on either side of a hole that must have held an enormous square stone. "I can't believe this! It must have been horrible for her!"

Each box revealed a similar story – a gold bracelet was just a series of empty links that had apparently held large expensive gemstones. A matching necklace was a mere gold chain without the jewel which should have hung from it. The long thin box held the skeleton of the choker that Sarah recognized from the pictures

Woody had shown her. Now it was just a series of empty holes.

"Maybe Winnie did this herself," Tyler mused quietly, leaning back in his chair. "Maybe she needed the cash."

"But the pieces must have been more valuable in their settings, don't you think? It just doesn't make any sense. Why would anybody mutilate heirlooms like these?" She shook her head in confusion, the thought recurring over and over again that her father had abused her mother, so why not her possessions as well.

"There must have been a reason. What doesn't make sense to me is why she kept them in a vault. They aren't worth much of anything like this." Tyler was waiting impatiently for Sarah to open the red velvet bag. Instead she just sat there with a dazed expression on her face, staring down into the palm of her hand at what must have been an exquisite pin in the shape of a blossoming peony, now just a worthless outline of its former glittering beauty.

Finally, he picked up the antique bag himself, prying at the knotted tassels of faded gold thread that tied it shut. At his insistent pulling, the ancient threads finally disintegrated under his fingers and the contents of the bag spilled out onto the table.

"Oh, look, Sarah!" Tyler spoke on an intake of breath. Half a dozen pieces of jewelry lay there, still intact. A string of cultured pearls, a large gaudy brooch of twisted gold, another inlaid with jade in the shape of a nightingale, a pair of cloisonné earrings in an intricate enameled design, a ring of silver filigree set with pink blister pearls and a pair of engraved gold bangles.

"My grandmother wasn't crazy, she wasn't," Sarah murmured over and over again, laughing in amazement as she gingerly touched the beautiful old earrings and then ran her fingers the length of the pearls.

"Here, put them on." Tyler hooked the pearls at the back of Sarah's neck as she pinned the brooches to her sweater and slipped on the ring and bracelets. Watching her slip her own silver hoops out of her ears, he frowned suddenly.

"I feel like a little girl playing dress up." Sarah giggled. "What's the matter?"

"It's all the valuable pieces that have been dismantled," he said, holding up the empty links of a bracelet. "There are no gemstones here really, unless you count the pearls. If the jewelry on this side of the table were intact, you'd be a fucking heiress! Pardon my language, but do you see what I mean? I mean these earrings are very nice, but they're really not worth much."

"Tyler!" She grabbed his hand to make him look at her and the expression he saw in her eyes made him pause. Although she appeared close to tears, when she spoke it was with exasperated amusement. "It doesn't matter to me if any of this stuff would bring a good price at a jewelry shop. These were my mother's, and her mother's and her grandmother's treasures and that makes them worth more to me than any flashy diamond."

"Of course." He looked away, embarrassed, but she pulled on his hand to get his attention again.

"And if it weren't for you, I would never have found them." Now the tears did spill over in gratitude and she threw her arms around him, mumbling "Thank you," into his shoulder. "Look at me, crying like a baby." She laughed a little and tried to pull away from him but he held her close, slipping his hands under the back of her sweater so he could make contact with her skin. She felt fiery to his touch.

"My God, you're burning up. Let's get out of this sweatbox." Reluctantly he let her go. "Shall we take this stuff with us?" he asked as he replaced the gem–less jewelry back into its respective boxes. "Boy, it sure makes you wonder though, doesn't it?" Dangling the choker from his fingers, he sat down again. "Who do you think would even know what stones were in here in the first place?"

Sarah did not reply, not wanting to voice the name that they both were thinking.

"He would know. And it certainly would give us a good excuse for a trip to Atlantic City."

She flashed him a dirty look and swept the boxes off the edge of the table into her open shoulder bag. Tyler shrugged and gave a last look into the safe deposit box.

"Look, this was in the bottom." He held up a navy blue bankbook with a few pieces of paper folded inside of it. "We'd better bring it along so you can close out the account."

Sarah did not speak to him again until they were outside the bank. Then he grabbed her arm and said, "All right, I'm sorry I suggested it. But I don't get why you're so against it."

"You don't understand—"

"Well, why don't you help me to understand? It's got something to do with what that doctor said to you, doesn't it?"

She sighed and pulled away from him. "If you really want to know what that jewelry looked like, although I doubt that's your motive for wanting to visit my father, there is someone else who would know. And you could really travel to the ends of the earth to make that visit."

"Who's that?"

"My Aunt Roberta."

Tyler snapped his fingers. "The missionary! Of course! Where does she live now?"

"Jakarta, Indonesia." Sarah laughed at the expression on his face. "Come on, let's go find a travel agent and book you a ticket."

Tyler spent the afternoon photographing the damaged jewelry. Sarah wrote a letter to Aunt Roberta explaining why she was being sent the enclosed pictures

153

by express mail and was there any chance she might remember these pieces of jewelry from her childhood.

"I haven't seen her since I was fifteen. She didn't even come to grandmother's funeral. Well, I guess by the time she found out about it, it had already happened, but even so. She did call and tell me I was welcome to visit her in Indonesia any time."

"I hear Bali is a pretty happening place. You sure you wouldn't want to come with me and deliver this stuff in person?" Tyler stretched out on the couch and closed his eyes, visions of Sarah in a batik bikini dancing through his head.

"Another day, Tyler. I have to get ready for work." She disappeared into the bedroom.

"What nights do you have off?" he called after her.

"Tomorrow and Sunday. There's a guy who's worked Saturday nights for years and Woody closes down on Sundays. Why?"

"Oh, nothing."

She peered through the door at him. His eyes were still shut and he was grinning like a Cheshire cat, the deep crevices in his cheeks hidden by his beard. Shit, she thought, turning back to the mirror over the dresser. Sometimes she found him so attractive that it made her stomach ache. But she knew there was no point in getting involved; eventually he would just leave and go back to New York and his snooty long–time girlfriend. And yet since she'd come to West Jordan, she hadn't met anyone who'd made her feel this way.

As she passed by him on her way to the kitchen, he stuck out an arm and deftly grabbed her around the waist, pulling her down beside him. "You look pretty in pearls." He gently brought her face down so that he could kiss her on the lips.

"Tyler–" She began to protest and then changed her mind. What did it matter; she would enjoy herself now and cry later when he was gone.

"What?"

154

"Nothing." Much to his surprise, she returned his kiss with wholehearted passion. When she sat up at last, she felt lightheaded and woozy. "If you are taking that film into Jordan Center, you'd better hurry." She looked away abruptly so as not to drown in the response of his amber–colored eyes. "Drugstore sends the film out at 4:30 for next day developing."

Friday night always started off in full force at the Night Heron lounge. Most of the customers attributed the high color in Sarah's cheeks to her hustling pace as she served drinks and dinners to the rowdy crowd. Only Woody raised an eyebrow and commented. "Tyler said he spent the night at your place."

"On the couch, Woody. On the couch. I suppose he failed to mention that."

"No, actually he did say that. I just wanted to see if it was true or not." Woody laughed at her indignant reaction as he filled two bowls with homemade chili and placed them on a tray for her to carry out to the bar. "But you two certainly spend a lot of time together."

"He's helping me track down my past." Despite great efforts at self–control, Sarah could feel herself blushing. "Look." She held out her hand so he could see the ring she wore and then held up the pearls and pointed to her earrings. "He found an old safe deposit box my mother kept in Potter's Falls."

"What? Really? Here, tell me later. This food is getting cold." He shoved some rolls and butter on the tray with the chili. In a practiced motion, she swept it up onto her shoulder and went through the swinging doors.

Nearly everyone had heard about her burglary and offered their sympathy. A few people commented on the jewelry she was wearing and she felt a glow when she announced, "It was my mother's."

Tyler spent most of the night playing chess with old Pete and drinking Dos Equus while casually chatting

155

with him between moves about the old days in West Jordan. More than once, as Sarah passed by them, she heard Dora Evans mentioned.

Around midnight, Lyle and Bo became so belligerent that she had to shut them off and give them black coffee to drink.

"Forget it, Sarah." Lyle spat the words at her. "We'll go give our business to someone else. Look at her," he said to Bo. "She thinks she's better than us just because her momma was rich and left her a lot of jewelry."

Sarah slammed a green slip of paper down on the bar in front of him. "Your bill is twenty–three dollars, Lyle. Now pay up and get your ass out of here before I call the police."

"His brother never busts him." Bo guffawed into his sleeve. "He'd just put him in the cruiser and drive him home."

"Shut up, Bo. Let me just pay Miss Hoity–Toity and we'll get out of here." As Sarah took the money he left on the bar, he said loudly, "No point in leavin' a rich bitch like that a tip. She comes from more money than you and I'll ever see, Beauregard. Now let's boogie."

After they left, Sarah went into the bathroom and splashed cold water on her face. It shouldn't matter what a jerk like Lyle said, but his remark brought back the whole reason she had hidden her identity for so long after arriving in West Jordan. It reminded her of being back in high school in White Plains and the girls who had pointed and talked about her from behind their locker doors and seemed to take great joy in the fact that her cheap shoes and pocketbook came from the discount department store. She never understood the perverse pleasure some folks got from seeing rich people grow poor. Not until she and her grandmother had moved to Arizona and nobody knew who she was, had she been relieved of the curse of her family's past.

When she went back to the bar, Tyler was waiting for her, a weary expression on his face. "I'm just beat," he said. "Will you be all right alone tonight? Call me if you're scared, okay? I can hear the phone from my room."

She assured him she would be fine and then spent the next few hours assuring herself as well. It was nearly two by the time she got home and nearly three by the time she stoked up the fire, had a nightcap and got into bed. The only thing that made Friday night worth the effort, she thought sleepily, was the bundle of money she could count on making.

When she heard the squeak of the front door, she abruptly sat upright in bed before she was even awake. When she opened her eyes, she realized it was dawn and that she had already slept a few hours.

Tyler stood in the bedroom doorway, a sheepish grin on his face. "I was worried about you. I couldn't sleep."

"For crying out loud, what time is it?" She threw her head back down onto the pillow before looking at the clock. "You'll have to excuse me, but I don't usually entertain visitors at 6:30 in the morning when I didn't get to sleep until 3:30 the night before."

"Do you want me to leave?" He stopped with a hand poised to unzip his jacket.

For a moment she said nothing, feeling the cold air on her face contrasting with the warmth of the flannel sheets and quilts on her bed, remembering the dream she had just been having about the very same man who stood at the foot of her bed, ready to go or stay.

"No, she replied, looking at him finally. Her sleepy, solemn eyes were as heavy as the covers she lifted from one side of the bed. "Why don't you get in bed and keep me company while I sleep?"

For the first two hours they both pretended to sleep, nestled together like spoons in a drawer, warm flesh against warm flesh. Eventually coziness gave way to overpowering arousal and Tyler was more than ready for her when Sarah rolled over at last to face him.

"How does a journalist from the city keep in such good shape?" she murmured as she sat astride him, running her fingers across the taut muscles that covered his lean frame.

"I work out. At a health club. Oh, Sarah." He groaned and closed his eyes, his hands tightening about her waist as she moved on top of him. "I've dreamed about this," he gasped.

"I have too." And as she whispered, she felt his warmth explode inside of her.

"We'll do it again in a little while," he said softly as she stretched out on top of him, laying her face against his damp brow.

"Good," she replied, pulling the covers up over her shoulders.

They both dozed for a while. Sarah awoke to the sensation of Tyler's tongue doing circles around her nipples. She reveled in the warmth of the morning sunlight on her face and the warmth of his mouth as he explored her body to find out what excited her. "How's this?" "Nice." "And this?" "Mmmm. Nicer." "How about this?" A shudder and a shriek and then uncontrollable laughter answered his last question.

"You really like doing this, don't you?" he asked her at one point in the early afternoon, as they made love again amid the crumbs and stains of coffee and muffins in bed.

"With the right person. One who can keep up," she teased, rubbing the muscles of his buttocks as he hovered over her on his knees.

"How old were you when you first did it?"

She had never held a conversation during intercourse before but accepted the challenge. "Young, very young, fourteen. Junior high school. My grandmother was old, wasn't able to discipline me

158

much." She stopped talking and breathed heavily for a few seconds.

"Go on."

"So...I had an older boyfriend...taught me everything...we did it every day after school until he went away to college. It was exciting...fun...better than homework...oh, Tyler, stop, no, don't stop, oh..."

"How about you?" she asked, curled up in the crook of his arm a few minutes later.

"I was too young. An older cousin who was bored at a family reunion dragged me off into the bushes and showed me how to do it. Maybe that time doesn't even count. God, Sarah, you win. I'm exhausted. Isabel and I never–" He broke off, not having meant to mention Isabel at such an intimate moment. "I'm sorry, I didn't mean–"

She pulled away to look at him from a distance with more perspective. "Isabel and you never what?"

His already flushed face reddened even more. "We never did it like this. For hours. With such..." he gestured wildly in the air over the disheveled bed, "...abandon. It was always very methodical, controlled, we knew what moves brought what responses in exactly what amount of time. She even knew how many calories she was burning up!"

Sarah could not keep from bursting into a laugh. "Well, I'm ready for a shower, how about you?" Before he could reply, she was in the bathroom, running the hot water.

When they both stood clean and dripping on the bathmat, Tyler snapped his fingers suddenly. "Wait. Before you get dressed. I have something in the car for you." Wrapping himself in a towel, he raced outside barefoot, marveling at the coolness of the afternoon air, which even the pale November sun could not seem to warm.

Sarah watched him through the window as she combed her wet hair over the wood stove, droplets of

159

water sizzling as they landed on the hot cast iron. Although dizzy with hunger and fatigue, she had an overall feeling of contentment, as though she had accomplished something very important. When Tyler ran back in and handed her a garment bag, she accepted it with a kiss and a dazzling smile.

"What's this?" she asked, unzipping the plastic cover and pulling it back to expose the contents. She held up a very old, dark green wool dress. It had a fitted bodice with a white lace collar and a black velvet string bow at the neck, long tapered sleeves and an accordion–pleated skirt.

She laughed. "Uh, thanks, Tyler, but it's not really me. Now this I might wear," she went on, removing a short, gray Persian lamb jacket from the garment bag. But when she saw the matching pillbox hat with its black net veil, her smile faded into a frown. The frown deepened at the sight of the clear plastic bag that contained green suede pumps and a clutch purse the same shade as the dress, as well as a pair of short white gloves.

"This is like a whole costume! What's it for? Tyler, if this is part of your plan, forget it, because it's just not my style."

"I know it's not YOUR style," he replied, taking the dress from her and undoing the buttons at the back. "But thirty years ago it might have been. Look, just do me a favor, okay, and go into the bedroom and put it on."

She looked at him suspiciously. "I don't know about you, Tyler. You're so eccentric sometimes." She took the dress from his outstretched arm and went into the bedroom muttering loudly, "If this is some kinky sexual idea of yours..."

The dress had a zipper that made the fitted waist even more fitted, as well as zippers at the wrists of the snug sleeves. By the time Sarah had figured this out and done them up, she couldn't reach around to do up

160

the back. "Oh, for Christ sake." She stomped into the other room. "I don't know how they used to stand it. Button me up, will you?"

"My god, it fits you perfectly, that's amazing."

"Really." Her tone was very sarcastic. "How did you manage it?"

"Well, I hate to say it, but Isabel has a very good eye for this sort of thing. Now don't say anything just yet. Just stand still for a minute and let me do something." He picked up her hairbrush from the dresser and clumsily brushed her hair up off her neck, twisting and pinning it to the back of her head. He carefully set the little hat on her head, pulling down the veil so that it just covered her eyes, and then led her over to the mirror.

"There. Now you tell me what you see."

Sarah swallowed hard as she stared at the uncanny reflection in the mirror. She knew she was looking at herself dressed up in vintage clothes from the fifties but the effect was startling. "I– I look just like her."

"Bingo!" Tyler sat down on the bed and the, realizing he was still dressed only in a towel, began searching the bedroom for his own clothes as he talked. "It was this idea Isabel and I cooked up while I was back in New York. One day when I was working on the story at my computer, she kept looking at the pictures I had of Winnie Scupper and commenting on what a remarkable resemblance there was. She thought that if we dressed you up like your mother and visited a few of the old–timers around here, we might jolt a few forgotten memories. When we visited Maude Alfred and she mistook you for your mother, I realized Isabel had probably been right, but I figured you would think it was unreasonable. I couldn't think of an appropriate way to approach you with the idea until now."

Picking up one of the jewelry cases from the end of the dresser, he came up behind her. She was still staring at her reflection and did not protest when he hooked the gold chain around her neck from which dangled the empty gem setting or when he replaced the cloisonné earrings with the dangling ones full of holes.

"What do you think he would say if she came walking through the door like this?" he whispered in a soft, hypnotic voice. "Don't you think it might jar his memory a little?"

Color flooded into Sarah's face and she gripped the edge of the dresser to keep herself from striking out at Tyler for what she thought was a perverse and cruel idea. "You crazy fool. You won't stop at anything until you get what you want. If you think I would go with you to visit that abusive—"

But her tense, angry words faded away as she suddenly saw herself as her mother in the mirror, only now she had puffy purple circles around one eye, a raw bruise leading into a cracked and bleeding lip, and one arm in a cast. The image was so painful, it gave Sarah a throbbing tightness around her heart. She could not imagine waiting patiently for a man to come home and hurt her. She would have swung back at him and been out the door in no time flat.

What would she do if she ever came face to face with the man who did that to her mother? For thirty years he'd gotten away with what he'd done, destroying a woman, her property, her legacy, leaving his own daughter with nothing. How many more women had he brutalized over the years since then?

What would he do if the image of Winnie Scupper walked through his door to haunt him, demanding an explanation and an apology?

"Sarah?" Tyler touched her on the shoulder, frightened by the expression on her face. "Listen, forget the whole thing, okay? You can wear the dress on Thanksgiving, give Woody a thrill. I'm not going to force you into doing anything that you don't—"

"I'll do it."

"What?"

162

She turned away from the mirror at last and through the veil he could see her gray eyes flashing with a grimness that was frightening. When she spoke her voice had a hard edge to it that he had never heard before. "I said I'll go with you to Atlantic City to see my father."

Sarah's tension broke the spell between them and although it was his victory, Tyler was almost sorry he'd brought the idea up. The intimate atmosphere quickly reverted back to their peppery working relationship as Tyler feverishly dialed 800 numbers for airlines and Sarah interjected cynical comments from the kitchen as she cooked up a couple of omelets.

"This would go so much faster if you had touch tone dialing," Tyler complained.

"But just think of all the calories you can burn up dragging your finger around a rotary dial." She was almost sorry for that remark, since it brought back a reminder of what he had said about having sex with Isabel.

"Well, it looks like next weekend is out. Thanksgiving weekend every flight out of Burlington is booked solid with college students, I guess." Despite this news, Sarah thought she glimpsed a flicker of a grin as he sat down at the table. "But I did finally manage to get us on a flight with Continental to Newark."

"And when is that?"

"Tomorrow morning at 6:30 am."

"You're out of your mind! Tomorrow?"

"Tomorrow is Sunday, you don't have to be back at work until Monday night. We'll fly back Monday morning and as long as we're in Burlington, we can stop at Maude's daughter's house and I can photograph that lamp."

He had it so well planned already that, although she felt exasperated with him, she had to laugh. "And how do we get from Newark to Atlantic City?"

"We'll rent a car at the airport."

"And what if we can't find him in the twenty–four hours we're there? What if he's not home?"

"Then we'll have a little vacation. Just you and me. I'm sure we can find something to do to entertain ourselves." He reached beneath the table and caressed her thigh. Neither the intensity of her mood nor the heavy denim of her jeans could protect her from feeling the magnetic force of their physical attraction. "Even in Atlantic City."

CHAPTER EIGHT

With his pen poised on 39 Down of the New York Times Sunday crossword, Tyler stole a secretive glance at Sarah as she sat rigidly in the seat next to him. She was sipping coffee from a Styrofoam cup and staring grimly out the oval window of the plane. He was glad he had been able to find the Sunday Times at a newsstand at the Burlington Airport; it gave him something to bury himself in and an excuse not to carry on a conversation with Sarah.

Ever since her decision the previous afternoon to make the trip to Atlantic City, she had been moody and silent. He had left her for a few hours to go down to the inn and pack a suitcase. Sarah had not wanted Woody to know where they were going, so Tyler told him they were just getting out of town for a couple of days, probably going to Montreal via Burlington. Although she had little to say, they went to bed early and made love with a forceful intensity. Afterwards she fell asleep clinging to him in a way that made him feel secure in her need for him, even if she couldn't express it.

Finally, during the long drive to the airport and under cover of the pre–dawn darkness, he had stopped trying to cheer her up with small talk. She had every reason to be dark and apprehensive about this visit. Even at his most persuasive, he had not been able to talk her out of wearing the outfit he and Isabel had concocted in an imaginative moment. She had stubbornly insisted that if they were going for the surprise effect, why not make the most of it. So at 3:30 AM he had clumsily done up the covered buttons at the back of the green wool dress, noticing even at that hour how beautifully the color of the fabric brought out the green in her gray eyes.

Although she carried the shoes, purse and hat in a large shoulder bag, and the Persian lamb jacket covered the outdated style of the dress, there was still something exquisite and unique about her appearance that had turned heads as they hurried through the small airport.

Looking at her now, he noticed that her knuckles were white as she gripped the armrest between them. Her lips had become a thin, determined line slashing across a very pale face. Sensing his gaze upon her, she turned from the window. Once again he was startled by the fierce anger that burned in her eyes. He had been so excited by the prospect of Sarah finally meeting her father (not to mention the literary possibilities that this dramatic encounter promised), that he had not stopped to really consider what might happen when Winnie Scupper's daughter came face to face with the fortune hunter who had gambled away both the family's past and future. The look in her eyes scared him; just what did she have in mind? He had engineered this journey, but what was he becoming an accomplice to?

He swallowed the lump in his throat and said, "The capital of Switzerland, four letters."

"Bern," she replied and one corner of her mouth turned up ever so slightly in reaction to his astonishment.

Southbound Sunday morning traffic was light on the Garden State Parkway as they sped along in their economy rental car, a lemon yellow Ford Escort that made Tyler shudder if he looked at it for too long. He passed the time trying to focus on the road without looking at the hideous color of the hood, wondering what he could say to ease the tense atmosphere that was becoming heavier by the mile.

"So. I guess you traveled through Switzerland when you were in Europe."

"Mmmm."

"Did you like it?"

"Mmmm."

"How about Greece? Did you go there? I spent a few weeks on Corfu a few years ago when Isabel and I—" He gulped back the words as Sarah shot him a black look.

A moment of uncomfortable silence passed before Sarah spoke. "After college I wanted to travel to Europe more than anything so I spent a year working as a flag girl on a highway construction crew. I made a ton of money, we had to work 60 or 70 hour weeks sometimes. You know, lots of overtime pay and no time to spend it. I was able to take off the entire next year and travel through Europe and North Africa. But I'll tell you about it another time."

Over the next several miles Tyler thought about his own trip to Europe and how easily it had come to him. It had been a birthday present from his parents for the summer between his freshman and sophomore years, all expenses paid. When he had run out of money, another check had been waiting for him at the American Express office in Rome. He wondered how different his life would have been if he'd had to work as hard for everything as Sarah had. He'd never had to take a job just to make money; there'd always been someone willing to support him while he expended his creative energies at the keys of a typewriter or word processor.

Lost in self–reflection, he nearly missed the exit for Atlantic City. When he rolled down the window to pay the toll on the Atlantic City Expressway, the salty smell of the ocean was in the air. "I'm starving," he said suddenly. "Let's get some brunch and figure out what to do next."

"I guess this is it." Tyler slowed the car down as they passed a six–story apartment building of beige concrete. There were cars parked in every space on the shabby block of the narrow, one–way street that dead–ended at the boardwalk. "Walking distance to the beach."

"And the casinos."

Tyler was almost relieved by the characteristic sarcasm of Sarah's remark. She had eaten nothing at the restaurant where he had gorged himself on waffles and eggs. She had excused herself to go to the ladies room, returning with her hair twisted up and pinned to the back of her head, a more skillful version of the hairdo Tyler had produced the day before. The lipstick and eye makeup she wore made her likeness to Winnie even more profound.

As he searched for a parking spot, her nervousness was still apparent in the way she twisted the white gloves she had found in the pocket of the jacket. With a considerable amount of skill and swearing, he managed to squeeze the car into half a space between a Cadillac and a Buick. "There, goddam it."

When he turned the engine off, neither of them moved for a moment. "What if, after all this, he's not home?" Sarah said softly.

Tyler turned to her. She sat there so stiffly, the pillbox hat perched on her head, her long legs crossed demurely at the ankle. "Then you've dressed up so beautifully just for me. We'll rent a motel room with a hot tub and you can fulfill my fantasies. But it's Sunday morning," he added quickly as she opened her mouth for a quick retort. "Where would he be?"

"Church?"

They both laughed and in that moment of temporary release, Tyler quickly got out of the car and ran around to open her door for her.

"Don't be ridiculous," she snapped. "Just because I'm dressed like this, doesn't mean I'm helpless." As she

168

stepped out into the street, a strong breeze blowing off the ocean lifted the hat right off her head and blew it into a gutter. "Oh, for crying out loud. How did women ever keep these stupid hats on their heads, anyway?"

Tyler reached the hat first. As he handed it back to her, he tried to give her a kiss but she pushed him away. "Don't. You'll smear my lipstick."

"I think I hate you dressed up like this. Come on, let's get this over with so I can touch you again."

Sarah tried to walk with a purposeful stride but it was difficult in the green suede pumps which were a size too small and squeezing her toes. Isabel may have guessed her dress size but she'd been way off on her feet. Or maybe she'd done it on purpose, Sarah thought cynically, feeling the comforting pressure of Tyler's arm where his elbow was linked through hers.

They pushed open the heavy, swinging glass door that led into the lobby of the apartment building. Except for a wall lined with mailboxes, the only decor was a ragged strip of ash–brown carpet that ran across the linoleum–tiled floor to the elevator. The air was heavy with the industrial smell of Pine–Sol.

While Tyler studied the names on the mailboxes, Sarah hung back by the door as if she were ready to make a run for it at any moment. "Here he is, T. Monroe/C. Ferrera, #516. I guess he has a roommate."

Fear of one more unknown element made Sarah physically faint and she leaned back against the outside door for support. At the same moment, the elevator door opened and an elderly couple stepped out. They were short and stooped and moved with the uncertainty that comes with the brittle bones of old age. For the first time she realized that her father would be in his seventies by now; he might well be as frail and bent as these two.

It was Tyler's willpower, not her own, that moved her into the elevator. As the doors closed, she thought she might suffocate in the airless, creaking box, but before she had time to die, Tyler was leading her out of the elevator and down the dark corridor of the fifth floor. A cavalcade of cooking smells assailed their nostrils as they passed the closed doors; baked ham gave way to garlic and tomatoes and then faded into fried shrimp.

"Sarah? Sarah! This is it." Tyler shook her a little until her eyes lost their glazed appearance and focused on the door. He could see that the flaming anger of the last day had been replaced by a deep–seated fear of the unknown.

"Oh, God, Tyler, I can't do it, I'm sorry, let's go–"

"You can do it. I'm right here, I won't leave you." Before she could stop him, his finger was pressing the black button of the doorbell. On the other side of the door, a distant buzzer rang. "You're strong, Sarah, you're the strongest woman I know–"

They could hear locks snapping and turning. The door opened and the silhouette of a large woman filled the doorway. It was hard to determine her age; a bright floral print dress covered an ample figure that had probably been svelte and curvaceous at one time. Her dark hair was piled in a skyscraper upon her head; equally dark eyes watched them suspiciously beneath eyebrows plucked into unnaturally thin arches. Her high cheekbones suggested that, before the creasing lines of old age had set in, she had unquestionably been a beauty.

"Yes, can I help you?" Her English was accented with Spanish overtones and there was no friendliness in her voice.

When it was obvious that no sound was going to come out of Sarah's mouth, Tyler stepped in quickly. "We're looking for Travis Monroe. Is he in?"

The woman frowned. "He is expecting you?"

"Probably not. Tell him Ms. Scupper–Monroe is here to see him." Tyler pushed Sarah to the forefront, letting the woman get a good look at her. The frown deepened as she took in Sarah's outdated clothing.

"Consuela! Quien es?" The gruff voice came from the next room and was followed by a racking cough.

"Una Senora Scupper–Monroe."

"What?"

Consuela stepped away from the doorway, giving them a quick glimpse of a tiny living room full of heavy furnishings that had seen better days. Coming towards them, across the worn Oriental carpet was a tall, white–haired man. With the addition of a perfectly trimmed white moustache, a deeply furrowed brow and the crow's feet crinkling the corners of his eyes, the face was the same as that of the wedding picture on Sarah's mantel. A gold silk ascot was knotted at the open neck of his white shirt. His erect carriage and style of dress gave him a distinguished appearance that contrasted with the shabbiness of his surroundings.

Travis's steel blue eyes peered shortsightedly at Sarah. "My God," he gasped and then clutched at his chest. His face turned ashen gray as he fell to his knees. "Consuela, my medicine. Pronto!"

"Madre de Dios!" Consuela hurried out of the room, returning in seconds with a bottle of pills. Kneeling beside Travis, she expertly placed a pill under his tongue and held his mouth closed.

"Shit. We nearly gave him a fucking heart attack." Sarah spoke in amazement as she and Tyler moved into the room, staring down in horror at the pained expression on Travis's face.

At the sound of her voice, Travis's eyes fluttered opened and tried to focus on her.

"I can't stand this, Tyler," she said bluntly, removing her hat and then frantically pulling out the hairpins that held her hair up.

"You're...you're not Winnie." Travis passed a hand over his eyes. "Winnie would never use language like...For a moment there...but when you spoke...your voice is much lower...I'm sorry, you reminded me of someone–" As he watched her hair fall around her shoulders his eyes fell suddenly on the cloisonné earrings and he choked on his words, turning a shade paler. "Oh, God, I must be seeing things." He fell back onto a pillow that Consuela had efficiently placed beneath his head. "Where did you get those earrings? Who are you?"

"I'm Sarah." His expression did not register any recognition of her name. "Winnie's daughter. YOUR daughter."

"Sarah. Oh, my God."

Consuela suddenly loomed between them threateningly. "This is too much for him. You had no right to come here without invitation. He has a bad heart; strain and surprise can kill him."

"No, wait, just give me a minute." Travis struggled to a sitting position and took several deep breaths. "It's been over thirty years since I last saw you." His voice became sharp suddenly. "Consuela, what are you just standing there for? Where are your manners? We have guests. Take their coats and make them some coffee."

It was hard to tell at whom Consuela's sour look was directed as she swept out of the room with Sarah's wooly lamb jacket over her arm. Tyler declined to have his sweater and tape recorder removed.

Grabbing the arm of a chair, Travis pulled himself to his feet and cleared his throat. "Won't you sit down?" He indicated a rather threadbare, mauve brocade couch as he sank into a matching armchair.

Sarah seemed rooted to the floor, her round eyes following Travis's every move. Tyler forcibly took her arm and moved her to the couch, before turning back to Travis. "I don't believe we've met. Tyler Mackenzie." He offered only his name and his hand.

"Travis Monroe. Now tell me, Sarah, how did you track me down after all these years?" Travis seemed to be regaining his composure quickly and now he gave Sarah a thorough once over as he spoke.

Sarah cleared her throat and the three of them froze for a moment at the eerie similarity of this gesture to Travis's. "Tyler did it actually. He discovered the house in West Jordan was still in your name."

"Really?" Travis removed a cigar from a box on the table next to him. "And how did you ever find out that obscure piece of information?"

"I've been living in West Jordan for the last year and a half. Since my – since Grandmother Charlotte died."

Travis raised one eyebrow. "Well, old Mrs. Scupper certainly lived a long life, didn't she? I hope you don't mind cigar smoke," he remarked as he puffed into the air. He looked lovingly at the cigar in his hand. "A terribly unhealthy habit I picked up during my years in Cuba and a hard one to break. So you're here to try and make a claim on the old family homestead, is that it?"

"Well, no not exactly–" Sarah sputtered nervously, a bit taken aback by his blunt approach.

"That, among other things." Tyler's voice overrode hers and he reached for her hand, entwining his own sweaty fingers with her icy ones.

Travis threw back his head and laughed. The sound cut through the atmosphere like a bitter wind and made Sarah shiver. "Well, unfortunately you'll never get the house," he said. "It's only mine in name. I lost it years ago, in a card game in Havana, to a couple of fellows named Sampson. I owed them a lot of money and being friends of mine–" the word "friends" was ripe with sarcasm– "they agreed to let me pay it off by turning the house into apartments and sending them the proceeds. The monthly income has enabled them and their families to live comfortably in Mexico City in the years since they were forced to flee from Cuba. They hired an agency in New York to take care of it all, maintenance, tax escrow etc."

"So what happens when one of you dies?"

Travis looked sharply at Tyler, unable to guess his interest. "The arrangement continues. It's quite possible that one if not both of the Mr. Sampsons are already dead. The family is quite powerful and does not let anything stand in their way to keep them from taking what they believe is rightfully theirs. It was a plan that suited everybody. I had no use for that old house in the middle of–" He stopped suddenly and stared off into space above their heads at some distant point in his past.

"It sounds totally illegal," Sarah commented softly.

"I'm sure it is but that's never mattered to the Sampsons. If you value your lifestyle, whatever it may be," he added with a condescending look at Sarah's vintage clothing, "You won't try anything stupid, like claiming the house for your own." His gaze drifted away again and his eyes narrowed as though he were trying to remember something. "Who did you say told you where I lived?"

Sarah looked helplessly at Tyler. At the same time Tyler's brow burst into beads of nervous perspiration at the thought of revealing his New York source to a man with underworld connections. "I think it was that woman who lived in the hollow, wasn't it?" he said, hiding his uneasiness by making a big deal of removing his sweater and laying it carefully across the arm of the sofa. "The one that took care of Sarah as a baby. What was her name, Sarah?"

He glanced up at Travis and was surprised to see the angry expression that was spreading across his face, causing his ashen face to redden. "She had my address?" Travis spoke in a flat, tight voice. "What was her name – Donna?"

"Dora. No, it wasn't her, Tyler." Although she addressed Tyler, Sarah was watching Travis's face carefully. "It was through the clerk at the county courthouse, remember?"

The flush cleared itself from Travis's face in reverse of the way it had spread, starting at the ears and ending with the nose. He cleared his throat and puffed on his cigar. "I see. And was Dora happy to see you after all these years, Sarah?"

"Actually—"

"Did you know Dora very well?" Tyler abruptly cut Sarah off.

"Not at all. We only met briefly once or twice. I used to travel a lot, was away from home most of the time..." His words faded away.

In the awkward silence that followed, Sarah tried to recall the original anger that had brought her to this auspicious meeting. But looking at the well–manicured fingers of her father's slender hands, it was hard to imagine him using them to hurt somebody in a cruel, unnatural way.

"Have you ever married again?" Always the interviewing reporter, Tyler pressed on, eager to get the most from these moments.

Something flashed in those eyes of steel, glinting like a sharp blade, as Travis looked from Sarah to Tyler and back again. He seemed to come to some sort of personal decision and he leaned forward in his chair as he spoke. "Yes, I had another wife in Havana. Three sons. After the missile crisis in the early sixties, she was not permitted to join me in the States."

Sarah had never pictured Travis's life after Winnie and she had trouble digesting this new information. Was he saying she had three half–brothers in Cuba?

"And Consuela? Is she your wife now?"

Travis chuckled. "Consuela? I've known Consuela for decades, since the days she worked as a –uh– dancer, shall we say? – in an exclusive nightclub in Old Havana I used to patronize. She got out of Cuba just in time, lived in Miami, worked on one of those offshore party cruises, you know, the floating casinos that sail across the three mile limit into international waters and then anchor for the night. That's where I met her again and we've been together off and on ever since."

Consuela entered the room at this point. On her shoulder she had a heavy tray laden with coffee, cups, cream, sugar and pastries, which she unloaded with practiced ease. "No mas esta manana, senor," she said sternly, offering coffee only to Sarah and Tyler.

"Yes, I knew I'd met my match in Consuela. Only woman who could ever–" he broke off, Sarah's likeness to Winnie reminding him of who his audience was. "Well, and what about you, Sarah? What do you do in that quaint village in northern Vermont?"

"I tend bar at the West Jordan Inn." Sarah heard herself speaking, but it was as though she were a wind–up toy performing her part. Inside her mechanisms were grinding away, trying to absorb all this new information about her father. She wondered what he had been going to say about Consuela, what it was she could do. Gamble away as much money in one night as Travis? Abuse him as much as he abused her?

"Well, now, do you really? The Fosters still own it, do they? I have some pleasant memories of that bar. Back in the fifties, if there was a good time to be had in West Jordan it was at the inn." But before Travis began drifting off into his memories again, Tyler quickly brought him back.

"And what about you, sir? Do you still work or are you retired?"

Consuela gave a snort and then, adjusting her bra through the fabric of her dress, crossed the room to peer through the crooked Venetian blinds at the street below.

"Retired," was Travis's response. "Doctor's orders. I do a little investing now and then but I don't get out much anymore."

Sarah wondered what "investments" meant to him – horses, drug smuggling, money laundering perhaps. She was beginning to doubt the wisdom of this visit.

Perhaps it would have been better to have continued fantasizing what her father would be like.

"It's hard to imagine you came all this way just for a social call," Travis remarked, helping himself to a half cup of coffee while Consuela's back was still turned.

"Why? Although you've obviously never shown much interest in me, it's not unusual that I should be curious about the father I've never met." Sarah's comment expressed more than she had intended and Tyler's eyes flashed warning signals at her as he tried to smooth over the conversation.

"Actually, we brought some things along with us, some family heirlooms, that we thought you might be able to help us with. Where are they, Sarah? In your bag?"

"All the more reason to wonder why you should want to look up a parent who abandoned you." Travis ignored Tyler, referring back to Sarah's remark. "I'm sure your grandmother, my ex–mother–in–law, had nothing but good things to say about me."

"Actually, she had very little to say about you. In fact, I learned a lot more about you from Dr. Wilder in West Jordan than I did from anywhere else."

"Did you now?"

Tyler's hand froze on the antique bag inside Sarah's purse. The tension in the room was escalating dangerously, but he was not sure if he should change the topic now or if Sarah might be about to reveal what the doctor had told her. Travis's lips were sculpted into a one–sided smirk, his eyes daring Sarah to go on, but Sarah's expression, which had changed to pure hatred, was the more frightening of the two.

"Yes, I did."

She seemed to be willing him to remember for himself, staring at him darkly, her fists clenched as though she would be ready to defend herself physically if necessary.

"And?"

Her face flushed, her eyes filled with tears, and she couldn't bring herself to say it. Not in front of Tyler and especially not in front of Consuela. She could not admit that her mother had let him beat her and for some unknown reason had been too dependent on him to leave.

"Where were you when she died?" She changed the subject abruptly, focusing on a spot on the wall above his head, not able to meet his gaze.

"What?" Travis was startled by her sudden tack. "Where was I when Winnie died? Is that what you just asked me?"

"Yes. I've just been curious. How did they find you and contact you to come home?"

"Police found me. By my license number. I was headed home at the time but I had stopped in Providence to visit a friend. Believe me, I was as shocked as anybody that Winnie had jumped off that bridge. I always thought that perhaps it had been accidental, I mean, it was muddy, she might have slipped, or the dog might have pulled her over."

"Have you ever been to that bridge?" Tyler asked curiously.

"Well, I've driven over it but not for thirty some years. Why?"

"Don't you think it would be pretty hard to fall off it accidentally?"

Travis shrugged. "Probably. By the time I got there it didn't really matter how it had happened, just that it had."

"I guess she wasn't very happy."

"Well, if you don't mind my saying so, I always thought she was slightly unbalanced, emotionally, that is. She didn't seem to understand how to have fun and she was afraid of trying anything new. I tried to teach her, but she never seemed to get the hang of it. I bought her beautiful, expensive clothes and she gave them away to that housemaid, Dora. She had a lot of fine old

178

jewelry that she never wore; I don't know what she did with it."

Tyler took the word "jewelry" as a cue and by the time Travis had finished speaking, he had emptied the velvet bag onto the coffee table. The open settings of Winnie's antique finery seemed to stare blankly, like so many empty eye sockets, out of the skeletal remains.

Despite years of practice at concealing his emotions, Travis could not mask his astonishment at what he saw. "What the...how could...after all those...son of a bitch. Where did you get these?" With shaking fingers he picked up a gold bracelet.

"Winnie had put them in a safe deposit box in my name up in a bank in Potter's Falls. We wondered if you could tell us anything about them."

Travis laughed bitterly as he laid the bracelet gently across his knee. "The little minx," he said softly. "So that's what she meant." He looked up, suddenly aware that Sarah and Tyler were watching him closely. "What happened to the stones? They're not worth anything like this."

"We were hoping you might know."

He shook his head, speaking half to himself again. "She didn't understand the value...what a foolish thing to do."

"Mr. Monroe, do you remember any of these pieces? We wondered what kind of gemstones might have filled these holes. Sarah and I thought it would be nice to at least repair them with simulated stones, until someday we could afford the real thing."

The pressure of Tyler's leg against her own warned Sarah not to give him any funny looks and to just play along for a moment.

"Why, certainly I recognize a few things. This piece here was all cut diamonds, that necklace there was its mate. That one must have been the choker that was set with those large rubies..." He identified nearly all the pieces before closing his eyes and shaking his head again. "They were priceless. What a shame. I wonder who managed to get them."

"Any ideas who or why..."

"I really don't have a clue but I daresay your mother herself was crazy enough at the end to do a thing like this."

"At the end?" Tyler pushed the question curiously.

"Well, Christ, she jumped off a goddam bridge, didn't she?"

The conversation stopped abruptly as a loud click sounded from the pocket of Tyler's sweater, indicating that the tape had ended. Travis eyed it suspiciously. "What was that?"

"Oh, uh, just an alarm, a beeper, to let me know it's time for my medicine." Tyler hurriedly picked up his sweater from where it had hung neatly on the arm of the couch and stood up, hugging it to himself protectively. "Diabetic with a hyper–active thyroid. I'm always taking something. Is there a bathroom I could use?"

"Consuela!" Travis shouted over his shoulder. "Show him where the john is, will you?"

Before anybody could move, however, there was a rattle of keys in a lock and then the sound of the apartment door opening. "Es Maria," Consuela announced before gesturing to Tyler to follow her into one of the other rooms.

"Maria is Consuela's daughter," Travis explained. "She always brings us the Sunday papers on her way home from, uh, church."

"Hello – what's this? I didn't know you and Mama were having company today?"

Sarah looked up at the young woman who stood towering above her on four inch spike heels. Maria's heart–shaped face was exotically beautiful; her dark hair had been swept high in a jeweled clip and then braided into one long braid that hung down her back. Her short, fuzzy, white jacket hung open, revealing her "church" attire. She wore a very short and shiny, royal blue dress, cinched at the waist with a wide belt that dramatically displayed a tiny waist and generous curves. It was easy to imagine that Consuela had been similarly attractive in her heyday.

"This is my daughter, Sarah, who dropped in unexpectedly for a surprise visit. Sarah, Maria."

"How nice! But I didn't know you had a daughter." Maria extended a hand to Sarah, who noted the long fingernails polished to match the blue dress, before turning back to Travis. "I brought you the Sunday Times, querida."

As Maria bent down to kiss Travis on the cheek, Sarah saw two disturbing things from her vantage point on the couch. When Maria leaned over, her mini–dress flared up just slightly revealing matching black and blue marks that extended in a narrow band across the back of both of her thighs, dark enough to be seen through the sheer nylon of her pantyhose. At the same time Travis's hand reached out to caress the curve of Maria's behind and rested there for a moment in a suggestive way that was too familiar to be casual or spontaneous.

"Mama is not home?" Maria's innocent inquiry had a hint of the cautionary in it.

"Yes, she was showing Sarah's friend to the bathroom. I don't know what is keeping her. Consuela! Maria is here!"

Sarah's head was spinning, not so much from the unspoken messages she was picking up, but from the inevitable result of what those signals added up to. She felt suddenly hot and nauseous, as though she might suffocate in the airless apartment. She wanted to leave immediately, before she accidently discovered anything else about the depraved life of this man who was her father.

Blindly she began scooping the jewelry up off the coffee table and tried clumsily to stuff it all into the bag at one time. She could feel the old velvet ripping under her fingers but she didn't care.

"What are you doing?" Tyler asked in concern as he re-entered the room.

"We have to go. I have to go. I can't stay—"

"Hi, I'm Maria, Consuela's daughter." Maria straightened up at the sight of Tyler and extended one of her hands in all its nail-polished glory. The two of them stared at each other for moment, each assessing the other's youth and beauty. Tyler broke the gaze as he became aware of Sarah struggling painfully to her feet in the high heels that were too small.

"We're not really ready to leave yet, are we?" He muttered under his breath to her.

"You can stay if you want to. I've learned enough." She knew she should show some manners, thank Consuela for the coffee, say goodbye to the father she had just met and would never see again. But as Maria bent down to place the newspaper on the coffee table, Sarah caught another glimpse of the bruises on her thighs and she could not keep from making the connection with Dr. Wilder's story of her beaten and abandoned mother.

She did not wait for the elevator, but ran down the five flights of metal stairs, unaware of the pain in her feet until she was out on the street. As the cold salt air hit her in the face, she realized she had left her jacket in Travis's apartment. She limped to the car only to find that, of course, it was locked. Howling with frustration, she kicked off the offensive shoes, one of them etching an arc over her head to land in the street behind her. Tears of disappointment streamed down her face as she ran down the cold pavement until, through the thin nylon of her stockings, her feet made contact with the rough boards of the ramp up to the boardwalk.

The Atlantic looked bleak and uninviting, as dingy as the sand it washed up against and as gray as the sky it reflected. An icy wind whipped through her dress as she descended the stairs that led to the beach, but she didn't care. Her only thought was to put as much distance between herself and the past hour as she possibly could.

When Tyler finally caught up with her she was sitting in the sand, staring out to sea, shivering with the cold but too numb to care. He wrapped the Persian lamb coat around her shoulders and held out her red Reebok high tops.

"Put them on!" he insisted when she ignored him. "Listen, I don't know what happened back there, and I don't even care, but I'm not going to let him make you as miserable as he made your mother."

She stared at him expressionlessly for a second; her round blue eyes seemed as gray as the sea. Then her gaze moved back to the crashing waves as she said, "He abused her, you know."

"What?" As the wind blew his query away, he knelt quickly before her in the damp sand, anxious not to miss a word.

"Travis. He beat her. Winnie." He noticed she was not referring to them in the usual parental terms.

"How do you know?"

"He broke her arm, he pushed her down the stairs, he punched her in the stomach and broke her ribs and made her lose a baby—"

"Dr. Wilder told you all this?"

"And he said it was just as well that she lost the baby because Travis had given her gonorrhea on their honeymoon!" She burst into tears and laughter at the same time. "Can you believe it? What a bastard! And she only went to the doctor a couple of times, when it was totally unbearable. Can you imagine how much else he did in between? Why do you think she was wearing sunglasses in that picture of her in the bar at night? She probably had two black eyes!"

"Why did you let me bring you here if you knew all this already?" Tyler asked quietly.

"I don't know, I think I wanted to tell him off, or slap him in the face. Maybe I just wanted to meet him so I could convince myself it couldn't possibly be true. I almost did at one point. But then I decided there was no purpose in accusing a broken, shabby old man at the end of his life of ancient depravities. But when Maria came in..." She shook her head and buried her face in her knees.

He stroked her hair and kissed her dirty hands. "What happened when Maria came in?"

She explained to him what she had seen. "Maybe she fell on something hard, I don't know. But it looked just about the width of his belt..." She choked a little. "He looked so weak, it's hard to believe. She probably has to let him do it because it's the only way he can get a hard–on."

"Sarah–"

"I'm sorry, but it just makes me sick to think I'm related to him. He never wanted to have anything to do with me and the feeling is certainly mutual now. Damn him and damn you too, Tyler, for stirring all this up!"

He sat in the sand with his arms around her and rocked her until she had drained herself of tears and emotion. Occasionally a tear slid down his own cheek, but he was ready to blame this on the biting wind that blew in off the ocean if she had looked up and questioned it.

Sarah was only vaguely aware of Tyler walking her back to the car and checking them into a motel on the edge of town. She did not begin to think clearly again until she was up to her neck in a bathtub of steamy water and her cold skin was tingling as though someone was pricking her all over with hot pins and needles.

Opening her eyes, she saw Tyler sitting on the lid of the toilet seat next to her, wrapped in a blue blanket and scribbling furiously in his notebook. It took her a moment to see that he had headphones on and that he was listening to his tiny tape recorder. When he realized her eyes were on him, he quickly shoved his gear aside.

"How do you feel?" From somewhere in the depths of his blanket he brought out a paper cup. He took a sip before offering it to her.

She sputtered a little as the brandy lit a fiery path down her throat. "Where did you get that?" she asked, sinking back into the water as the liquor infused her body with a relaxing warmth.

"Oh, I brought it along. Never know when you might need it."

"Why are you wearing that blanket?"

"Well, I was pretty damn cold by the time we got here but I thought you needed the hot bath more than me."

She didn't reply, feeling like a heel for her behavior and yet knowing it could not be helped. "Well, come on in," she said at last, sitting up. "There's room for two."

"Two what? Sardines?" But he dropped the blanket and stepped into the deliciously hot water, creating a tidal wave that soaked the tiny bathroom as he attempted to sit across from her. Finally they ended up side by side, their long legs hanging over the edge of the tub, intertwined at all the places where their arms and legs met.

"Well, how would you like me to show you the sights of Atlantic City?"

"And what makes you an expert on this lovely vacation spot?"

"Oh, I used to come here with my grandparents as a child, when it was a dying beach resort, before all the casinos moved in. In those days you could ride up and down the boardwalk in these wicker carriages pushed by black men–"

"Oh, come on. You expect me to believe that? How old are you, fifty–five?"

Tyler was glad to see Sarah warming back up to her usual sharp–tongued self. "No, this was in the early sixties, believe it or not. We would hire one of these guys to push us up and down the boardwalk and we would buy salt water taffy and rock candy and stop at Steel Pier and take in a few of the rides. Then, if you got up early enough in the morning, you could ride bicycles on the boardwalk. My brother and I would rent a tandem bike and ride like maniacs to see if we could get all the way to Ventnor and back before nine o'clock when bicycle riding was forbidden again until the next morning."

Sarah closed her eyes and listened to Tyler talk about his own childhood, realizing how little he spoke about himself, always concentrating on her past instead. She absorbed the details of his typical upbringing, wondering if he appreciated how lucky he was to have had a family to vacation with. She thought perhaps he kept much of it to himself because the happy ordinariness of his life contrasted so sharply with her own.

Eventually Tyler worked himself into a frenzied depression over the fact that Atlantic City and all of America had changed so much since his childhood. They ended up spending the evening in bed, eating Chinese take–out and watching TV, until Tyler discovered that the bed vibrated when quarters were put in a box on the nightstand. Then, of course, they had to see what it was like to have sex on a bed that vibrated, and by the time Sarah fell asleep she could only vaguely remember why they had come to New Jersey in the first place. Travis hadn't been mentioned all night.

When she woke up a few hours later, she was surprised to see that the light was still on. Tyler was sitting in a chair across the room. His eyes were closed and he was listening intently to his tape recorder, an expression of extreme concentration furrowing his brow. She rolled over and went back to sleep.

The next time she awoke it was 6 a.m. and Tyler was gone. She figured he had gone off to satisfy some nostalgic curiosity about bicycling at dawn on the boardwalk and tried not to concern herself over his odd behavior. A brief search told her immediately that he had taken his tape recorder and notebook with him, but she convinced herself he was just too neurotic to be without them.

Sitting on the edge of the bed, she observed her reflection in the large mirror that ran along the wall across from the foot of the bed. Her tangled hair stuck out at odd angles, still caught in a few stray bobby pins she had missed. Her eyes were a bit puffy from all the crying she had done the day before. The woebegone image in the mirror reminded her too much of her mother. She wanted to be done with all that now.

Tyler gasped at the first sight of her when he walked in the door a half hour later. Sarah was sitting naked on a chair in front of the mirror, hacking away at her bangs with a pair of nail scissors. Clumps of black hair lay all around her feet, contrasting dramatically with the orange shag carpet. The ragged haircut she had given herself was somewhere between punk and pixie and altered her appearance impressively.

"My God, what have you done? Stop it!" He came forward and tried to take the scissors from her but was hampered by the bulky white bakery bag he was carrying which held coffee and bagels. She pulled away from him and put the scissors down on the dresser with a resounding smack.

"What's the matter, Tyler? Don't you like me when I look like myself?"

Her sarcasm stung him and he flushed as though he'd been slapped. "That's not fair, Sarah," he said quietly, turning away from her to put the bakery bag on the nightstand. But he could not keep from looking back at her over his shoulder. She was using a hand towel to brush off the stray hairs that had stuck to her shoulders and breasts.

"I'm sorry, Tyler. But I needed to make a loud statement. Something declaring that I'm done with searching for the history of my life and ready to get back to the future. Do you understand?"

"Of course." He took off his sweater, unable to meet her frank gaze.

"Are you still with me?" She came up behind him, kneeling on the bed and wrapping her long arms around him. He could feel her breasts pressing into his back, her nipples becoming two hard points as she kissed his neck the way he had kissed hers that first time at the cabin.

"Of course." He could not give up Sarah Scupper any more than he could give up working out the mysteries of her mother. He would just have to figure out how to keep his two current passions separate from now on.

CHAPTER NINE

"Maybe you should get some snow tires put on this car," Sarah remarked as the back wheels spun out around yet another icy curve.

"It's not my car, it's my brother's," Tyler replied tersely, his concentration taxed by the sleet hitting the windshield as he inched his way along the last ten miles to West Jordan.

Because of the adverse weather conditions, they had not spoken much on the ride home from Burlington. After the plane had skidded to a stop on the runway, it had been Tyler's idea to spend a few hours in Burlington waiting for the weather to improve before starting for home. He suggested dropping Sarah at a beauty salon to have her hair re–cut professionally and Sarah had reluctantly agreed, wondering what he was up to. Somewhere between the shampoo and the rinse she remembered Maude's daughter, the one who had Winnie's lamp and lived in Burlington, and she knew that was where Tyler had disappeared to.

She was not happy that Tyler was still pursuing his story and Tyler knew this, but neither of them mentioned it on the tense journey back to West Jordan. They slid into town barely a few minutes before Sarah was due at work and headed directly for the inn.

"You guys are in hot water," Woody said as way of a greeting when they came wearily through the front door. He was sitting behind the desk going over some paperwork and pulled off his reading glasses to get a better look at Sarah. "Sarah! What did you do to your hair? My God, you look like–"

"Like I used to."

"Exactly." He turned to Tyler. "You missed a phone call yesterday."

Tyler's jaw dropped and then he slammed a fist against the desk. "Shit. Isabel. I forgot I told her to call on Sunday."

Woody laughed. "I guess you forgot. That was one angry broad. Said you should call her the moment you got in. I believe her words were 'a matter of utmost urgency'."

"Right. Her mother needs to know how many place settings of silver to polish for Thanksgiving."

Sarah threw him a look of indeterminate meaning and headed for the lounge to set up for the evening.

"Ah, yes. Which brings us to another matter of 'utmost urgency'." Woody put down his reading glasses again. "I didn't realize how long you would be staying or I would have advised you about this in the first place."

"What's that?"

"I need your room. Months ago I rented all the rooms out to the Stevenson family for Thanksgiving. They're having a big family reunion and didn't have enough beds up to their house for everyone. Anyway, they're due in tomorrow night." Woody put his glasses on again and looked down at the desk. "I didn't think it would be a big deal for you seeing as you haven't been sleeping here much anyway..." He peered up at Tyler meaningfully from beneath his bushy gray eyebrows.

"Sure. No problem." He rubbed his beard and wondered what Sarah would say when he told her. Worse than that, he wondered what Isabel would say when he told her. "Mind if I use the phone for a credit card call?"

"Be my guest."

Tyler pulled the phone as far away as it would go and managed to get it almost around the corner into the living room. He sat on the floor with his back against the door jam, trying to create an illusion of privacy, knowing Woody was listening in with a curiosity of the best intentions.

"Felicia, hi, is Isabel around? It's Tyler...Listen, Isabel, I know I'm a shithead, you're right, I'm sorry, I should have called you... I was away. Doing some out of town research...Yes, Sarah was with me...Isabel!...It's coming, slow, but it's coming...No, I'm going to stay here for Thanksgiving...Now calm down, Isabel, it's not the end of the world...I know you miss me...Well, of course I do...I've been busy, I haven't had time...I can't understand you when you sniffle like that..."

Tyler looked over his shoulder at Woody, who quickly averted his eyes and shuffled the invoices on his desk.

"Look, I've been doing a lot of thinking and we'll talk when I get back...What do you mean you talked to him? He called?...Wait a minute, you called MY editor and he told you I wouldn't have a job if I didn't get back soon? Why the hell did you call him in the first place?...Why would I have called him and not you? Stop crying, I can't understand you...Well, I think you've hit the head of the nail, sweetheart, and I'm glad you said it and not me. I think it is coming to an end between us but now is not the time to discuss it. I'll try to get home next week...What? No, don't, can't you wait— Isabel! Isabel! Hello? Shit."

He slammed the phone down and stood up to carry it back to the front desk.

"Everything okay at home?" Woody asked cheerfully.

"Yeah. Great." Cursing under his breath, Tyler stomped up the steep stairs to his room.

Sarah's haircut was the main topic of discussion in the Night Heron that evening. Because of the constant buzz of conversation directed at her, Sarah was not always aware of what Tyler was up to. He bought Lyle several beers and spent a couple of hours talking to him, which Sarah found very suspicious. But after Lyle left, the only reference he made to their conversation was an offhand remark to Sarah about Lyle's missing finger.

"I never noticed it before. I mean, the whole pinky finger is missing from bottom knuckle up."

"Yeah, he hides it pretty well. Nobody really says anything about it."

"How'd he lose it? Logging accident?"

Sarah shrugged. "Guess so. Probably drank a six pack for lunch one day and lopped it right off. But believe me, I never thought it was worth asking him about. You never know how he'll react."

Tyler suggested he go up to the cabin and get a fire started so that it would be warm when Sarah got home. He convinced her he knew how to run the woodstove and she reminded him that she had no vehicle. They parted a little stiffly with him promising to come back in a few hours. Tyler still hadn't mentioned that Woody had asked him to move out of the inn. Nor had he told her how furious Isabel was and that she was threatening to put his belongings out in the street if he didn't return to the city soon. He figured it would all be better said in the cozy and familiar surroundings of the cabin.

The cabin was in darkness, so he left his headlights shining on the porch while he fumbled for the key to the padlock. He was surprised to find once he was inside that the temperature felt nearly the same as outside. Sarah had left the faucets running to keep the pipes from freezing, but a trickle of water on the floor near the bathroom door indicated that this old trick might not have worked.

He jumped as the bedroom curtains fluttered suddenly and then settled back into position. Frowning, he walked slowly to the window and pulled back the curtains to reveal the shattered pane of glass that was responsible for the breeze. Someone had punched a hole with a rock or a fist just beneath the sash, to gain easy access to the lock.

Sinking down on the bed, he looked around the room trying to determine what had been disturbed. Contrary to the last break–in, it looked virtually untouched this time, but Sarah would be a better judge of that. The least he could do was call the police so they could dust for fingerprints again.

He started a fire and made the phone call before he went into the bathroom to inspect the damage. He flicked the switch and looked immediately at the floor, following the stream of water to the bottom of the toilet. Consequently, he had been in the bathroom for a minute or so before he looked up and saw what was written on the mirror.

The message scrawled in black magic marker did not make any sense – "MONROE TAKES WHAT BELONGS TO MONROE."

Tyler hovered over the woodstove, alternately holding out his hands in front of him and then turning to warm his behind. His mind was racing rapidly. He wanted to figure out what the words on the mirror meant before the police arrived. It was hard to believe that Travis's arm could reach as far as West Jordan and so quickly, but perhaps he had connections nearby. After reading the message Tyler had known exactly what had been stolen, but had not wanted to touch anything until fingerprints had been taken.

Before he could think any further, headlights appeared in the driveway and then Brian Evans' face peered through the glass of the front door. Tyler motioned for him to come in, momentarily surprised to see that he was alone, until he remembered that Brian was the entire police force for West Jordan.

Tyler showed him the broken window and the bathroom mirror, and Brian's expression darkened as he

193

read the bold capital letters. "What do you think it means?" he asked.

Tyler shrugged and led him back into the bedroom. "I think whatever's missing came out of there." He pointed to an inlaid wooden box on top of the dresser where he knew Sarah kept the pieces of jewelry from the safe deposit box along with a few other important keepsakes. Using a clean handkerchief, Brian lifted the lid, confirming Tyler's suspicions.

"Sarah had the earrings and the nightingale pin with her, so that leaves a string of pearls, a ring, a gold pin and a couple of gold bracelets." Tyler tallied it up on his fingers.

"Who knew about this jewelry besides you?"

"Well, just about everybody in town, I guess. She wore nearly all of it to work at the bar the night we discovered it." He thought that would give Brian enough suspects to go after and he could get by without mentioning their visit to Travis. A trip to Atlantic City could easily be explained as a spontaneous idea between new lovers who wanted to have a good time. "Look, I've got to go back down into town and pick Sarah up. Maybe I can stall her long enough so that you can be done by the time we get back. She's barely over the first break—in and I think this is going to upset her a lot."

Brian agreed and Tyler left for town, wondering what he was going to say to Sarah. Much as she wanted it to be a dead issue, the mystery seemed to be very much alive.

One thing was for certain, Tyler mused to himself. He was watching Sarah as she slept beside him, looking pale and fragile in the frosty light of dawn that seeped through the opaque sheet of plastic that covered the bedroom window. She had been more than happy to let him move in with her for the next few days. She had tried to be tough and disbelieving but when she saw the message on the mirror, her resolve had crumbled and for the rest of the night she had clung to him, saying with her body what she couldn't put into words.

Even now, as he lay propped up on one elbow looking at her, she rolled over and threw one arm around his waist, snuggling her face against his chest. The warmth of her breath against his skin aroused him but he fought the urge and gently pulled away, slipping out from under the covers.

Wearing a pair of wool socks and a sweatshirt, he squatted in front of the open door of the woodstove, stirring the embers with an iron poker, watching them grow bright in the draft of cold air. When the flames were finally happily licking at the new wood, he tiptoed back into the bedroom, returning with his tape recorder and notebook.

He was sure that somewhere in all the information he had gathered were clues, if not the answer, to who was harassing Sarah and how that person was linked to Winnie Scupper's death and the missing jewels. He had a feeling that if he could answer just one of those questions, everything else would fall into place.

Besides, it wasn't just idle curiosity now that urged him onward. Who knew what would be next in the game of "Monroe Takes What Belongs to Monroe"?

Shuddering at the possibilities, he pulled a chair over by the fire and settled down to work.

By the time Sarah awoke, Tyler was gone, having left her a note that said he had gone down to the inn to pick up his belongings. Next to the note were a few sheets of paper ripped out of his notebook, covered with lists and phrases that had been scratched out and scribbled over. Despite the fact that he had more than enough material for his article, he was obviously still working on her mother's story.

"Jewels are where?" she read. Turning the paper sideways, she tried to decipher a list of names under a heading. It looked like, "Monroe's W.J. Connection," whatever that meant. "Probably over 50. Who caretakes the house? Talk to 1.Woody, 2.Maude, 3.Mrs. Wilford, 4.Red, 5.DORA." A dark circle was drawn around Dora's name and a couple of stars were next to it.

Sarah sighed. She knew he had left this out purposely for her to see. When she said she didn't want to deal with the past anymore, he had vowed not to talk to her about it again. This was his way of letting her know what his plans were for the next few days without having to say a word.

Probably she should have said no when he asked if he could move in for a few days. Then maybe he would have packed up and gone back to New York and she could get on with her life.

The sound of the wind rattling the plastic covering on the bedroom window reminded her that it was not over yet and that, like it or not, Tyler had become part of her life now.

Tyler looked up and down the deserted road and then checked the lock on the trunk once more. He did not like leaving his car here in the middle of nowhere with all of his stuff, particularly his laptop computer, in the trunk. But it was easier than dropping it off at the cabin and evasively answering Sarah's questions about where he was going.

Zipping up his jacket, he headed off through the woods in the direction of Dora Evans' house. There was still a light covering of old snow in the darkest shadows beneath the trees but most of the ground was soft and damp. Occasionally he heard the crackle of ice breaking as he stepped on springy piles of dead leaves and pushed his way through the dry underbrush and fallen branches. A couple of gun shots in the distance made him pause for a second, before he remembered it was still deer hunting season.

Through the trees he glimpsed the roof line and then the faded pine boards of a tumbledown shack. He approached the abandoned building cautiously, knowing he must be on Evans property now. For several minutes he peered through the window at the rusty metal vats and the enormous woodstove, visions of moonshine operations going through his head. A stack of metal buckets finally enlightened him to the fact that all he had stumbled on was someone's old maple sugaring shed.

The path he followed led him out onto the hillside just above Dora Evan's house. He went as close as he dared, until he had a good view into her kitchen window. Then he settled himself and his binoculars behind a large spruce tree.

He didn't really know what he was looking for; some sort of clue that would gain him access to the house and the woman he had convinced himself held the answers to a thirty–year–old mystery. Maybe if she left the house he could sneak in and snoop around but he wasn't sure he would have the guts to do that. Particularly since she had one son that was a cop and another that was very protective of his mother. He knew that Brian Evans had his own house on the other side of the road where he lived with his wife and daughters. There was also a chance that Lyle might come home for lunch although he doubted it.

He wasted the better part of the morning kneeling in the mud, watching Dora through the binoculars as she washed dishes and sat at her kitchen table watching TV, consuming close to a dozen glazed doughnuts during a talk show and two game shows. The telephone rang once. Looking at the sagging electric and telephone lines that ran to the house from a homemade pole that leaned at a precarious angle, Tyler thought of a way to at least gain access to the other side of Dora's front door.

It took the better part of the afternoon to prepare for his return to the Evans property. He drove to Jordan Center and outfitted himself in some basic gray work clothes from a thrift shop and a discount department store. He also bought some cheap tools to heighten the effect.

Luckily Sarah was out when he got back to the cabin. He quickly unloaded his belongings from the trunk of the car and then sat down at the telephone. His heart was pounding as he dialed the number he found under Evans, D., in the telephone book.

"Hello? Hello? Who's there?" He could hear Dora's voice coming from the earpiece of the receiver as he carefully unplugged it from the telephone. From his own experience he knew that this would tie up Dora's phone line, making it virtually unusable until Sarah's receiver was put back on the hook, severing the connection.

He slipped Sarah's telephone beneath the couch where she wouldn't notice the receiver was missing and where the buttons would not be accidentally pushed, thereby disconnecting the call. Hanging the black receiver from his belt, he looked at the cord dangling from it, trying to decide what to do with it. By the time he left a few minutes later, it was cleverly attached to his tape recorder which also hung from his belt, but face down so that it was unrecognizable as the most important tool he carried.

The sun was almost setting as he parked his car around a bend, just outside the hollow where the Evans clan lived. Tyler knew that he had a couple of hours at least before Lyle arrived home from his inevitable visit to the Night Heron for a couple of beers. Judging by Lyle's physical appearance, it was fairly obvious that he never stopped home first.

Dora answered the door with a surly expression on her puffy face. She was wearing a pair of men's rubber boots and a purple nylon ski jacket that vied for attention with the color of her hair and didn't come close to meeting across her oversized chest.

"You from the phone company?" She scrutinized his face and he was grateful that he was wearing a cap and had not shaved off his beard yet, hoping that she would not recognize him from his previous visit. The name embroidered over the pocket of his used work shirt was "Don."

"That's right, Mrs. Evans. We got a report that something was wrong with your phone."

"Well, I was just going down to my brother's to call you. That's the quickest service I ever got. Usually takes days." She chuckled to herself and moved aside. "Come on in. The phone's in the kitchen."

Tyler stepped inside and looked quickly around at the living room before she moved him on. It was garishly furnished in bright greens and oranges; there was fake paneling nailed to one wall decorated with a clock shaped like the state of Florida. It was nearly four o'clock. On an end table, in the place of honor between two Naugahyde recliners, was a framed photograph of a young, shapely Dora wearing a rhinestone tiara and a winner's sash over her prom dress.

He found the telephone on the wall beside a calendar from the West Jordan gas company. "What seems to be the problem?" he asked, taking in at close range what he had already seen through binoculars.

"It rang and I answered it and nobody was there. I couldn't get a dial tone after that. It just went dead," Dora shouted from the living room where she was struggling to get her boots off.

"Hmmmm. Nice place you got here. You lived here long?"

"I grew up in the house down below, but I've lived in this house for about 25 years." Puffing a little, Dora sank her bulk into a kitchen chair, helping herself to the last doughnut in the box on the table.

"Your husband build the place?" Tyler unscrewed the mouthpiece of the phone, inspecting the inside of it.

She snorted. "That bastard? No, he left me with two small boys and barely a cent to feed them with."

Tyler studied the receiver, trying to mask his surprise at this reply. It was only natural that a woman like Dora would invent a husband to cover up an unsavory past, but he pursued the point anyway.

"That's too bad. Where'd he light off to?"

"I don't know, some place down south. He wasn't a good man, I think he had to leave the country, you know, what do they call it? Defect?"

"Really? So. You live way out here all by yourself?"

"Nah, I got my boy, Lyle, still lives at home with me. My other son lives acrost the way, you've probably heard of him, Brian Evans, he's the town cop."

"Oh, sure." Tyler chatted amiably with her, trying to win her over as he took the telephone apart on the kitchen table, laying the pieces out in what he thought was a professional manner. He complimented her on anything he could think of, from the cleanness of her kitchen window, to the size of her large striped tom cat.

"That photo in the living room, is that you?" he finally asked, as casually as possible.

"You betcha. Back in my youth before I lost my figure." She patted her torso forlornly.

"Hey, weren't you the one lived with that artist woman? Somebody Scupper?" He asked the question without looking up, pretending to concentrate on reassembling the receiver.

"How do you know about that?" Dora asked suspiciously. "That was a long time ago, you probably weren't even born yet."

"Oh, people have been talking about it lately, ever since her daughter found that stuff in the safe deposit box up in Potter's Falls."

"What stuff?"

"I don't know, a bunch of old jewelry I think. Was she some kind of rich miser or something? From what I heard her daughter didn't end up with anything." He risked a glance up at Dora from beneath the rim of his cap. She was staring off into space, her face hardening into an angry expression.

"And where'd you hear that?"

"Oh, down at the Night Heron. The daughter works down there as a bartender, you know."

"No, I didn't know." Dora seemed to be slipping further away from him. She was staring at one of her plump hands, nervously twisting something on her smallest finger. When she stopped for a second, Tyler could see it was ring that was so tight it seemed to disappear into the flesh surrounding it, never to come off except with a hacksaw.

"Do you have any other telephones in this house?" he asked abruptly.

"Yes, one in the bedroom." Dora seemed to snap back to the present. "But the bedroom's a mess. Let me go in and straighten up a little, it'll only take a second."

When she had lumbered into the bedroom, he took the opportunity to quickly scan her calendar. From what he could tell, she had a hairdresser's appointment on Friday morning at 10:00. The day before that was Thanksgiving. Before she returned, he reached over and unlocked the kitchen window, slipping a pencil into the storm window behind it so that it couldn't lock. He didn't know if Dora locked her doors but he wouldn't take any chances.

"Okay," she called. "It's ready."

"So you having your family in for Thanksgiving?" he asked as he crawled around on the floor beside her sagging double bed looking for the phone jack into the wall. The room had a stale odor of old perfume and unwashed socks and he gagged a little as he worked.

"No, we'll be going over to my son, Brian's. His wife has a big do with her side of the family and all. Saves me the trouble of cooking."

"Oh, I bet you're a good cook. Are you one of those families that has an early Thanksgiving supper or a late one?" He pushed the bed away from the wall a little bit to get a better angle on the phone jack, dislodging the mattress from the box spring in the process.

"Oh, we usually eat around one. We're not the kind of family that can wait for..." Dora continued talking but Tyler did not hear what she said. His eye had caught the corner of a brown manila envelope that was protruding from the head of the bed from underneath the mattress where it had moved an inch or two off the box spring.

"Mrs. Evans, would you mind picking up the phone in the kitchen? I need to see if the line is clear between these two phones."

As soon as Dora was out of the room, he tugged the envelope out of its hiding place. It was a large size, probably 8 inches by 11, and he froze for a moment, frantically trying to figure out where he could hide it. Finally he unbuttoned his shirt and slipped it inside, against his chest, buttoning it up again. It made an odd bulge but if he kept his arms down, she probably wouldn't notice.

"Hello, can you hear me?"

Tyler's hand shook as he picked up the bedroom extension. "Yes, Mrs. Evans. I hear you loud and clear."

It was dark by the time he got back to the cabin. Sarah had gone to work, but had left the porch light on for him. The telephone was still under the couch where he had left it and he quickly hooked the receiver back up to it and dialed Dora's number.

"Hi, Mrs. Evans? Don from the phone company. We found the problem on our end. Just checking to see if your phone is working."

"Yes, thank you, it seems to be fine now. Look, if this wasn't my fault, am I going to get a bill for this?" Dora's voice crackled a little and the connection sounded rather tinny after Tyler's reconstruction.

"No, of course not. Have a nice holiday." He hung up the phone, gazing nervously at the envelope that lay on the couch next to him. It was outright theft, but he would replace it on Friday morning while she was at the hairdresser and she would never have to know. It felt like photographs and he assured himself it was probably something stupid anyway, like autographed pictures of Hank Williams or Barry Manilow.

A moment later he was staring open–mouthed at the black and white photographs that lay in his lap. Eight by ten glossies of a voluptuous naked woman who was unquestionably Dora in her younger years. In a couple of the pictures she appeared to have posed coquettishly for the amateur photographer, but instead of erotic the effect bordered on vulgar as she smiled for the camera, lifting her oversized breasts to improbable heights and spreading her legs. The remaining shots were purposely obscene and Tyler thought they may have been taken without her consent. They made his stomach churn; Dora in outlandish positions, performing unnatural sex acts on herself with objects, occasionally dressed in sheer, skimpy undergarments, her eyes closed, her mouth open and panting in painful ecstasy.

Tyler could feel his face burning with embarrassment, not for Dora but for himself, that he had been foolish enough to violate someone's darkest personal secrets thinking he might learn something from them. His fingers shook as he unfolded the white sheet of writing paper that had come out of the envelope with the photographs. He could barely make his eyes focus on the words, his gaze stealing back again and again to the array of pornography spread across the couch next to him.

"I thought perhaps these photographs might be worth more than the thousand words I could write to you describing what I will do to you if you bother me for money again. They bring back pleasant memories, don't they? I'm sure you have friends and relatives who would take a great interest in these photographs of you, as well as several magazines I could sell them to which specialize in this sort of thing. Or perhaps if you are really as desperate as you say you are, you can sell them for some quick cash.

"It is unlikely that any letter you should write might reach me at this point, but in the unlucky event that it does, don't forget that I have the negatives. In any case, don't threaten me again. You wouldn't want to put the lives of your children in danger now, would you?"

There was no question it was some sort of blackmail but Tyler was not quite sure who was trying to blackmail who. Although there was no signature, he was certain the letter was from the "ex–husband" Dora had mentioned. It was hard to imagine why Dora had held on to these pictures and this letter for so many years but perhaps she had her reasons. One thing was painfully obvious; it certainly had nothing to do with Winnie Scupper.

He looked at the offensive photographs closely one more time before slipping them back into the envelope. He noticed that each photograph had the date it was developed printed on the white border, in the same manner he had noticed on old snapshots of his own family. He could read the year clearly, it was 1957, but he could not make out what he thought should be the abbreviation for the month. It looked like ENE; perhaps it was the initials of the photography studio that did the developing.

1957...two years after Winnie's murder. From what he could remember of the Evans chronology, Lyle had been born in 1956. He would have been a baby at the time these pictures were taken. Brian would have been five or six.

Tyler wondered what Dora's children had been doing while she performed for her lover. The thought made him shudder. Nothing was turning out the way he had hoped. Instead of the answers to an exciting mystery, he was just unearthing one gruesome detail after another about the people in Winnie's life.

CHAPTER TEN

"I love watching you cook," Sarah remarked. She sat perched on a high stool in the center of the tiny kitchen, watching Tyler create a casserole for Woody's Thanksgiving supper. "I mean, you never use a recipe, you throw in anything that looks good, it's sort of like modern art."

Despite her lighthearted chatter, she was worried about Tyler. She was usually a very sound sleeper, but Tyler had woken her several times in the last two nights, mumbling and thrashing restlessly. Once in the middle of sex, he suddenly turned away and said, "I'm sorry, I just can't do this right now." When she asked if it was because of Isabel, he denied it.

But something was definitely on his mind and she assumed it had to do with his further investigations. For the last couple of days she had made a point of not asking him what he did with his time and he had not offered any insights. Although she never mentioned it to Tyler, Sarah felt they were putting their relationship to the test, seeing if there was anything to it without the common ground of Winnie Scupper's story. Their sexual attraction was still so strong, however, that it pleasantly filled any silent spaces and Sarah, in her analytical way, found it curiously interesting how pleasant it was to just lay intertwined on the couch with Tyler and do nothing.

"How many people does this have to feed? Ten, twenty?"

"Something like that. I have no idea, but I wouldn't worry about it. Just make a lot." Sarah hopped off the stool. "I guess I better figure out something to wear."

"Sarah, would you mind if we went in separate cars?"

She bit her tongue to keep from asking why and swallowed hard before replying. "I guess not. In that case, I might as well get dressed and go. Woody can probably use some help. Don't forget, he wants to eat around two."

Tyler watched through the window as Sarah drove off down the driveway and once again he was struck by the contrasts between her and Isabel. Isabel would never have let the matter rest until he had told her why he wanted to stay home and there was no way she would have agreed to go off alone without a fight.

But when he drove down to the hollow on the other side of Dalton Mountain, he realized it was foolish to think he could pull this stunt off today. It was a warm day for November and there were Evanses outside everywhere. To reach Dora's house, he would have to troop through the woods again and risk arriving at the inn for Thanksgiving dinner suspiciously wet and muddy. He couldn't even be sure that Dora would have left for her son's house yet.

Swearing, he stuffed the manila envelope into the pocket on the back of the passenger seat and he turned the car around, headed back for town. Despite his immediate revulsion, he found he had a haunting fascination with the pictures of Dora. Not because of some sexual obsession, but because he thought he might glean some stray detail in the background that would enlighten him in what was beginning to seem like a hopeless quest.

All he had come up with was that the pictures had been taken in a well–furnished bedroom that did not match up with Dora's own as far as taste or furniture. There was a window with lace curtains and a drawn shade. The wallpaper had an unusual colonial pattern of what appeared to be Grecian urns with lilacs spilling out of them. In one shot, the framed picture of Dora as homecoming queen appeared on the nightstand next to the bed along with what looked like a snapshot of a small boy. This seemed to identify the room as a personal one, probably that of Dora and her ex–husband. In the background of another photograph there was a mirrored dresser, littered with hair curlers and makeup in a manner that spoke of Dora.

Well, maybe he could get Woody alone for a moment to talk about it after the Thanksgiving meal. Woody still seemed interested in helping him get to the root of Winnie's secrets, even if Sarah did not.

When he arrived at the inn, he found that the supper was being held in Woody's personal part of the building, a place that most patrons never saw. It was bigger than he expected and furnished in an old–fashioned style that Tyler suspected dated back to Woody's mother's youth. A highly polished oak table was covered in an antique lace tablecloth and set with heavy silver. Several people were standing around sipping wine and eating hors d'oeuvres. He made his way through them to the kitchen, where he found Sarah stirring the gravy and Woody cursing the slow baking yams.

"Anything I can do to help?" he asked, feeling slightly out of place and a little homesick suddenly.

"Yeah, find me a gravy boat. Where can Tyler find a gravy boat, Woody?"

"Out in the big sideboard in the dining room or maybe in the glass cupboard. Get the one that matches the china."

Tyler went back out into the dining room and found the sideboard. It held china and silver and cloth napkins and some fancy matchbooks that had the name of the inn embossed on their covers in gold. A tall cupboard with glass doors seemed to hold the more unusual pieces like sugar bowls, creamers and gravy boats. It also held delicate knick–knacks like little glass camels, carved wooden giraffes and ivory elephants.

As he shut the door, something caught his eye through the glass. It was off to the side on the bottom shelf, shoved behind a porcelain ballerina wearing a porcelain lace skirt. He almost dropped the gravy boat in his anxiety to reach it quickly.

"I found the gravy boat," he said placing it on the counter next to Sarah, "and I also found this."

She looked at him oddly. "What do you mean? Why did you bring my kaleidoscope here?"

"This isn't your kaleidoscope, this is its twin!" His voice was falling into the fast–paced rhythm it took on when he was excited. "Woody, where did you get this?"

Woody looked up. "Oh, I made that a long time ago. I haven't seen it in years. Where did you find it?"

"You made this?"

"Yeah, I used to do some woodturning when I was younger. Don't look so amazed." Woody laughed. "There are lots of things about me you don't know!"

"Did you know that Sarah has one just like it?"

"What?" Woody put down his potholder and turned to Sarah with a strange expression on his face. "You do?"

Sarah nodded. "My grandmother gave it to me. My mother had sent it to her for a birthday present."

"She did? I always wondered what happened to the other one." Woody was staring at the kaleidoscope in Tyler's hand with a distant look in his eyes. "It was an idea we came up with together. I made the kaleidoscopes and she fitted the ends out with frosted glass and then filled them with bits of broken colored glass. I had made two of them, one for each of us...God, I haven't thought about this in years. But now I can remember it so clearly."

Woody sat down heavily in a chair and reached for the kaleidoscope, turning it over in his hands reflectively. Tyler cursed himself for not bringing his tape recorder along – he had no idea anything like this would come up at Thanksgiving dinner.

"So when was this?"

"It was during the time she was pregnant with Sarah. I used to come out and help her quite a bit. We got pretty close."

"But isn't that when Dora lived with her?"

"Yes, but Dora couldn't drive and she was pretty useless when it came to anything beyond house cleaning. I used to take Winnie to her monthly doctor's appointments and afterwards we would go food shopping and we got to be very good friends." Woody looked up in time to see the meaningful exchange of glances between Tyler and Sarah at his last remark. "Oh, for Christ sake, we were just friends. She was pregnant and it was 1955! I admit I was quite infatuated with her and had naive dreams that she would get divorced and marry me. I mean, there she was, getting bigger by the day and I was the one going through it with her, not her husband."

"I thought you said you weren't around when my mother died."

"Well, I wasn't. When were you born, May? Well, it was sometime in April that Travis finally showed up again. Winnie and I were down in the cellar, that's where her workshop was, putting these kaleidoscopes together when we heard Dora talking to someone upstairs. A moment later Travis came walking down the cellar steps, six tanned feet tall, wearing this light colored suit that made him look even darker. But I swear his tan faded away when he got a look at Winnie, big as house and laughing away with me. She didn't have many pregnancy clothes so a lot of the time when she was home she didn't get dressed, she just wore a nightgown with this big old flannel bathrobe over it.

"It was easy to imagine what passed through his mind once he got over the shock of the pregnancy. It was hard for me to believe that she had never written to him about it but maybe she had wanted to surprise him."

"Or maybe she didn't have his address," Tyler remarked.

"Could be. In any case, an ugly scene followed. I don't know if you really want to hear about it." Woody looked sideways at Sarah.

She shrugged and turned back to the gravy. "Go ahead. It can't make me like him any less and I'm sure Tyler is just dying to hear it."

"Well, I said my goodbyes thinking they would probably want to be alone after all those months. But I was barely up the stairs before he started yelling at her and accusing her all of sorts of filthy things that involved me. In my naive, young way I thought I should go back down and defend her reputation. I got back down just in time to see him give her a smack that sent her backwards into the cutting table. I didn't think twice about going at it with the guy. But he was a good bit bigger than me and before long he had me face down on the dirt floor with my arms twisted behind me, making me promise never to set foot in the house again. He assured me he had ways of making me comply if I wouldn't listen.

"In the end, the only way I could make it work was to leave town. I knew that if I stayed around I would have to see her. I learned from Dora that Travis only stayed a couple of nights and that Winnie was okay after he had gone. So I bought a Harley and rode it to Mexico."

"What?" The tension was broken as both Tyler and Sarah burst out laughing at the idea of Woody dressed up like Marlon Brando, taking a motorcycle on a wild joy ride south of the border.

"I told you there was a lot you didn't know about me! Yes, I disappeared for about six months. By the time I got back, well, you know the rest."

"Woody, are we eating or what?" A couple of hungry looking guests popped their heads through the kitchen door.

"Right away." He stood up and undid his apron. "The story is over. Let the meal commence!"

Tyler realized there would be no way to talk to Woody alone unless he volunteered to do the dishes. He knew Woody well enough to know that, although he might not actually submerge his hands in the soapy water, he would hang around the kitchen, making sure everything was taken care of properly.

"Woody, let me ask you something." Tyler spoke in a low, confidential tone that he knew inspired interest on the part of the listener. "I can't reveal my source but somebody showed me some nude shots taken of Dora back in the fifties. You ever hear anything about that?"

Woody gave a soft whistle and his gray curls bounced as he shook his head. "No way. You're kidding me. Who was it?"

It was Tyler's turn to emphatically shake his head. "I can't say. I just wondered if it was another one of those small town secrets."

"Well, I guess it is because I never heard tell of it. But it doesn't really surprise me. Hard core pornography?"

Tyler nodded. "1957 was the date."

"Now that's odd." Woody's brow wrinkled. "What did she look like? Was she already getting fat?"

Tyler laughed. "Not exactly. Except that she had those really mondo, out–of–proportion tits. Why?"

"Well, I'm trying to remember. It seems to me that after Lyle was born she never really got her shape back. And I believe he was born in '56."

"Really?"

"Yeah, he was one enormous baby, she probably gained a hundred pounds during her pregnancy. In fact I think they had to take him out of her, you know,

212

Caesarean, but I'm not certain. Men didn't talk about that stuff in those days. All we knew was we never saw her sunbathing in a bikini after that."

"Really." It didn't make a lot of sense but Tyler had a feeling that this piece of information would answer more than one question if he just put his mind to it. "You ever hear of her having a husband that left her?"

"Hell, no. Where'd you hear that one?"

"Just a rumor someone mentioned. Hey, what herbs did you put in that stuffing? It was excellent." Tyler smoothly changed the subject. There would only be trouble if he went any further with it.

He found Sarah down in the lounge by herself. She had built a fire and pulled up a small rag rug in front of the fireplace. Although it was only five o'clock, the room was already in darkness, lit only by the flames. Sarah sat cross–legged on the rug, her dress hiked up around her thighs, and her long legs in their white tights appeared endless. Looking up at Tyler framed by the doorway, she patted the rug next to her and said, "Come be romantic with me in front of the fire."

"God, you're beautiful." He sank down next to her. "Let's do it right here, right now."

"Ouch! What's this– a pistol in your pocket or are you just glad to see me?" She pulled Woody's kaleidoscope out of Tyler's jacket pocket. "Tyler. What are you still doing with this?"

"I just wanted to take it home and compare the two of them. Woody knows I have it."

Sarah held it up to her eye, pointing it toward the light of the fire. "It's different," she said, turning it a few times. "It doesn't seem to have as much glass in it as mine. The patterns are much sparser."

"Well, it sounded as though Woody had to leave in an unexpected hurry. Maybe it wasn't quite finished. Let me see." Tyler looked through the kaleidoscope and understood what she meant. He was impatient to get home now and look at the two of them together.

Putting down the kaleidoscope, he reached for Sarah, massaging, stroking and kissing until she gasped a little. Slipping her hand down his pants, she said, "Maybe we'd better go home now. You drive."

But when they got outside, Sarah said, "Oh, we can't just leave without saying goodbye." So contrary to Tyler's plan, they ended up satisfying their lust in the back seat of his brother's car, amid much squirming and laughter. "I haven't done this since high school." Sarah rested her head against the padded velour armrest of the door on the driver's side. "How about you?"

"I don't think I ever did it in a car. We always found a bed or a couch somewhere. You sure you don't want to go home now and do it like grown–ups do?"

"No, let's go back inside and visit a little more. It'll be fun to try and act like normal, bored Thanksgiving guests knowing that we just screwed our brains out like teenagers in the parking lot. Here." Sarah shoved her underpants into Tyler's jacket pocket before pulling her tights back on. "That will remind you of the animals we really are every time you stick your hand inside your pocket."

As they walked back across the parking lot to the building, the outdoor light came on suddenly and Woody's shape appeared in the doorway. "Oh, there you are. Where have you been? You've got a call from New York, Tyler."

"Isabel?"

Woody nodded.

As he headed for the telephone, Tyler's hand instinctively closed around Sarah's underpants in his pocket, still warm from the heat of her body.

He managed to avoid thinking about the conversation with Isabel until the following morning as he sat in the cover of the underbrush of Dora Evans' backyard, waiting for her to leave for her hairdresser's appointment. Isabel had made things pretty clear to him and there was no getting around it. There were too many details left hanging in his life there, bills to pay, appointments still dangling. He was going to have to leave on Sunday for New York and he was going to have to decide what he was going to do when he got there.

The sound of a pickup truck roaring up what he had thought was an untraversable driveway ended his speculation. Lyle bumped his way to the back door in four wheel drive and honked the horn. Dora appeared almost instantly and a few seconds later they were gone.

Tyler breathed a sigh of nervous relief. Picking up the manila envelope he headed for the house. He would be glad to be rid of those pictures for good. After talking to Woody, he had given them another once over and had determined there was definitely no scar from a Caesarean delivery obvious in any of the pictures. It made him realize that the date etched in the border was merely the date of printing, not the date when the pictures were actually taken. They could have been taken years before.

In any case, he was sure the photographs had no relevance to Winnie Scupper or anything about her. But perhaps something else in Dora's house would.

Dora had left the back door unlocked in the habit of most rural people and Tyler let himself in quietly, thankful he did not have to use the window over the sink. The Florida–shaped clock ticked loudly, reiterating the emptiness of the house and reminding him of his limited amount of time. In a few moments he had the manila envelope wedged securely under the mattress in the same place he had found it.

Looking around, he wondered where a person like Dora kept important papers and precious keepsakes. He went carefully through the bedroom, looking in bureau drawers, under the bed, and through boxes in the closet. He hated himself more by the minute; even though he left everything exactly as he found it, he felt that he was no better than the burglar who had torn Sarah's house apart.

The desk in the living room seemed a likely target for search. At the end of an hour he knew how much Dora had paid for gas, electricity and telephone, what her property taxes were and how much money she had in the bank. But all of it told him nothing. Sitting down heavily in one of the Naugahyde recliners, he contemplated the problem. Where would a person keep things from thirty years ago?

His eyes strayed to the ceiling where a squared off area indicated a trapdoor to the attic. No doubt that was where Dora's important mementos were kept; her homecoming queen's dress, old Christmas cards, her son's baby shoes. But he would need a ladder to get up there and the thought of finding one was overwhelming.

It was time to give up. He might as well go back to Sarah's and start writing the story as he now knew it. Maybe someday he would be able to fill in the missing pieces.

As Tyler stood up, he noticed a couple of photo albums lying sideways on a bookshelf across the room, sandwiched between stacks of old magazines. It couldn't hurt to spend a few more minutes looking around. He would never get the opportunity again, that was for sure.

He tugged on one that had gold lettering on the side announcing it as "Baby's First Year." As it came free of the pile, some folded papers fluttered to the floor. Frowning, he read through report cards, birthday cards, and immunization records, trying to find some useful information. He finally opened up the album and there on the first page was a special pocket marked "Baby's Birth Certificate". He had just unfolded it and begun to read when the sound of Lyle's pickup truck reached him as it began the return trip up the driveway.

In a panic, he shoved the papers back into the album and shoved the album back into the pile of magazines on the shelf. The truck was already rounding the corner of the house and he realized he was too late to make it out the back door. His only chance was to go out the front door and make a mad dash for the woods while Dora was getting out of the truck.

For a brief second the front door stuck from disuse and Tyler's throat closed with fear at the thought of coming face to face with Lyle. But on the second pull it opened, and then he was leaping off the front steps and running as fast as could in the opposite direction from the driveway, diving for cover behind the biggest tree he could find.

He leaned against it for a long time, unaware of the snow that was beginning to fall thickly from the sky, his heart and brain pounding with the craziness of what he had been doing. But as he sat on the cold ground, trying to control his breathing, his mind ran over the documents he had just been reading. It came to him that he had at last found what might be a significant clue to a story kept secret for thirty years.

Brushing the snow from his clothes, he headed back through the woods to his car. He wanted to get it all down on paper before he decided whether or not to share his suspicions with Sarah.

When Sarah went off to work, she left Tyler sitting at the kitchen table playing with the two kaleidoscopes. He had been acting strangely all afternoon, saying very little and appearing restless. She had been glad when he finally focused his attention on the kaleidoscopes.

"Woody's is much more colorful and changes shape easier," was his only comment. "Maybe Winnie's mood changed by the time she put her own together."

When she said goodbye to him, he was holding both kaleidoscopes up to his eyes and looking through them at the same time. She managed to get an absentminded promise from him to come down to the inn for dinner in a few hours.

Sarah did not have much time to dwell on Tyler's mood as she drove to work. Snow was falling thickly and it took all her concentration just to see the road. She wondered how business would be on a night like this; sometimes when the weather was bad people came pouring in, laughing in the face of nature's desire to triumph over man.

She had forgotten it was a holiday weekend and that Woody had a full house of guests as well. From the moment she unlocked the door, the lounge was packed. As well as local merrymakers, carloads of skiers from Massachusetts and Connecticut filled the place. By the time Tyler walked in, the bar was three deep, all the tables were filled and Sarah was in high gear with no time to chat amiably with anyone.

"Sarah–" Tyler grabbed her arm to get her attention, "I've discovered something really amazing–"

"Tyler, do you see how many people are in here?" She pulled away from him. "I'm really close to losing it. I absolutely cannot talk to you now." She was irritated that he should come in when she was so busy with that excited tone in his voice and that sparkle in his eye, thinking she should drop everything to talk to him.

Her anger melted when she next caught a glimpse of him. He had tied the other bartender's leather apron around his waist and was clearing glasses off tables, handing out menus and writing down orders. For the next two hours he served food and drinks, glazing over his inexperience with smooth talk and impeccable manners, keeping everyone happy, especially Woody who could barely keep up with the orders in the kitchen.

It was close to ten o'clock when Tyler finally pulled a stool up to the bar and sat down to a bowl of chili and cornbread. Sarah came over and put her arms around him and kissed him on the cheek. "You were great. Woody thinks you were fabulous. I bet you could make

218

more money as a waiter than as a magazine writer. Now what was it you wanted to tell me?"

In contrast to the din of the previous hours, the Night Heron seemed strangely quiet now. Sarah could see Tyler was having second thoughts about speaking. With his eyes focused on Lyle and Bo who sat at dead center of the bar, he said mysteriously, "It's waited thirty years, it can wait another few hours until you get home."

"Roads are getting really bad out there," Bo commented loudly to the entire bar.

Tyler looked out the window at the swirling snow. "Maybe you should shut down early, Sarah."

"Oh, I'll be all right." She lowered her voice and said conspiratorially, "Why don't you take my car home since it's better in the snow? By the time I'm out of work the roads will probably have been plowed."

It was an outright lie – she knew that the snowplow usually didn't go by until five in the morning – but it was easier than telling him she thought she was a better driver in the snow than he was. She was sure she had a better chance than he did of making it home in his car without snow tires. After some argument and a long, unfulfilled search for an expensive leather glove that had fallen from his pocket, Tyler finally left for home in Sarah's battered red car.

But later, as she waded through the snow on her way to the dumpster with the garbage bags, she wondered if she hadn't made a mistake. Probably she should have asked Tyler to wait for her; it was going to be impossible to drive home without snow tires. Her common sense got the better of her and a few minutes later she was on the phone, asking him to come down and get her.

Turning out all the lights, she sat in the darkened bar wearing her boots and coat, sipping tequila. The room was illuminated only by the emergency exit signs and on impulse she flicked the switch for the light behind the Night Heron window. She always felt comforted by the colored glass presence of those solemn birds who kept watch over her every night with their red eyes.

Forty–five minutes and two more shots of tequila went by before Sarah began to get really worried. She called the cabin knowing, even as she dialed, that there would only be endless, unanswered ringing. She paced back and forth for a while, sure that Tyler must have slid off the road on his way down into town. She was unable to decide whether to stay and wait for him to walk down or to risk taking his brother's car out into the storm.

Finally she could not stand waiting any longer. She locked the door and started up the engine of the car. As she drove slowly out of the parking lot, she took one last look at the inn. Through the window of the lounge, she caught a glimpse of the brightly lit, stained–glass herons and realized she'd forgotten to hit the switch.

The snow was slowing down now and visibility was better than it had been. Inching her way along, Sarah sat tense and upright in her seat, her hands tightly clutching the steering wheel as though it were a life preserver. The car did okay until she started on the uphill grade out of town. The tires began to spin and lost their grip on the road; she slid to the bottom of the hill and tried again. After a few tries, she managed to fishtail her way to where the road leveled off. Sighing loudly, she tried to relax a little. The first mile was behind her and she'd made it up the first hill.

The windshield wipers thumped ominously as the car crawled around the curves of the winding country road. Another mile crept by and still no sign of Tyler.

Around the next bend her headlights caught the gleam of a red reflector up ahead, pitched at an odd angle to the road. Within seconds it became obvious that the reflector was mounted on the rear fender of a car. As she drove past the disabled vehicle, Sarah gasped and without thinking, slammed on the brakes. Immediately the car she was driving spun crazily out of control, stopping at last with its front end in a snow bank on the opposite side of the road, pointed back towards town.

Cursing, she flung open the door and leaped out into the deep, virgin snow. Then suddenly she was shouting Tyler's name and running. Her own red car, the one Tyler had been driving, was dark and silent. It had smashed head–on into a large maple tree at the side of the road.

CHAPTER ELEVEN

Snow had covered the car's windows and Sarah couldn't tell if Tyler was inside. She tugged on the driver's door, but the impact of the crash had bent the front fender back so that the door wouldn't open. Brushing the snow away with her sleeve, she peered through the window into the dark interior. She could just barely make out the outline of a body slumped over the wheel.

The door on the passenger's side opened quite easily and a little sob escaped her as the overhead light came on. Tyler appeared to be unconscious; his body was held up by the steering wheel and his face was against the dashboard, one cheek resting on the defrosting vent. He had apparently struck the windshield but it had not shattered; there was an enormous lump on his forehead but no blood.

"Tyler!" Sarah tried to say his name sharply but it came out as a tiny squeak. She reached over and shook his shoulder and he moaned loudly. "Oh, God, Tyler." She burst into tears, overcome with relief that he was still alive, but deathly afraid of what might be wrong with him.

Kneeling on the seat next to him, she took off her gloves and touched his face. "Tyler, can you hear me? It's Sarah."

His eyes fluttered open for a moment and then closed again. "I'm so glad you came." His voice was a hoarse whisper. "Go back to town, get an ambulance."

"Tyler, what happened?" She tried to sit him up, but when she grabbed hold of his shoulders and pulled, he howled piercingly.

"No! Don't! I think my collarbone is broken. This is the only comfortable position. I turned off the engine. Didn't want to die..." His face was contorted with pain and his fists were clenched tightly to the cuffs of his jacket.

"You're freezing. What am I going to do? I can't leave you like this." She looked around for something to cover him with. "Oh, God, how did this happen?" There was an old sweater in the back seat that she draped over his back.

"I think someone shot at the car."

"What? What did you say?"

"I heard...a gun shot and then...one of the front tires was flat...then another...another shot and that was when I lost control and saw the tree coming. I guess I hit it."

Sarah swallowed hard, unsure of what to do. "Why would someone– who would do such a thing?"

"Same one probably. Same one smashed into you before, same one's being doing it all along. It wasn't my fault, Sarah. I'm a good driver."

"Yes, dear, of course, it wasn't your fault." Her voice had slipped to a whisper that matched Tyler's as she tried to mask her fear. Whoever had caused this accident must have thought she had been driving her own car. But if they had discovered it was Tyler instead, then maybe they were still out there somewhere, waiting for her.

"Sarah. Go."

She didn't want to leave him but she knew it was the only way. "Tyler, listen, I may have to walk back to town. I skidded into a snow bank when I stopped here and I don't think I can get out of it." She spoke slowly, trying to sound calm and reassuring. "I'm going to look in your car for something to cover you with and then I'm going to go."

"The trunk. Clothes in the trunk."

Backing out of the front seat, she ran through the fine, sparkling snow back to the other car. She found the clothes and as she carried them back she wondered why he had been driving around with the work uniform of someone named "Don."

In the end, it made more sense to wrap him in the down jacket she was wearing and put on the work clothes herself. She was going to run back to town; she would only overheat in a down jacket.

She started off at a medium–fast jog down the middle of the road back to town, more frightened than she'd ever been before in her life. She found herself praying that just maybe somebody would be out on a night like this, reasoning that if a car had not gone by in the last two hours, the laws of probability dictated that one should be coming along soon. A hidden patch of ice beneath the snow caused her to take a tumble and she rested for a moment, her head full of the sound of her heart pounding and her lungs heaving. The damp feel of her clothes, half–wet and half–frozen, forced her to move on.

The thud of her own footsteps echoing in her brain prevented her from hearing the rumble of the approaching vehicle. Suddenly she saw a shaft of light illuminating the trunks of the trees on one side of the road. She turned around, waving her arms to stop the car that was coming up behind her, panting too heavily to shout at it.

A pickup truck roared to a stop beside her. Running up to it, she opened the door on the passenger side. "Oh, Lyle, thank God it's you," she gulped between breaths. "I need a ride into town quickly." She climbed up into the high cab of his four wheeled drive pickup. The heavy smell of liquor filled her nostrils, but she had no choice other than to take this ride.

"Sarah, what are you doing out here this time of night?" he asked, peering curiously at her face, wet with a mixture of snow, sweat and tears.

"Tyler had an accident, you must have passed the car on your way. But you might not have seen it. It was off in the woods and covered with snow." She wiped her forehead on the arm of the work shirt as her breathing came easier. "I don't know what you're doing out carousing on a night like this, but I'll owe you a few beers for this one."

"Yeah, I guess you will." Lyle was driving too fast for the slippery condition of the road and Sarah felt for a seat belt to fasten around her waist. Something hard was poking uncomfortably into her lower back from the crack of the seat and she grabbed for it, thinking it might be the seat belt buckle. The object came loose in her hand and she held it up to the dim light coming from the dashboard controls.

It was a fat black magic marker. The top had come off when she had tugged on it and a thick, indelible black line ran across her palm. "Shit," she muttered, looking for a place to put it down. Then suddenly it occurred to her where, not long ago, she had seen big ugly letters written in black magic marker.

She dropped the marker to the floor as though it was on fire and the short hairs prickled on the back of her neck. She looked over at Lyle, driving like a maniac through the storm, and then behind him to the gun rack that hung on the back window between the two of them. Two shotguns rested there, a common enough sight in pickup trucks during deer hunting season, but it finally occurred to Sarah to wonder why Lyle happened to be out at 2 a.m. driving around in a blizzard.

Gripping the door handle, she stared dead ahead at the swirling flakes, trying to swallow her fear and figure out what to do. She had no idea what Lyle was planning; all she knew was she had to get out of the truck. As they bounced along, she realized her only chance was the stop sign where this road met the main one into West Jordan. Even if he didn't stop, he would have to slow down to make the turn.

She didn't have to wait that long. As they came down the hill towards the stop sign, the truck skidded sideways and then spun around, doing a 360 degree turn in the middle of the road before coming to stop. Sarah was out the door heading for the woods at the side of the road, crashing through the trees in the direction of Main Street. Behind her she could hear Lyle shouting her name. She could see the headlights of his truck as he moved along slowly, looking for her.

What would he do when he caught up with her? He must know she was on to him by the way she had bolted. Once she got out onto Main Street she would be exposed and easy to find. If she stopped to knock on the door of the nearest house, she would have to wait for the people inside to wake up and let her in and he might catch up with her by then. The only thing to do was head for the inn. She had the key and could let herself in and lock him out. Then she would call the police, the ambulance and wake up Woody.

Colliding hard with a snow–covered picket fence, she realized she had made it to Main Street. Otto Jensen's yard lay still and silent, his vegetable and flowers gardens put to bed for the winter under a thick blanket of snow. Sarah felt her way along, using the fence as a guide. On the other side of the house she could see the road lit up by the headlights of Lyle's truck as he drove slowly down the street. He was shining a powerful flashlight through the open window, searching for her. Sarah ducked behind the corner of the fence until he had passed.

She could not remember how many properties lay between the Jensens and the inn, five or six maybe. She had covered half the distance when she saw Lyle make a u–turn in the parking lot of the inn and head back towards her. She managed to hide behind a small stand of fir trees, struggling to catch her breath, warming her frozen hands beneath her armpits until Lyle had driven by.

Only two more houses to go. If she used the street instead of slogging through the deep snow of the West Jordan back yards, she could probably make it to the inn before Lyle made his return patrol in search of her. Taking the chance, she took off as fast as she could. As she neared the inn, she could see the warm colors of the Night Heron window beckoning from the interior and a fresh burst of tears blurred her vision as she fumbled with cold fingers for the pocket of her jacket where she kept the keys.

"Oh, no, shit, NO!" She screamed in frustration as she realized that the keys to the inn were safe in the pocket of the down jacket she had so carefully wrapped around Tyler back in the car. Sobbing, she pounded on the door, shouting for Woody, knowing that in his third floor bedroom on the opposite side of the building, he would never hear her.

The rumble of Lyle's engine and the sound of his voice calling her name spurred her into action. Picking up a large rock that was used as a doorstop in the summer, she heaved it through the square of glass on the door. Gingerly reaching through it, she turned the handle from the inside and let herself in as Lyle's headlight swept the parking lot again.

Sarah made a beeline for the wall phone behind the bar, leaving a wet trail of melted snow in her wake. She could barely make her icy fingers dial the number for the police as she heard the door to Lyle's truck slam. Turning she saw his flashlight shining through the broken window of the door.

"West Jordan Police." Brian Evans' familiar but sleepy voice spoke into her ear.

"Brian, sorry to wake you, this is Sarah Scupper, I mean Monroe, and this is an emergency. Tyler's had an accident up on the old South Jordan road, before the crossroad, he's hurt, he needs an ambulance and the ambulance probably needs a snow plow—"

Her words caught in her throat as she saw Lyle's unsteady form appear in the doorway. He was holding his shotgun to one shoulder, aiming it right at her.

"Hang it up."

Sarah stood rigid. She was unable to speak, but her mind became suddenly as clear as spring water. Here was a man training a shotgun on her, a man who apparently had been pursuing her for weeks now for some unknown reason. Each time something happened, the police had been called. The one–man police force of West Jordan would come out to investigate and yet never turned up any suspects. But what man would arrest his own brother if he could keep from doing so?

"Sarah?" Brian's voice calling her name was tiny and far away. "Are you still there? Where are you?"

"I said hang it up," Lyle hissed from across the room.

She stared at him, trying to gauge whether or not he meant to shoot her or just scare her. His eyes seemed glazed into a demented expression; she had no way of judging what he would do next. She wondered if his brother would be able to cover up for him if Lyle actually shot her. In a split second she decided that Brian was probably the only one who could get Lyle under control. He'd probably been doing it for years.

"Lyle, if you put the gun down, I will hang up the phone." She spoke quietly and distinctly, holding the receiver out in the air as though she were about to hang it up.

"Sarah, where are you? Is my brother there?"

"I said hang it up or I'll shoot the damn thing out of your hand."

"Okay, Lyle, I'm hanging it up right here on the wall behind the bar. Would you like a beer? It's on the house." She made sure her last remark could be heard clearly before the weight of the receiver in the cradle severed the connection. She leaned on the phone with her eyes closed, wondering what to do next. She figured he probably couldn't hold a beer and shoot a rifle at the same time.

"Sure, give me a Bud. But you know, Sarah, you are a lousy bartender."

Sarah's hands were shaking too much to get the top of the bottle into the bottle opener. "Why's that, Lyle?" Wrapping her shirttail around it, she wrenched the twist cap off. Beer suds overflowed onto the bar as she set it down on the corner nearest to the door.

"The reason you're a lousy bartender is–" Lyle lurched forward and tossed something at her before he picked up his beer. "–Is that you've never carded me once in all the time I've been coming here."

Sarah laughed nervously. "Why should I, Lyle? I know you're old enough to drink."

"But you should card everybody at least once." He took a large swig of beer and some of it ran down his chin. He dashed it away with his sleeve. He still had not put the gun down. "You see, if you'd ever looked at my driver's license, you'd realize that you and I have something in common."

"We do?" Sarah laughed again and shivered, wishing she could take off some of her dripping clothes.

"Yeah, pick up my license and read it. See my middle name there? Now how about that, huh?"

Sarah gave a little sigh of relief. "Oh, you're middle name is Monroe, same as my last name. Well, that's nice, Lyle." She shoved the license back at him.

"Nice?" He slammed his beer bottle down so hard that she jumped back in alarm. "It ain't no coincidence, Sarah. You know the reason my mother gave that to me as a middle name?"

"N–no, Lyle. Why?"

"Because that was my father's last name and she was hoping that someday it could be my last name too."

Sarah stared at him in confusion. "Your father's last name was Monroe too?"

"Funny thing about that, huh? You know why? Because your father and my father are the same man."

Sarah let out another laugh that verged on hysteria. "Don't be ridiculous, Lyle. That's impossible."

"Why? Because I'm not as high class and rich as you?"

"Oh, come off it, Lyle. I'm not rich. I probably don't even have as much money as you." Sarah picked up the license again. "It's impossible because my father was long gone from West Jordan by the time you were born in 1956."

"Well, he sure as hell was here in August of 1955 when he fucked my mother." Lyle lifted the beer to his lips and finished it off in one long gulp.

August of 1955...Sarah leaned on the cash register for support, realizing that there could be some truth in what Lyle was telling her. Travis had certainly showed up in West Jordan a week or so after Winnie's death. It was altogether possible that he and Dora Evans had gotten together at that time.

"I never would have figured it out if you hadn't gotten that speeding ticket. I mean Monroe's a common enough name. Brian came over that day and told me who you were and then I knew I finally had my chance to get a part of what should rightfully be mine." Lyle spat on the floor. "Give me another one, Sarah. You owe me."

"Owe you? For what?" Sarah slid another beer across the counter at him. If he kept drinking maybe she would be able to get the shotgun away from him.

As if reading her mind, Lyle's hold tightened on the gun. "For all the grief your father caused my family back in the fifties and for all the trouble your boyfriend is causing now." His hand disappeared inside his grease–stained down vest for a moment and returned with a leather glove which he flipped onto the bar.

"Tyler's glove. When did you get this? When you shot holes in the tires of the car a couple of hours ago?"

230

"Don't you get smart with me, missy. Your pansy–ass boyfriend left that on my living room floor this morning."

"What? Tyler was at your house this morning?" Sarah fumbled in a drawer for the pack of cigarettes she kept there, unable to understand what Lyle was getting at.

"You know damn well he was. You probably sent him there. I found out that he's been bugging my mother, posing as a telephone repair man, trying to stir up trouble for us again."

"Look, Lyle, I don't know what you're talking about. I don't know anything about Tyler being at your house and I don't have any idea what my father did to your mother. Now why don't you just calm down and drink your beer and go on home? Tomorrow we can pretend this never happened."

"No way, sister." Sarah shuddered at the implied truth in his snide remark. "Only place you and I are going is back to your house to get the rest of that jewelry that rightfully belongs to my mother."

"Now how the hell did you ever make that connection?" Sarah could not keep the anger out of her trembling voice.

"He promised my mother he would marry her." Suddenly Lyle no longer seemed like a menacing bully, but more like a small boy swallowing back his tears. "He told her everything would be hers, that we would be rich and could move off of Darby's Mountain...He was a liar. He ruined my mother."

"He WAS a liar. He ruined my mother too." For a brief moment the two of them sat there, each grieving in their own way for the sadness resulting from Travis Monroe's ruthless greed.

Then Lyle let out a roar and threw his empty beer bottle against the wall. "Your mother had everything! MY mother had nothing! When she asked him for money for his own son, he gave her nothing and he

231

made them hurt me." He was crying now, great hiccupping sobs. "WE had nothing! Well it's time I got a piece of the inheritance, a piece of the action you found up in that bank in Potter's Falls."

"Lyle, you're crazy." The words slipped out in amazement before Sarah realized what she had said. She ducked down behind the bar as, with another bellowing cry, Lyle sent the second beer bottle sailing her way. It smashed against the beer keg built into the wall behind her.

Sarah crouched on the floor, trembling, wondering what to do next. The best she could do was make a run for it, dash up the stairs to Woody's apartment, and hope that Lyle was too drunk to catch up with her. But before she even stood up, she saw the dim outline of his shadow on the floor next to her. Looking up, she saw Lyle looming unsteadily in the open gateway to the bar.

"Get away from me, Lyle." Using her most threatening voice, Sarah pulled herself to her full height, looking around desperately for something to defend herself with. Picking up an unopened bottle of vodka, she swung it over her shoulder like a baseball bat.

Lyle laughed demonically. "You don't scare me, Sarah," he taunted, swinging his rifle over his shoulder in an imitation of her stance, as he approached.

The loud creaking of a floor board overhead made them both look up at the ceiling. Heavy footsteps and the sound of a toilet flushing made Sarah's knees weak with relief. She had forgotten that the Stevensons' relatives were staying upstairs.

"Now you've done it, Lyle," she said with false confidence. "You've gone and woken up the guests. Woody will be down in a minute to see what's going on. Maybe you'd better just leave peacefully while you can."

"The hell I will. I'll finish what I came here to do first." In one sudden move, he had his left arm around

Sarah's neck and was tugging at her earring. "For starters, I want these earrings for my momma."

"Ouch. Stop it! You're hurting me!" Sarah screamed loudly, hoping to disturb the guests upstairs enough that they would actually complain.

"Shut up, you little bitch." He slapped her face and she struggled with him, waving the bottle of vodka wildly in the air, trying to come in contact with some part of his body. She managed to knock him off balance and he reeled backwards, crashing into a shelf full of wine glasses. As she raised the bottle over her head, he lunged at her madly with all his weight.

The force of his body striking her own pushed Sarah back into a row of liquor bottles that lined the wall beneath the Night Heron window. But the heavy vodka bottle, which she was still holding above her head, continued to fly backwards. Sarah, reluctant to let it go, let the pull of gravity take her with it.

There was a deafening crash as the vodka bottle splintered the glass of the Night Heron window with Sarah's head close behind. Instinctively she threw her arms across her face as shattered pieces of stained glass rained down on her head and shoulders.

Through the ringing in her ears she heard the familiar sound of Woody's voice booming from somewhere. The room seemed to be spinning around her. "Sweet Jesus, son of Mary, what the hell is going on in here?"

CHAPTER TWELVE

"It can be reconstructed. Don't worry about it. I know a guy in New York who does excellent work." Tyler squeezed Sarah's hand as it rested on the edge of his hospital bed.

"This is ridiculous!" Sarah let out a fresh burst of tears. "You're the one with the broken collarbone. I should be consoling you."

"Shh! Stop crying or they'll hear you and make you go back to your own bed. Didn't they give you a tranquilizer or a sleeping pill to take?"

"Yes, but I haven't taken it yet." She touched the bandage covering the stitches on her neck, trying not to think of how long it had taken the doctor to remove the tiny glass slivers that had been embedded there. "I wanted to see you first. I feel so awful about this. If I hadn't asked you to come back and get me—"

Sarah stopped her guilty tirade suddenly. Her eyes narrowed as she remembered something. "Wait a minute. I take it back. This is as much your fault as it is mine. Tyler, what were you doing poking around in Dora Evans' house? Lyle said he found your missing glove there."

Unable to turn his head, Tyler shut his eyes and sighed. "Looking for something to connect Dora to your mother's death. But it seems like Lyle has already told you what I found out."

Sarah gave a bitter laugh. "That Travis Monroe sowed another of his wild and fertile seeds? Ironic, isn't it? All my life I thought I had no family. Turns out I've got more than any one person deserves."

"Sarah—"

"Was that the 'amazing' thing you wanted to tell me when you came into the bar last night?"

Tyler snapped his fingers and then winced in pain. "Jesus. I can't believe it even hurts to snap my fingers. No, that wasn't what I wanted to tell you. With all this rigmarole I forgot all about it."

"Ms. Scupper, what are you doing in here?" The floor nurse stood in the door with an annoyed expression on her face. "Mr. Mackenzie needs his rest as much as you do. You'll have plenty of time to chat during his recuperation."

"Sarah, it's the kaleidoscopes," he whispered as the nurse came forward to lead her away. "Take them apart when you go home tomorrow. They're on the kitchen table. I think you'll be pleasantly surprised."

It was late afternoon by the time the effects of the sleeping pill wore off and Sarah awoke. Her eyes felt gravelly and stuck together. Every muscle in her body ached. Woody was sitting in a chair by the window, reading a People magazine, waiting to take her home as soon as she was ready to go.

"You're going to stay with me for a few days," he announced. "Doctor's orders – no arguing."

"What about Tyler?" She sipped the coffee he gave her, grimacing at the taste but enjoying the feel of the hot liquid on her dry, swollen throat.

"I don't know what to do about Tyler. He's going to need someone to take care of him full time for the next two months. He'd probably be better off down in New York with his family if we can figure out some way to get him there."

Sarah pursed her lips and said nothing. She knew he was right. A two room, wood–heated cabin in the mountains was not the ideal place to recuperate for a man in a body cast to his waist.

"Woody, I'm sorry about the window. Tyler says he knows someone who can put it back together—"

"Will you cut it out? There you were last night, dripping with blood, terrified, and the first thing you do is apologize for destroying the Night Heron window. As though it was even your fault!" As the tears started to fall from Sarah's eyes again, Woody angrily pulled her blood stained clothes out of the closet and threw them on the bed. "Here, put these on and let's get out of here. Hospitals are so depressing. You'll feel better once we get home."

Someone had pulled Tyler's car out of the snowbank and driven it back down to the inn. The sight of it in the parking lot brought the events of the night back into sharp focus and made Sarah weak and shaky again. She felt rooted to the seat of Woody's station wagon.

"What did they do with Lyle?" she asked in a tiny voice.

"He's in jail. He won't bother you anymore." Woody came around to Sarah's door and helped her out of the car. Normally she would have shaken his arm off, but today she felt like an eighty–five year old lady.

"Won't he get out on bail?"

"Held without bail. County sent in someone else to handle the case instead of Brian. I guess Brian's pretty embarrassed about the whole thing."

Although she had slept all day, all Sarah wanted to do was go back to bed. Woody tucked her into his own high colonial bed and made her take another sleeping pill, assuring her that he would be more than comfortable on the pull–out sofa bed in the living room.

"Woody, did you know?" she asked as she watched him putter around the room putting together a few days worth of clothing for himself.

"Did I know what?"

"That Lyle was my half–brother."

Woody stood motionless for a few seconds with his back to her. "No, I did not." He slammed a drawer shut.

236

"I'm not sure whether I even believe it's true. Dora just might have thought Travis would make the best provider of all the possible guilty parties."

Sarah snorted and sank back on the pillows. "Yeah, right. Lyle was a better provider for his mother than a leech like Travis ever could be. Her house is much nicer than his apartment."

"What? Whose apartment?"

"Travis's." She closed her eyes so she would not have to see his reaction. She didn't care who knew what now. "Tyler took me there, you know. The other weekend. It was a mistake. It's all been a mistake. I should never have come here to begin with." She was suddenly overwhelmed by an image of her trip across the country from Arizona to Vermont in her little red car, completely unaware of what lay in store for her. The car was totaled; she would have to think about getting a new one. But she was too tired to think about that now.

I think it's Tyler who should never have come here," she heard Woody growling under his breath, but his voice sounded fuzzy and it faded away as she drifted towards sleep. "And maybe it's time we sent him home."

Another twenty–four hours passed before Sarah felt good enough to drive up to her cabin. She told Woody she needed to pick up some clothes to bring back down to the inn and to get a few things Tyler wanted in the hospital. The compelling force behind the trip, however, was to find out what Tyler had meant about the kaleidoscopes.

Inside the cabin she could see her breath, but Sarah was pleased to see that someone had taken care of replacing the broken window and draining the plumbing. She sat down immediately at the kitchen table to examine the two wooden kaleidoscopes. She was not really sure how to dismantle them and tried to remember Woody's story about how they had been constructed.

Picking up one of them, she tugged on the large end that turned around the main cylinder, the part that held the bits of colored glass. She was surprised at how easily it came off in her hand and looked at it carefully, trying to decide whether it would be easier to take off the frosted glass on the outside or the clear piece on the inside. Tyler had left a serrated steak knife on the table and Sarah picked up his tool of choice and tired to pry the inside glass away. After a moment it popped out almost effortlessly, and tiny pieces of broken colored glass spilled out into a pile on the table.

"Well, big deal. What am I supposed to do, assemble them like a jigsaw puzzle?" Sarah half–heartedly sorted the pieces into piles by color. Then, pushing them aside in disgust, she picked up the other kaleidoscope. "This better be good, Tyler," she muttered as she disassembled the second one.

The inside glass did not come off as easily on this kaleidoscope. She finally put the small, round rattling piece on the table and came down hard on it with her fist. When she picked it up again, she found that inside glass had dislodged itself at last. The contents of the second kaleidoscope sat in a little heap on the table, sparkling in the late afternoon sun that filtered through the frosty kitchen window.

Instead of the flat, broken fragments of brightly colored glass which had created the shifting patterns of the first kaleidoscope, this one was filled with tiny, faceted jewel–like pieces. Some of them were delicate little chips almost too infinitesimal to be seen. Trembling, Sarah picked up one of the larger pieces and held it up to the light between her thumb and forefinger. Blood red in color, it was shaped like a teardrop and intricately carved with hundreds of facets.

"The jewels," she whispered to herself, staring in awe at the gemstones on the table in front of her.

"Grandmother had them all the time and never knew it."

Laughing and hooting, she jumped around the kitchen, not knowing what to do next. But she sobered up a moment later, realizing that this had to be only a small portion of the precious stones that were missing; the largest ruby would fall right through the settings in the choker they had found.

Retrieving the heirloom jewelry from the bedroom, she laid their remains out on the table, trying to match them up with the emeralds, rubies and diamonds. Within seconds she knew that these jewels were just trimmings, the complimentary stones that surrounded the larger ones, the diamond chips that were used to set off the really expensive stones.

Rubbing her icy hands together, she closed her eyes and tried to picture the scene that Woody had described of the day when Winnie finished the kaleidoscopes in her basement studio. His had been completed before Travis arrived. Winnie had filled her own afterwards. But with Travis in the house would she have dared to go upstairs and possibly expose her hiding place? Or was it possible that the loose jewels would have been right there in her workshop, perhaps in a box alongside the other boxes of cut glass pieces, hidden in plain view?

It would have been an easy thing to carefully scoop up a handful of the tiny gems and place them into the kaleidoscope. She could have done it right in front of Travis and he would never guess. But if that was what she had done with the smallest jewels, where had she hidden the significant ones?

Sarah held up the little oval ruby again as she pondered this question. When it caught the sunlight in just the right way, it seemed to wink at her like an eye. It reminded her of the red eyes of the stained glass night herons. Only in miniature.

"Oh, my God." Sarah stopped breathing suddenly.

Of course. It made perfect sense. Anything resembling faceted or cut glass could easily be incorporated into Winnie's three–dimensional textured glasswork. No one would ever question it.

"Oh, my God." She repeated. "Oh, no."

She made a beeline for the phone. Still holding her breath, she dialed the number for the inn. "Woody, when you cleaned up the broken pieces of the Night Heron window, you– you–" She stopped to inhale before fearfully blurting out the rest of the question. "You didn't throw them away, did you?"

Woody laughed. "Sarah, you are obsessed. No, I didn't. I saved them so that the colors could be matched for the replacement window. What kind of fool do you take me for? And where are you, anyway?"

But Sarah's merry laughter was all he heard before the line was disconnected.

Sarah was surprised to find Brian Evans standing in Tyler's hospital room when she arrived. It was apparently an official visit; he was in uniform and filling in a form on a clipboard. When he saw Sarah, he reddened uncomfortably and closed his clipboard abruptly. "I'll be down in the ER for the next hour or so if you think of anything else, Mr. Mackenzie," he said before leaving.

"What was he doing here?" Sarah asked in bewilderment. "I thought he wasn't allowed to handle this affair because of Lyle."

"Relax, Sarah. He just needed to fill out his accident reports. Nothing else."

"Oh. Well, I brought you your work," Sarah announced brightly, kissing Tyler on the cheek. "I thought it might give you something to do until you're out of here."

"That was nice of you," Tyler answered in a puzzled tone as Sarah dumped his notebook and tape recorder on the white bed sheets between his legs. "But very out of character. I thought you didn't want me to do this anymore."

Sarah grinned mysteriously at him. "Change of plans, inspector. When my head cracked that window, I think it cracked your case as well."

"I think what you cracked was your brain. What are you talking about?"

She sat down on the bed, facing him, her leg pressed against his beneath the sheet. "I'm sorry that I've been so uncooperative and unsupportive," she said contritely with just a shade too much sarcasm. Then she laughed. "But now I need your help."

"You witch! Did you open up those kaleidoscopes?"

"Yes, I did. Did you?"

"Well, I couldn't get the clear piece of glass out of yours, but when I shined a flashlight into it I could see those little babies pretty clearly. I figured I'd wait until you got home that night and we could open it together."

While he was talking, Sarah had pulled the kaleidoscopes out of the bag she had packed for Tyler. She showed him the jewels and told him her theory about the eyes of the night herons. "I think that's what she did with them all," she went on excitedly. "I think she hid the jewels in all the windows she made for people she knew around here. Remember what Dr. Wilder's wife said about that strange window in her hall? She said something about Winnie saying she wanted to come back and change a few things but she never got a chance to."

"That ugly window with the green...You think those are emeralds?" Tyler laughed in disbelief, but he was already reaching for his notebook, flipping through the pages.

"So we need to go over all the windows you've looked at. All I could think of was Dr. Wilder's and the library. Didn't you take pictures?"

"The library...Jesus, Sarah, you're either crazy or a genius. But you may be right. Think about how Mrs.

241

Winslow kept raving about how the stars seemed to sparkle in that one winter window."

"Up above the world so high—"

"Like a diamond in the sky!" They both laughed. "Oh, Sarah, I wish I could hug you! I wish I was out of here and out of this cast. There's so much that needs to be done now. Speaking of which—" he sobered up – "They want me to check out of here in the morning. Woody came by yesterday and told me you guys think I ought to go home."

"Well, Woody thinks that, not me." Sarah said nothing for a moment, and picked at the leg seam of her jeans as she searched for the right words. "He seems to think I won't be able to take care of you adequately if I have to work nights. He's probably right. I mean, you wouldn't be able to keep the stove going and what if you fell or something when I wasn't there."

"I was supposed to go back today, you know."

Sarah looked up to see if he was joking, but his handsome features were etched with seriousness.

"Isabel told me my job was on the line if I didn't get back by Monday with something to show for my time. I guess I've got something to show for it now." He rapped on the solid plaster of his cast.

"You would go back and live with – Isabel?" Sarah spoke slowly, disliking the taste of the words in her mouth.

"No, she more or less threw me out the last time we spoke. Besides, she works more than you do," he teased weakly. "No, I guess it's home to Mom and Dad for a while. Guess I've got a good six weeks to put this story together, don't I?"

"Tyler – don't put anything in it about where the jewels were hidden, okay? I mean, what if it gets back to Travis?"

"Oh, come on, Sarah, what other angles have I got? We still haven't got a clue as to what happened the night Winnie was murdered, or if she even WAS murdered. My story is pretty thin without that or the missing jewelry." Irritated, he flipped through his notebook, stopping suddenly on a page where something was circled in red ink. "Who was this Clara Dobrinsky Dunbar, anyway? You never did tell me that?"

"She was a nurse who took care of my mother in the hospital before she died. Dr. Wilder thought she would be the only person who might know if Winnie spoke at all in those last couple of days following the accident. But I guess she moved to Florida years ago with some rich old man. She's probably dead herself by now."

"A nurse! Shit. Here I've been lying around in a fucking hospital for two days, the very same hospital where she worked, I've seen a dozen nurses and I haven't asked a single of them whether they ever heard of Clara Dobrinsky!"

"Oh, for pity's sake, Tyler—"

"No, I'm serious. It's something constructive I could have been doing. I mean, look, who else is there who might know something about what happened that night?" He counted off the possibilities on his fingers, slapping each one down disgustedly. "Woody was in Mexico, Travis was where...Rhode Island? The cops who handled the case are dead, Dora won't talk about it, you were only three months old. I mean, who else is there?"

In a desperate and defiant gesture, he grabbed her hand and pulled on it to make her look at him. "I don't know, Tyler," she answered him, trying to control her anger. "Who else could possibly have been there that night?"

He dropped her hand as suddenly as he had picked it up, his amber eyes widening with an expression of enlightenment. "I can't believe it. I can believe we never even thought of it all this time. You know who was there. Think about it. Dora didn't come alone to live with your mother. She brought her little boy with her. Hand me the phone, quick."

243

Dumbfounded, Sarah passed it over to him.

"Hello? Yes, get me the emergency room, will you? This is Tyler Mackenzie in Room 204. I need to talk to Officer Evans."

Brian Evans' freckled face appeared in the doorway. "You remembered something else you wanted to tell me, Mr. Mackenzie?"

Tyler was struck suddenly by Brian's resemblance to the old bearded man named Red he had talked to at the Night Heron. "Queen of the Quickies", that was what Red had called Dora. Brian was apparently the result of one of those "quickies."

"Actually, I wanted to ask you about something you might remember, Brian. Why don't you close the door and sit down?"

Tyler was thankful the other hospital bed in his room had been vacated that morning, giving him the needed privacy for this conversation.

"Sarah gone already?" Brian looked around suspiciously as he shut the door behind him.

"She just left." Tyler resisted looking at the bathroom door to make sure it was closed enough to hide Sarah. They had both felt Brian might talk more openly about Winnie if Sarah wasn't there.

"So what's this about?" Brian stood at the foot of the bed and shifted his weight uncomfortably. "I'm not supposed to be discussing the actual case with you, you know."

"No, it's not about that. It's about this project I've been working on."

"About the Scupper woman?"

"Yes, about the Scupper woman. You lived with her for a while with your mom, didn't you, when you were little?"

"Well, yeah, but I was only what – like four or five years old at the time. I don't remember much." Brian laughed a little nervously.

"Oh, come on, everybody remembers something from that time of their life. I thought it might be an interesting angle, the memories of a town cop who knew Winnie Scupper as a kid. I mean, sometimes kids remember really basic things that evoke a mood beautifully. Like what color dress someone wore, what present someone gave them for their birthday, what kind of dog they had..." Tyler let his voice trail off suggestively. He could tell Brian was thinking about what he had said, flattered by the idea of his own words in print.

"Well, I remember the dog all right." Brian gave another nervous laugh and sat down on the chair Tyler indicated by the bedside with one hand, while the other hand nervously checked the tape recorder hidden beneath the bed sheets to make it sure it was running. "All right, listen, Mr. Mackenzie—"

"Call me Tyler."

"Tyler then. I'll make a deal with you. I'll tell you a few things I remember from my childhood, if you promise to leave my brother Lyle out of your story. He's had enough psychological problems in his lifetime without raking up any more dirt for him."

"Sure, it's a deal," Tyler agreed hastily. "What kind of psychological problems are you talking about?"

"I'm not at liberty to talk about them, you know, because it's what his lawyer is using for a defense. Now let's just get one thing clear — everything said here between you and me is strictly off the record and you will never print a word about my brother."

"Right. Now. What about that dog?" Tyler would agree to anything. He had no intention of using Brian Evans' actual story unless there was some relevance.

"Greta. Her name was Greta. I use to play with her a lot because there were no other kids around. Especially after the baby was born—"

"You mean Sarah."

245

"Well, yeah, Sarah. We always just called her "the baby" though. I never remembered her name until the day I stopped Sarah for speeding and saw her license. The name Scupper brought it back – it's a funny name, you don't forget it."

"So you played with the dog because everyone was busy with the baby."

"Yeah, and I'll always remember that morning when Greta wasn't there when I got up. Then they found her down in the streambed with Miz Scupper... She always walked Greta before she retired for the evening. I remember looking all around the house, looking in every room. It was early. I was always an early riser as a kid."

"Like how early?"

"You know, five, five thirty. It used to drive my mother crazy because she liked to sleep late."

"Did you have your own bedroom there?" Tyler hoped Brian wouldn't think it an odd question, but Brian seemed carried away by his own reminiscing.

"Hell, yes, it was a big house. They gave me some room that had horses on the wallpaper and I thought that was the greatest." He laughed in embarrassment. "Is that the kind of stuff you want to hear? It sounds so dumb to talk about the horse wallpaper. I haven't thought about it in years."

"It's great, perfect. It's very evocative." Tyler looked out the window at the twilight gathering on the hospital parking lot. "Can you remember any of the other wallpaper in the house?"

"Nah. The horses were the only one that made an impression on me. The rest of it was kind of old–fashioned, flowery stuff. What are those purple bushes that bloom in the spring?"

"Lilacs?" Tyler's voice squeaked with suppressed excitement.

"Yeah, lilacs. I think the wallpaper in my mother's room had something on it like bowls with lilacs in them." He closed his eyes, trying to remember. "I didn't go in there much. I wasn't allowed to." He chuckled to himself. "She was afraid I might see who her boyfriends were. What she didn't know was I always knew because I would see them leaving in the morning anyway, because I was up so early."

"So the morning that Greta wasn't there, did you see a man leave then?"

Brian was silent for a moment. "We're talking about thirty years ago, you know. Yes, I think there was someone, but I was too busy looking for Greta to pay attention. I couldn't say for sure."

"There was someone else in the house that night? Why don't any of the newspaper articles ever mention that?"

Brian rolled his eyes. "Why do you think? It was 1955. Besides, the whole thing was very upsetting for my mother. To this day she hates to talk about it. Well, you know that. I think she always felt a little guilty."

"Guilty?"

"You know, guilty because maybe she should have walked the dog instead, maybe she wouldn't have slipped, guilty because she should have realized that Miz Scupper never came home that night. You know, she was supposed to be there to help her out and look what happens. Miz Scupper goes and falls off a bridge and dies!"

"Oh."

"Then all those newspaper reporters hounding her for her version of the story. She snapped a little after that. I went to live with my aunt for a few years until she recovered. Of course, during that time she had Lyle—" He shook his head. "Phew. I'm getting way off the track here. What else you want to know?"

"How about Winnie herself?" Tyler asked softly. "What was she like?"

247

"Nice. Real nice. She used to play checkers with me. Read to me. Let me play with her colored glass sometimes."

"Did you ever meet her husband?"

"Only once. Well, I don't think I actually met him. I just sort of remember him. He was quite big, well, who knows, I was only five. He wore a white suit and he yelled a lot. My mother told me to stay out of his way. I think I had to eat supper with my mother in the kitchen because they had a fancy dinner by themselves in the dining room, but it's all so vague, just sort of a picture..."

"Had Winnie had the baby by that time?"

"Christ, I don't know. I don't think so because I remember my mother always grumbling that the baby's father didn't come to see it. The reason I remember that is – oh, never mind." He waved his hand trying to brush aside an apparently unpleasant memory.

"What?"

"Nothing to do with your story. I just was remembering that I got spanked once when she was talking about the baby's father never coming. I asked her why she didn't care if my father never came to see me."

"Oh." Tyler shifted uncomfortably and tried to scratch his belly under the cast. He wanted to ask more questions about who Dora's lover might possibly have been the night of Winnie's accident. He was positive that it was the missing link in the story. He wondered if Brian had any idea what kind of sordid activities had gone on in that room with the lilac wallpaper. "So, what happened to Greta?"

"The dog? Well, she went kind of crazy and I think they had her put to sleep. I certainly was never allowed to see her again."

"Crazy? Like what, violent, you mean?"

"I think she bit somebody. I don't recall who. You'd have to ask some old timer about that one." Brian stood

248

up. "I've really got to get going. I hope you got some 'evocative' material you can use."

"You bet. Thanks a lot, Officer Evans."

"No problem. It was kind of fun actually, thinking about those years. It was one of the happiest times of my childhood, living in that nice house with the big grassy yard." He turned to go and then stopped. "If you have to mention my mother in this story, try to be kind. You know what I mean."

"Of course. Thanks again. You've given me a lot of insight. I understand your mother's reason now for not talking to me." Whether he meant it or not, it seemed like the right thing to say.

"Say, looks like your dinner is out here." Brian brought in a covered tray that been left sitting on a chair in the hall.

"Great. I can hardly wait. Thanks again." Tyler sat motionless, listening to Brian's footsteps as they receded down the hall. "Okay, Sarah. He's gone."

Sarah emerged stiffly from the bathroom where she'd been sitting on the floor behind the door. "Was it worth it? Did you really learn anything?"

"What do you think? Of course, it was worth it. Now we know that there was someone else there the night that Winnie died. If only there was some way to find out who that person was." Tyler uncovered his dinner. "Yum, want some? I'll even let you have the dessert." He offered Sarah a square of red jello that wobbled on its plate.

"Get away! What was all that bullshit about wallpaper? What do you care what kind of wallpaper was on the wall of Dora's bedroom in my mother's house?"

In lieu of an answer, Tyler popped a forkful of dry mashed potatoes into his mouth.

"Well, I guess I'm out of here." Sarah slung her purse over her shoulder and picked up her jacket.

"Sarah, wait." Tyler washed down the sticky potatoes with a mouthful of water. "Do me a favor. See if Woody remembers anything about your mother's dog biting someone after she died."

"Tyler, does this detail really matter?"

"I think it means everything. Think about it on your way home. Maybe you'll realize what I mean. Hey!" he called after her as she headed for the door. "I love you. Give me a kiss before you go."

It was nearly nine o'clock when the switchboard put Sarah's call through to Tyler. The gray–haired night nurse whom he had been engaging in witty conversation about old days at the hospital handed him the telephone.

"Tyler, it's me. I didn't wake you, did I?"

"Of course not. Nurse Watkins and I have just been reminiscing about what it was like working here at the hospital back in the fifties." His tone indicated he was anxious to get back to the conversation before he lost her.

"Well, I just wanted to tell you that Woody did know who the dog bit. He remembers because everyone thought it was so strange."

"Really? Who was it?"

"It was Travis."

"No. You're kidding."

"I'm not. I guess Woody's father was taking care of the dog. When the police finally located my father and he came back up here, old Elwood brought the dog by the house to see if Travis would want to take her. And when Travis took the leash and tried to lead her into the house, she bit him."

"Good God. But that would mean–"

"I think all it means is that Greta was very protective of Winnie and had probably seen Travis beating on Winnie one time too many. He probably beat Greta too. She'd probably been dying to bite him for years. Look. I'll see you in the morning, okay? I may be a little late – I've got to take the Night Heron's eyes to the jeweler to be examined first."

Tyler listened to the dial tone for a good minute after she hung up, staring blindly at a coffee stain on his bed sheet. Either Sarah did not understand what he had been driving at or she just didn't want to see it. And understandably so. But now he had no idea what to do next.

WINNIE & DORA

AUGUST 25, 1955

"I'm going out to walk Greta, Dora. Keep an ear out for the baby."

"Okay." Dora cracked her gum and did not bother to look up from the movie magazine she was reading. She and Winnie had had this same exchange every night for nearly three months now. The baby never woke up; in fact, lately the baby slept until nearly six every morning. Being a mother's helper for Winnie was a piece of cake. Winnie liked to do everything for the baby by herself. All Dora had to do was hold her occasionally or watch her when Winnie went out, which was almost never.

As soon as she was sure Winnie was on her way, Dora flipped the magazine open to a picture of Rita Hayworth in her younger days. Red had told her once that she had a figure like Rita Hayworth's. Untying her bathrobe, she quickly slipped it off and pranced out into hall carrying the magazine with her. She was wearing one of the fancy nightgowns that Winnie had given her. It was made of sheer black nylon with a black lace bodice like a bra and Dora thought it was incredibly sexy. She could not imagine why high-minded Winnie would even own such a garment. Perhaps her handsome husband had given it to her on their honeymoon.

Pulling an antique chair over to the hall mirror, Dora perched on the back of it with her hand on her knees and her chest thrust out, trying to affect the same pinup pose as Rita Hayworth. Her breasts were much larger than Rita's and in this position they threatened to work their way free of the black lace cups. Through

252

the sheerness of the nylon she could see that her thighs were also heavier than Rita's.

Absorbed in her own image, she did not hear the front door opening quietly behind her. When she heard the click of the lock, she gasped and quickly stood up on the chair, crossing her arms over her chest.

"Well, well. Dora. What a surprise. I didn't think anyone would be awake at this time of night."

Travis was leaning against the front door with an amused expression on his face. His white suit was wrinkled from hours of driving and lines of exhaustion creased the tanned skin around his pale blue eyes. Dora still thought he was one of the handsomest men she had ever seen.

"Oh! Mr. Monroe! Oh!" Desperately she looked around for her bathrobe, but she had left it in the other room on the couch. "Oh, I'm so embarrassed–" As his eyes took in the sights beneath the transparent nightgown, she turned and darted into the living room.

"You shouldn't be embarrassed, Dora," he said to her as she reappeared, knotting the sash of her robe around her waist, her face several shades brighter. "You really have a lovely body." His eyes fell on the open magazine on the table beneath the mirror. "You remind me of Rita Hayworth."

"Do I really? Someone else thought so too!" She blushed deeper under the compliment and then said quickly, "Winnie's – I mean, Miss Scupper, I mean, Mrs. Monroe, your wife, is out walking the dog. She'll probably be back in half an hour or so. Would you like to see the baby?"

"The baby? Oh. Of course, show me the baby, would you?"

As he followed her upstairs, she chattered nervously, swallowing her words at the door to Sarah's room when he brushed up against her as he peeked in briefly at the sleeping infant.

253

"You'll have to excuse me but I'm bushed," Travis commented as he stopped outside the door to Winnie's room. "I'll see you tomorrow, Dora."

As Dora started back down the stairs, she heard Travis opening drawers and slamming them shut again and cursing loudly to himself. Moments later, as Dora was picking up her magazine, he appeared downstairs again.

"I guess I'm not as tired as I thought I was," he remarked. "Does Winnie still walk up Route 73 by the Sugartree? Maybe I'll see if I can catch up with her. You know, surprise her." Travis winked at Dora. "The way you surprised me."

"Mr. Monroe!" Dora giggled nervously. "Go on now or you'll never catch up with her."

Dora found her breath was coming in short gasps after he left. She knew it wasn't because she had been embarrassed to be seen in the black nightgown. It was because of the sexual way that Mr. Monroe had flirted with her. She knew he thought she was attractive and she found it very exciting to think about being sexy for a man like Mr. Monroe. He had flirted with her in that same open way when he had come for that brief visit in the spring. It had made her feel good to be admired by a man when she wore a tight sweater.

She also knew how Winnie felt about him. Maybe Winnie wouldn't put out for him tonight and then, with his passions frustrated, he would seek solace in Dora's own arms and she could show him what she felt about him. Then maybe he would divorce Winnie and marry her and she could ride off with him to whatever tropical place it was he went to in the winter.

"You bad girl, Dora," she scolded herself playfully. "Don't even think about it."

Winnie sat on the edge of the metal railing and breathed in the cool night air. This was usually the end of their walk; she would rest on the bridge and Greta would pick her way down the rocks of the ravine to where she could quench her thirst with the cool waters of the Sugartree River. When Greta came back up, they would start the walk back home.

It was such a warm night, and the shadow of the mountains looked so lovely etched in soft moonlight, that Winnie lingered a little longer than usual, enjoying the peaceful view. Suddenly Greta stiffened at the sight of something and began growling low in her throat.

"What is it, Greta? Not a bear, I hope." There had been some sightings of bear recently by the summer tourist population and Winnie prayed she was not about to make the acquaintance of one of them.

"Winnie?" A voice called her name from the darkness.

"Who's there?" She breathed a little easier. The voice was familiar but she couldn't place it.

"It's Travis." As he stepped onto the open area of the bridge, his shadowy outline came into view. "I stopped at the house. Dora told me I would find you here."

"Oh. Yes. Hello." Winnie was stunned. Since Sarah had been born, she had barely given a thought to Travis, filling her life with the love for her baby that she'd never had for her husband. Although she had known he would be back, she had secretly hoped he would never return after he had discovered she was pregnant. And now, here he was, at night...her body tensed up at the thought of his touch and tears filled her eyes. "I – I never expected to see you again."

"Oh, come now. I wouldn't just abandon you like that."

What once would have sounded like a soothing endearment to Winnie now seemed as cold and calculated as the ring of a cash register. He must have run out of money again, she thought. All the valuable jewels were safely hidden now, to be retrieved when she was ready; the rest of the jewelry she had managed to secure in a safe deposit box at a bank he would never find, along with the money her mother had sent when Sarah was born. After his last visit she had begun making plans in case she ever had to take the baby and run from him. Now that the life of her child was at stake, she could swallow a little bit of her pride if necessary, maybe even go back to New York.

"I only have about a hundred dollars in cash, Travis." She was glad that the darkness hid his features – it made it easier to talk to him.

"What about the jewelry, Winnie?" His voice had a hard edge to it. He had rarely mentioned the jewelry to her, never wanting to admit that he was selling her family heirlooms to feed his gambling habit.

"It's gone, Travis, all gone." Her laughter bordered on the edge of hysteria. She had been ready for this lie for months.

"What do you mean, 'it's gone'?" His shadow moved menacingly closer. "You would never sell it."

"I had to pay the doctor and buy formula and cereal for the baby. Some things are more important than old jewelry."

"I don't believe you for a minute."

"Oh, no? Well, why don't you look around the house and see if you can find them hidden anywhere?" Her thin arms trembled as she gripped the metal railing to steady herself and she was glad of the darkness once more.

"I already have looked." Travis grumbled. "So tell me where you hocked them."

"Travis, face it. This well has gone dry. You're going to have to dig for water somewhere else." Winnie flinched, unconsciously anticipating the blow across the face that usually followed such a bold remark. It came as expected but because of the darkness, Travis's hand only glanced off the side of her head as she ducked. Greta growled and Winnie reached quickly for the leash that was tied around the railing. Untying it, she pulled

Greta closer, saying softly, "It's all right, Greta. Stay. Good girl."

"I was hoping not to have to tell you this, Winnie, but in light of your last remark—" The blue flame of a lighter briefly cut through the darkness, leaving the red glow of a lit cigarette in its place. The smell of tobacco smoke was a harsh contrast to the freshness of the summer night. "I lost the house."

"What house?"

She could hear the sneer in his reply. "Our house, dummy. This lovely summer cottage you have been inhabiting year round."

She shook her head. "How could you lose our house? I don't understand what you mean. The taxes are paid—"

"You are so stupid sometimes. I lost it to some men in Havana that I owed a lot of money to. They want to turn it into an apartment house so they can collect rent. So I guess we'll have to move back to the other house we own. I always thought I would prefer living there anyway."

Winnie was speechless, staring in shock at the burning circle of his cigarette as it moved through the air to his mouth again. Although her backside was beginning to ache from sitting on the hard metal of the railing, she felt unable to move. Every time she thought she was finally in control of the situation, he managed to pull the rug out from under her. How was it possible that one man could ruin her life so thoroughly?

"I thought you would like the idea of moving back to New York. You must be tired of this provincial town by now. Your mother could help you with the baby."

In her considerations of going home to mother, Travis had never been part of the plan. The thought of Charlotte Scupper, stately and proper, watching her daughter humiliated daily by her smooth and ruthless husband was more than Winnie could bear. "No," she

257

whispered, the tears finally spilling down her cheeks. "If I move back there, you will not come with me."

Travis laughed and inched closer to her. "Don't forget who owns that house too, baby. If you're afraid we won't have enough privacy because your mother will be living with us, I'm sure we can arrange something. You know, give her a private apartment—"

"No!" Winnie would have shouted louder at him but a sob caught in her throat. "You can't do this, Travis! I've had enough!"

"There's my spunky little vixen." Travis was so close now she could feel his breath on the side of her bare neck. "Why don't we go back to the house and you can work off some of these vicious feelings in bed?" His hand, reaching out in the darkness, made contact with her forearm.

His touch made her flesh crawl and she jerked her arm away. "Go away," she said hoarsely, trying to sniff back the tears. "I've had enough. Leave me alone."

"You're my wife, damn you. By law I can have you whenever I want you." Grinding out his cigarette with his foot, he reached for her with both hands this time.

"No, Travis!" she screamed. As his hands connected with her shoulders, she kicked at him with her feet, pummeling him with her free fist. At the same moment Greta lunged at him and Winnie lost her grip on the leash. Thrown off balance by Greta, Travis fell forward, at the same time pushing hard on Winnie's shoulders. With her legs kicking wildly and her hands in the air, Winnie lost her grip on the bridge railing. With a terrified gasp, she went over backwards, disappearing into the darkness that filled the Vermont night and the rocky ravine below.

Greta was off like a shot, dashing down the gorge on the path she knew so well. Travis stood stunned and horrified, the metal railing of the bridge pressing into his hips, staring at his hands, which were still outstretched in front of him. He stood silently listening, hearing only the rush of the water as it flowed, dozens of feet beneath the bridge. Then slowly his hands fell to his sides as his mind began to work again. Flicking his lighter, he searched the ground with the small flame until he found his cigarette butt. Slipping it into the pocket of his pants, he walked quickly off into the night.

Dora had been just about to go to bed when she heard the sound of the front door being opened and shut very quietly. When she did not hear the familiar jingling of the leash or the clicking of Greta's nails on the wooden floor, she peeked out into the hall. Travis was standing there alone, his handsome face flushed from walking briskly.

"You didn't find her?" Dora asked in some surprise.

Travis shook his head. "Maybe she walked into town instead."

"Hmmm." Dora frowned. "She almost never walks any other way."

"Well, maybe she saw my car parked in the yard and walked the other way on purpose." Travis moved closer to lean against the doorway opposite Dora.

"What do you mean?"

"Oh, come on, you know as well as I do how she feels about me. Maybe when she saw that I was here, she decided not to spend the night at home." Travis's eyes left Dora's face and traveled boldly down the length of her body, before coming back up again to meet her gaze.

She giggled and fidgeted nervously. "Doesn't sound like Winnie to me."

"Last time I was here I told her how attractive I thought you were." Travis reached out and brushed a stiff red curl out of Dora's eyes. "She got mad at me and suggested I divorce her and marry you."

"No, she didn't! Did she really?" Dora wanted to believe what Travis was telling her. It was so close to the fairy tale she had been dreaming for the last fifteen minutes that it almost didn't seem possible.

"It's true." Travis calmly moved his hand down and untied the sash of Dora's flannel robe so that it fell open, revealing the black nightgown that accentuated her voluptuous curves. "Winnie gave you that nightgown, didn't she? I bought it for her, you know, but she wouldn't wear it. But you know what, Dora? I'm glad she gave it to you. It looks much better on you than it did on her. You fill it out in all the right places."

Dora's better judgment told her the right thing to do in a situation like this was to close the robe and run. But having the object of her sexual fantasies touch her and speak to her, in such an intimate way, was too overpowering a sensation.

"You look like the kind of girl who likes to dress up for her boyfriend in pretty clothes. Someone who likes to please with her beauty." Travis gave her another searching look. Then, brushing purposely against her, he turned to enter the living room. "Would you join me in a drink?" he asked, crossing to the liquor cabinet on the other side of the room. Without waiting for her answer he poured himself a stiff double shot of bourbon and knocked it back.

"I don't really drink hard liquor..." Dora began, thinking of the countless bottles of Budweiser she had consumed in cars with coarse adolescents who pawed her clumsily and without ceremony before shoving themselves inside of her. Maybe those days were finally over for her. "I mean, sure, I'll have whatever you're having. Winnie doesn't like me to drink, but it's your house." She giggled. "You're the boss."

"Now that's the kind of talk I like to hear. I bet you're the kind of girl who thinks of her man before herself, who really likes to give him a lot of – pleasure."

Dora noticed that Travis's hand was shaking as he handed her a shot of bourbon and she took it as a sign that he was nervous about approaching her like this. But she was ready to go through with it, whatever it would take. "What if Winnie comes back and finds us, uh, drinking together like this?" she whispered suggestively.

Although Travis smiled, his face seemed to remain deadpan, devoid of expression. He picked up the bottle of bourbon and whispered back conspiratorially, "Then why don't we go up to your room and shut the door?"

Dora laughed excitedly and led the way. "Does she really want to divorce you?" she asked as she flicked the light switch on and locked the door behind them. Her pretty room with lace curtains and flowered wallpaper had always seemed large and luxurious to her. But Travis's presence seemed to fill the space as he stood awkwardly by the door looking for a place to sit down.

"What do you think?" Travis finally put the bourbon down on the nightstand and sat on the bed. He glanced at his watch and then cocked his head, apparently doing some mental calculations.

Afraid that he was going to change his mind and ruin her plan, Dora let her flannel robe drop to the floor in front of him to get his attention. "I think I'd like to make you a happy man tonight," she said huskily, reaching for his belt buckle.

Travis threw back his head and laughed delightedly at her response. "Oh, we're going to have some fun together, aren't we, Dora?" She did not flinch when he pulled down the lacy bodice of the nightgown or when her vast soft breasts tumbled out and bounced provocatively in his face, mountain–like.

"I really like you," she whispered in what she hoped was a sexy voice. "I think you a very special man."

"Do you now? That's interesting." He undid his tie and then wrapped it around her waist, pulling her towards him with it. "Because I think you're very special too." One of her large, dark nipples seemed to find its own way into his mouth. Travis closed his eyes and sucked hard on it, as he slipped one hand under the *nightgown and between her receptive thighs. "And I bet you'd do anything for me, wouldn't you?"*

"I have found this very satisfying," Travis announced a few hours later. "When my divorce goes through, I think we will have a very exciting life together." He emptied the last of the bourbon into his glass.

"Do we have to wait?" Dora raised her head and gazed at him dreamily through a veil of disheveled hair. "Can't you just take me with you now? I don't mind living in sin for a while."

"No, I'm afraid we're going to have to keep this absolutely secret for the time being. You must never tell anybody we've been together tonight or I may lose everything in the divorce proceedings. Do you understand?" There was a sudden harshness to his voice that Dora found very threatening.

"But—"

"Do you understand?"

Dora nodded and rolled over on her back, resting her head against his bare thigh. She felt as though she wanted to tell the world about her good fortune, but if Travis wanted her to keep quiet about it for a while, she could do that.

"In fact, you better not even tell anybody that I was here tonight. I'll leave before dawn and no one will be the wiser for it."

"But I thought you said Winnie saw your car..."

"I put it in the garage when I came back from looking for her. If she, I mean, when she got home, she must have thought I already left. And she probably was glad."

Dora smiled sleepily. "Oh, Travis, you're so smart. I can't believe how lucky I am to actually hook up with a living dreamboat like you...Every girl I know is going to be so envious when they find out—"

262

A sharp tug on one of her curls made her cry out and brought her back to reality. "I said you were not to tell anybody yet. Can you manage that, Dora, or do I have to find some way to make you remember?" The cruel undertone of his words terrified and thrilled her at the same time. Having sex with him had affected her the same way. They had done things that had never crossed her mind, but even when it hurt her, she found it exciting.

"Travis, I'll do anything you say." She rolled away from him again and lay on her stomach, her cheek against the cool bed sheet. "Just knowing you're going to come back and take me away from this dreary place and treat me like a lady is enough to keep me quiet. Ouch, ouch, what are you doing? That hurts."

"But it feels good to me. Just tip your ass up a little and relax and then it won't hurt so much. See? Bite the pillow if you feel like screaming. Oh, Dora. Oh. You're the best."

A bright flash of light brought Dora out of the light sleep she had finally fallen into from sheer exhaustion. She sat up and held her hand to her eyes, squinting. "What was that?"

Travis was standing at the foot of the bed, holding something in his hand. When the spots in front of her eyes cleared away, Dora saw that it was Winnie's camera, the one she used to take pictures of the baby. "I want something to remember you and this night by," Travis was saying. "Something I can look at that will remind me of you and your gorgeous Rita Hayworth body. Would you mind getting up for a few minutes and putting these things on?"

"Oh, Travis, you're so sweet. What the...this is what you want me to wear?"

It was the sound of glass hitting glass that woke Dora up the next time. The pale grayness of dawn seeping in around the drawn shades showed her Travis, fully dressed, walking around the room, throwing any telltale signs of his visit into a brown paper trash bag.

"I have to go now, Dora, before Winnie wakes up and discovers I spent the night here with you." Travis spoke in a whisper. "Remember, not a word of this until you hear from me. If you see me in town in a week or two, pretend that nothing has passed between us. Okay?"

"How soon will it be until we can be together?"

"I don't know. Six months, a year..." Travis seemed almost frantic now, looking under the bed, lifting the rug, moving things around on the dresser. Finally he turned to Dora and grasped both of her wrists. "Just believe in me, Dora, and don't say anything about me being here last night. No matter what anybody asks you."

Her trusting eyes met his own troubled ones with a questioning look. He pulled her towards him and kissed her hard on the lips. "Just believe in me – I love you."

When he let her go, it was obvious from her rapturous expression that she had swallowed his words, hook, line and sinker. From the window she watched his car drive away in the gray dawn before sinking back onto the bed, hugging herself with excitement. She had never experienced a night like that before in her life. There were red marks on her breasts and an uncomfortable feeling in her backside that hinted at hemorrhoids, but she was glad of the pain. It reminded her of the man she was now hopelessly infatuated with.

Through her euphoric haze she could hear the insistent sounds of a crying infant. Wondering why Winnie didn't wake up and feed the damn baby, she threw on her bathrobe and slipped out into the hall.

"Mom, the baby's crying," Brian called from the bedroom next to hers.

"I know that. You think I can't hear her?" She hadn't mentioned Brian to Travis and now she

264

wondered how her son would fit into the picture. "Where the hell is Winnie?" she mumbled to herself.

Across from the baby's room, Winnie's bedroom door was tightly closed in a way that indicated she did not want to be disturbed. It wasn't like Winnie to ignore her baby's crying, but everything was a little topsy-turvy today. It was just as well that Winnie was sleeping in. Dora did not think she would be able to look at Travis's wife.

Sighing, Dora gathered up the sobbing infant in her arms. Plugging a pacifier into the little wailing mouth, she changed the baby's soaking diaper and then carried her downstairs to prepare her morning bottle.

EPILOGUE

When he came to the place where the dry white sand met the darker, wet sand, Tyler unrolled his beach towel and sat down, facing the ocean and looking at the fat envelope in his hands. He had stopped at the post office on the way to the beach, hoping that the paycheck his mother was supposed to be forwarding had arrived.

Shuffling through the mail in Sam's post office box, he had pulled out *The Atlantic* and *Newsweek* to read on the beach and then a letter had fallen to the floor. When he saw that the return address was West Jordan, Vermont, he had quickly pocketed it, preferring to read it alone, with the sound of crashing waves blocking out any background noises. A letter from Sarah was the last thing he would have expected to be reading today.

February 16th, 1987

Dear Tyler,

When I called your house, your mother told me you had flown off to Ft. Lauderdale the day before to visit your old college roommate and to let those recuperating shoulder blades soak up some warm, healing sunshine. She sounded as surprised as I was and we both agreed you probably had something else up your sleeve. All she could give me was this P.O. Box as an address so I decided to take a chance and write to you because I wanted to tell you all these things before I forgot them. Actually, I just wanted to tell you these things so I can forget them.

266

Since I last talked to you, Woody's over–protective father act finally got to me and I moved back up to the cabin. He also didn't like having a Labrador retriever puppy following me around when I was working and it was always getting into the kitchen garbage. He seems to think you gave it to me for Christmas just to bother him; in fact, every time I brought your name up, he seemed to resent your intrusion and influence on my life so much that I just couldn't take it anymore. Besides, my new four wheel drive Subaru is splendid in the snow and it easily makes it up the driveway.

Thanks to the detailed descriptions of Grandmother Charlotte's jewelry in Aunt Roberta's letter, most of the pieces were able to be nearly perfectly reconstructed; a few of the jewels were still missing, of course, but good fakes have been substituted. You were right about that old lamp that Maude Adams' daughter had. If she'd had any idea how valuable it really was she would never have let us borrow it for a few weeks! Winnie used it to hide all the emeralds and all the amethysts of two complete necklaces as a couple bunches of grapes!

What's really stupid is, now that I've finally got the jewelry, it's too valuable to just leave it lying around the cabin and I had to rent a new safe deposit box to keep it in. How ironic. I don't know what the hell good any of this did. I'll never sell any of that jewelry let alone wear it. I have to keep it locked up, and I'm no richer than before. By the way, your friend did a fabulous job on the Night Heron window; it looks almost as good as it used to. Just kidding, it looks perfect. Nobody can tell the difference.

The real reason I wanted to write to you is to tell you about what happened with Lyle. This whole story has come out about this weird thing that happened to him as a baby. They're using it as his defense to keep him out of jail and in the state mental hospital, where he is now. It turns out that he was kidnapped when he was less than two years old and his abductors scared Dora so much that she never told anyone about it. You know, saying that they would kill her baby if she went to the police, things like that. I guess they kept him for about two months, can you imagine? To prove that they meant what they said, they cut off half of his pinky finger – you know, the one we thought he must have lost in a logging accident. Nobody can figure out why anyone would kidnap Lyle; I mean, what could they possibly have wanted from Dora?"

Tyler looked away for a moment and passed a shaking hand over his eyes as he thought back to the letter that accompanied those old photographs of Dora. How had it ended...something about not asking for money again or the lives of her children would be endangered?

He had long since figured out that the 'ENE 1957' on the photographs was the abbreviation for 'Enero' which meant 'January' in Spanish. It had come to him in the hospital, when he had been lying in bed so bored that he had been watching Sesame Street and they had been having a segment on the names of the calendar months in Spanish. He suspected then that the pictures had been printed in Havana and after Sarah's phone call about Winnie's dog biting Travis, he was almost sure that he was right.

Tyler flipped over the letter and continued reading.

"I'm more than a little confused about what to do with our relationship. Despite what you think, I would never be happy living in the city again after living in West Jordan. And as we discussed at Christmastime, there is no job up here that would suit your high intensity, eclectic needs and you would get bored very quickly. I guess we'll just have to be satisfied with weekend visits now and maybe things will work out in the future for us. In the meantime, you don't have to worry about me looking at another man. Compared to you, everybody else seems so boring."

He smiled to himself and closed his eyes for a minute, picturing Sarah sitting at her kitchen table, her long legs tucked up under her, writing to him. It made his heart ache to think about her.

"Have you finished your story about my mother yet? Or are you still waiting for lightning to strike you with the answer to the question of whether or not she was murdered? Remember, you promised I could read it before it went to your editor. I certainly hope it turns out better than that article you did on pet graveyards! I can't believe you sent me that to read.

I have to go, it's time for work. Why don't you take your eyes off the teenagers strutting the beach in their bikinis and write me a letter while you work on your beauty tan? Tell me why you're REALLY in Florida.

Love,

Sarah"

Tell her why he was really in Florida? Tyler had tossed that one back and forth in his mind for the last two days and still could not decide what to do about it.

Reaching into his daypack he retrieved his little tape recorder. Putting on the headphones, once again he listened to Clara Dobrinsky Dunbar's voice as she recalled nursing Winnie Scupper in the hospital thirty years before.

With the help of the night supervisor at the West Jordan hospital, it hadn't taken much work to track down Clara's address in West Palm Beach. When he had finally found her, she was on the seventeenth green, tanned to a fine mask of wrinkles and incredibly trim for a woman of her age. She told him she would meet him in the clubhouse for a drink, which turned out to mean orange juice for her and a beer for him.

"However did you manage to find me? It doesn't matter, but I'm glad you did. I've been dying to talk to someone about this for years, but it doesn't mean anything to the people down here. I mean, they wouldn't have the faintest idea what I was talking about, now would they?"

"You've actually thought about Winnie Scupper since you left West Jordan?"

"Well, you see, I hadn't given much thought at all to those years I spent nursing in Vermont until Charlie had a stroke about ten years ago. You probably know I married a man much older than myself and I was prepared for the fact that I would most likely outlive him. Well, because of my background I was able to care for him at home during his last days, with the help of a few trained professionals. You must think I'm drifting here, but I'm not really. You see, Charlie's speech was affected because of the stroke and there were certain sounds he couldn't say. Hard consonants like *b* or *p* were nearly impossible for him. And that was what reminded me of Winnie Scupper."

"His speech? Did Winnie actually speak to you in the hospital?"

"My, you're an awfully excitable young man. Yes, that's what I'm going to tell you. I guess she had been in a coma for about forty–eight hours and she was fading fast. Her pulse was weak, she was a mass of broken bones and bruises, no one expected her to live. But late in the afternoon on the third day she opened her eyes when I was taking her pulse. I immediately spoke to her to see if she was coherent. When she tried to speak it seemed that part of her face was paralyzed. That, in combination with her bandages – she may even have had a broken jaw, I don't remember – made it almost impossible to understand her. She kept asking for somebody by name and I had no idea what she was saying. Looking on her chart I saw that her husband's name was Travis – funny how you can remember some things so clearly, isn't it? – and I asked her if she was trying to say her husband's name and she managed to say yes.

"So of course I thought she wanted to see her husband and I told her nobody had been able to contact him yet about her accident but that he would come as soon as possible. I'll never forget the big tears that welled up in her eyes and she kept trying to tell me something. At the time it sounded like 'He kissed me.' And silly me, all I said was something like, 'There, there, of course he kissed you. He loves you very much.' I thought she was a little delirious. Her eyes kept filling with tears as over and over again she tried to tell me something. Sometimes it sounded like 'he kissed me on the wrist' or 'lips.' I mean what she was saying was something like – 'e isst 'e awt ta is.'"

There was a silence on the tape where Clara had stopped speaking for a moment to watch someone tee off on the golf course. "Nice shot! Anyway, to make a long story short, when I was helping Charlie learn to speak again, I remembered Winnie Scupper. I was telling him

271

about her and suddenly it came to me, just like that, clear as a bell, what she had been trying so urgently to tell me."

Every time Tyler got to this part of the tape, a chill ran down his spine, the same way it had when he had actually heard Clara say the words the very first time.

"Why, she was trying to say 'He pushed me. He pushed me off the bridge!' She was trying to tell me her husband had pushed her off the bridge and I was too dumb to understand it. I mean, years later it was too late to do anything about it. By then it was just so much water under the bridge – excuse my bad pun – and well, it just wasn't worth it. They would never have been able to prove it anyway. Sometimes I feel very guilty about it but then I think that maybe my memory has just twisted her words into what I wanted them to be. If I recall correctly, her husband wasn't even around the night of the accident."

Tyler fast–forwarded the tape a few feet, through the embarrassing sounds of his own excited exclamations about what she had just told him. It was her last few lines that always stopped him from rushing to the nearest phone and calling Sarah.

"You say you're very close with the daughter? Well, take some advice from me, young man. Don't tell her what I just told you. I needed to get it off my chest, tell it to someone who could relate to it. But she doesn't need to hear that some old nurse thinks her father might have killed her mother. Now just be quiet and hear me out! I don't care how much evidence you have supporting what I just told you, it's not going to make her any happier to know the ugly truth. Just leave it be. It's part of the past and that's where it belongs. If you need to talk to someone about it, you can call me. I'll give you my home phone number."

Tyler clicked off the tape and solemnly removed the headphones. Clara Dunbar was right. Sarah did not need to know the truth. As he put the tape recorder away, he recalled his initial reaction to it.

At first the thought of not being able to publish the whole exciting story had driven him crazy. After visiting Clara, he had spent the rest of that day drowning his literary sorrows with a bottle of vodka and a can of grapefruit juice. By midnight he was over his personal disappointment. What began to bother him even more was the fact that Travis had literally gotten away with murder all these years.

Feeling angry at the circumstances and sorry for Sarah, he had an increasing sense of helplessness and confusion. Around 1 AM he reached for the telephone and dialed the number he had secretly copied from the wall phone of the shabby apartment in Atlantic City.

"Travis Monroe? I know what you did."

"Who is this?"

Until that very moment, Tyler had no idea what he wanted to say. But suddenly the words were tumbling out of him in a hoarse and threatening whisper. "You may have gotten away with it for thirty years, but I have positive proof now that it was you who killed Winnie Scupper. I have an eyewitness who saw you in West Jordan that night. We intend to prosecute. There is no way you can escape this time. We will see you rot in jail!"

"I don't know who you are or what you're talking about, but you must be deranged." The connection clicked off quickly.

Tyler closed his eyes, satisfied for the moment. He had no intention of taking Travis to court; even if he had wanted to, there wouldn't be enough evidence to make the charge stick. But Travis didn't have to know that. Let him suffer the mental torment of guilt. Let him lie awake the rest of the night remembering what he had done and wondering who knew. In a few hours Tyler would call him again. And again. The least he could do was drive the man crazy.

Slinging his pack over his shoulder and carrying his shoes, Tyler walked up the beach to the nearest high–rise hotel. Still barefoot, he followed the sun–baked cement of a path that led past the poolside bar to the back entrance to the lobby. He stopped at a pay phone to call the number he knew by heart after dialing it so many times in the last two days. For the last twelve hours it had been off the hook; he took that as a point of victory. But this time it was ringing and he prepared himself for his next threatening speech.

He was surprised when a strange woman's voice answered the phone. "Mr. Monroe, please." Tyler used an official, impersonal voice.

"I'm sorry but Mr. Monroe cannot take your call." The voice had a hard New Jersey accent; it was definitely not Consuela.

"I see. When would it be convenient to call back?"

"I'm afraid you will not be able to speak to Mr. Monroe at all. He had a massive heart attack early this morning and passed away before dawn. I'll have Ms. Ferrara return your call when she feels up to it, Mr...? Hello?"

Tyler was staring sightlessly at the receiver, a hollow feeling in the pit of his stomach. It's not my fault, he thought defensively. He did it to himself. He deserved it. It was what he had coming.

In a daze, he hung up the receiver and wandered outside. He should feel good about this, wasn't it what he had wanted? He had done it for Sarah. Anyone in his position would have done the same thing.

A blonde woman in a jungle print camp–shirt and shorts was tending bar. She looked cool and comfortable in contrast to Tyler, who was dripping with perspiration, unused to the heat and humidity of Florida.

"A shot of tequila, please," he said looking back over his shoulder in the direction of the sea. His fingers shook as he held the shot glass in the air, speaking softly but distinctly. "To Sarah." He clicked his glass against an empty beer bottle on the bar and drank the fiery liquid quickly.

"Who's Sarah?" the young blonde bartender inquired.

"Another bartender I know. Here, keep the change." Dropping a large bill on the counter, Tyler walked away swiftly, the hot cement of the sidewalk burning the soles of his feet.

Would he ever be able to tell her? He realized now that the sweat dripping down his face was not only from the heat. Well, there was nothing more he could do today. And it was definitely time for a swim.